DAUGHTER
OF THE
HUNT

Also by K Arsenault Rivera

Oath of Fire

DAUGHTER OF THE HUNT

K ARSENAULT RIVERA

FOREVER

NEW YORK BOSTON

This book is a work of fiction. Names, characters, places, and incidents are the product of the author's imagination or are used fictitiously. Any resemblance to actual events, locales, or persons, living or dead, is coincidental.

Copyright © 2026 by K Arsenault Rivera

Cover art and design by Nina Thomas. Cover images by DepositPhotos. Cover copyright © 2026 by Hachette Book Group, Inc.

Hachette Book Group supports the right to free expression and the value of copyright. The purpose of copyright is to encourage writers and artists to produce the creative works that enrich our culture.

The scanning, uploading, and distribution of this book without permission is a theft of the author's intellectual property. If you would like permission to use material from the book (other than for review purposes), please contact permissions@hbgusa.com. Thank you for your support of the author's rights.

Forever
Hachette Book Group
1290 Avenue of the Americas, New York, NY 10104
read-forever.com
@readforeverpub

First Edition: March 2026

Forever is an imprint of Grand Central Publishing. The Forever name and logo are registered trademarks of Hachette Book Group, Inc.

The publisher is not responsible for websites (or their content) that are not owned by the publisher.

Forever books may be purchased in bulk for business, educational, or promotional use. For information, please contact your local bookseller or the Hachette Book Group Special Markets Department at special.markets@hbgusa.com.

Library of Congress Cataloging-in-Publication Data

Names: Rivera, K Arsenault author
Title: Daughter of the hunt / K Arsenault Rivera.
Description: New York : Forever, 2026. | Series: Oath of fire ; book 2
Identifiers: LCCN 2025042201 | ISBN 9781538756706 trade paperback | ISBN 9781538756713 ebook
Subjects: LCGFT: Fantasy fiction | Romance fiction | Lesbian fiction | Novels
Classification: LCC PS3618.I8465 D38 2026 | DDC 813/.6—dc23/eng/20251114
LC record available at https://lccn.loc.gov/2025042201

ISBNs: 9781538756706 (trade paperback), 9781538756713 (ebook)

Printed in the United States of America

LSC-C

Printing 1, 2026

For Caroline Polachek.
Not because I know her but because I think she's cool and want to play Commander with her someday.

Content Guidance

This novel features extensive discussion of hunting, which necessarily includes animal death. No animals are harmed for pure sport, and everything is coming from a place of compassion. However, if you're sensitive to hunting, please proceed with caution.

This novel also features a protagonist struggling with depression and occasional suicidal ideation. No self-harm takes place over the course of the book. Still, some may find the discussion triggering. Please use your best discretion and remember there are plenty of resources for those in need.

Psyche, I've got a story for you, and I'd really like if you listened the whole way through. I know you've got other stuff to do. You're a god now, after all. There are plenty of people looking to curry favor with you. Dances to attend, prayers to answer, a horrible system to try to change from the inside. I might not know what it's like to be the god of the soul, but I've been around people like you enough to know that you don't have a spare moment.

I'm going to ask you to spare one anyway.

Not because we used to be friends (and I hope we still are). Not because I've spent my whole life serving gods—bending myself into shapes that best suited what they wanted from me. And not because I think this will be an easy request.

I want you to listen because my family has suffered enough—and so have I.

Let me explain.

Chapter One

In most cases we would start the story on the day I died.

This isn't most cases. We have to start a couple days beforehand.

The scene of our fair play will be my family's high-rise in Sydney. I know what you're thinking: *A high-rise? Didn't know you were rich.* And we are. I won't deny that. Nothing you're about to hear about my upbringing is normal.

Everywhere you go these days there's a Pelops Corp. logo. Not that it's very welcoming. A terrifying obsidian mask hardly leaves a warm and cozy impression. Our analysts have tried to get us to change it for *years*, and still it persists. Generations of my family have refused to change it.

That snarling mask is who we are.

But I'm getting ahead of myself.

We're starting in the high-rise at seven in the morning. I was awake not because I'm an early riser but because I hadn't gone to bed. The blackout curtains in my room were doing their best to help me maintain my awful sleep schedule; only a tiny sliver of light filtered in between them. That sliver of light happened to fall precisely across my monitors. I'd set it up that way on purpose. A cold cup of coffee and a YouTube LetsPlay were my only company at the time, but as the clock ticked over to seven, I braced for an onslaught of work emails.

Pelops Corp. was a complicated business with complicated needs, and most of them had to filter through IT at some point or another. Offices around the world meant tickets coming in at every hour of the day. I dealt with the American office overnight—but as dawn came to Australia I knew my headaches were just about to begin.

Sure enough, I saw the little red dot of a new ticket on my taskbar. Picking up my cold coffee, I opened it up and braced for another request.

You've got to help me, I was chatting with a coworker while I entered a purchase order and I accidentally added three extra 0s and if I don't get this sorted out before the transaction is finalized we're going to lose so much money—

Some tickets made you smile. Not all of them, of course; some were just so frustrating that you groaned under your breath imagining what steps you'd need to go through to fix them. But this one?

This one was funny. I couldn't help but imagine the guy on the other end of this pacing up a storm. *No worries, mate. Got your back.*

This sort of thing wasn't usually in my wheelhouse, but the good thing about being the eldest daughter of the CEO and president of Pelops Corp. is that you can make nepotism work for you. I picked up my coffee cup. Processing was two floors down from me. I might as well take a walk. Good for the old mental health, they said. Take a walk outside for ten to fifteen minutes a day! Reap the benefits!

The thought made the corner of my lip twitch. They had the big windows on the business floors. Maybe that would count for sunlight—but not in the way anyone meant it when they said you should take a walk. Still. It was all I had.

Out I went. The top few floors of the high-rise were penthouses for my family: my parents, then mine on the floor beneath, then my siblings sharing one below that. The tippy top of the building was my father's office. The gods—we liked to call them Guests while on the property—liked to be as close to the sky as possible in most cases.

The living area of my penthouse wasn't really mine. Not in the ways that mattered. My father's old things still littered the room: mounted fish he'd never caught, grassland vistas he'd never visited. My grandfather's bronze horse casts. Nothing I'd bothered changing when my father took over the company and I inherited the heir's room. It didn't feel right. Dad had spent all that time putting it together, after all, and it wasn't like we could make a quick trip outside to pick up new décor. Anything we wanted had to be ordered specifically for us. That fish up there on the wall meant something to him.

Even though I hated the way its beady little eyes stared at me, I'd never get rid of it.

Past the living room was the entrance to the lift. I swiped my card and waited for the private one to come up and get me.

When it did, I braced myself for terrible music. Dad was the one who picked what played in the private lifts my family used and he always chose—

Yeah. Terrible, forty-year-old rock music.

I groaned my way through a band of men playing guitar solos about wanting to date teenagers and hit the button for processing. Chances were no one would be in, but I could leave a note.

Except that when I thought it would go down to the business floors, it went up instead.

The door opened on my mother. She raised a brow and sighed. "Is it business that's got you out of your room so early?"

"Yeah," I said. I waved my mug. "And, you know, stretching my legs. Going on a heroic journey and all that."

She leaned forward. My mother had one of those faces people always thought of as severe. I didn't think so, though. She just felt things intensely. And what she felt right now was... "Iphigenia. How old is that coffee? I can see rings *inside* the mug."

I winced. "Oh, it's..."

"You can't remember, can you?"

"No."

She sighed. After kissing my forehead, she took the mug from my hand. "I'll have someone deliver a new one to your room."

"But, Mum," I whined, "it'll mess up my sleep schedule."

She stepped into the lift and pressed the Close button. "I'm your mother, not an idiot."

Well. She had me there.

But as the doors whirred shut I realized that I, too, was no idiot. "Wait a second. What are *you* doing up so early?"

My mother's eyes—the pale blue only my sister Elektra had inherited—stayed on the lift console.

"You're in full makeup, even," I said. "And that's one of your new gowns, isn't it?"

Like the opening of a switchblade, her eyes flicked over to me. "Taken an interest in more than just hoodies, have we?"

I pouted. "They're comfy, and it's not like anyone is ever going to see me outside of a meeting," I said. "I dress up for those. No need otherwise."

A pause. The pieces fell into place.

"You're meeting with someone, aren't you?"

The lift continued its slow descent; the rock music kept right on going. I lost track of which song's guitar solo we were listening to.

My mother let out a breath. "Your uncle is in town."

"Menelaus?" I said. My voice shot up about an octave. "Really? I haven't seen him in *forever*, I wonder if he brought any souvenirs—"

"If you would like, you can come along to greet him," said my mother. "I thought you might be busy with other things and, well…"

There was a strange pause that hung in the air, punctuated by snare drums and wailing. A couple of years lived in that pause. My shoulders went tense.

"I don't mind," I said. "Really, I don't."

She hummed. "It shouldn't be a matter of whether or not you mind, Iphigenia."

So many of these conversations. Was meeting up with my uncle really the only reason she was up so early? Ellie and Ori said Dad was skipping breakfast lately. The older I'd gotten, the more rumors I'd seen in the press about my mother. The lives of the rich should always be criticized, sure, but our family was odder than most. That meant more scrutiny...which meant reading more gossip about my parents' marriage.

I took a breath. Not here. Not in the lift, which might open any second, where people might hear. Being the Heir of Pelops wasn't something I could just change.

"...But if you would genuinely like to see him, I suppose it wouldn't do any harm," she said at length.

I smiled. Good to have the tension break. "I've got to stop first, but I'll head down right after."

A nod from her. "There'll be photographers. His new wife is..."

"Yeah, yeah," I said. It was the top thread on, like, every single gossip community. I could not tell you how many memes I had seen wondering what my new aunt saw in my uncle. Even I had to admit they were a little...unevenly matched. "I'll pull the hoodie up."

My mother sighed, but I wasn't sure it was a sad one. She pulled me in and kissed the top of my head. "Never change yourself for someone else's sake."

What a weird thing to say to someone in a lift.

Fixing our coworker's little fuck-up didn't take too long—not for someone like me. Once you know what a database looks like and understand the arcane whispers they use to communicate, you can get them to do things pretty easily. On some level coding and programming were always easier for me to understand than the business stuff. If something went wrong in your coding, you sat there and you figured it out, all on your own, explaining every little piece of it out loud until you found the problem. If you needed help, there were plenty of people on the internet who had usually had the same problem. You could talk with them if you wanted, but you didn't have to.

Didn't have to leave your little desk, your little world.

But the board meetings? Oh, I hated those. The new faces filing past. Lot of numbers talk was fine—I liked it, even—but everything about business felt so abstract to me. Other offices. Products I'd never see or use. Despite growing up in all that luxury, there was a whole world out there that just... wasn't for me. Couldn't be for me.

The second the Heir of Pelops left the land the gods allotted for us—the land on which our high-rise had been built—it was all over. All our fortune turned to misfortune.

I sent off an email to my panicking coworker. As I did, I wondered what it was like over in his corner of the world.

And I did something I maybe shouldn't have.

Remotely accessing a PC is easy if you know what you're doing. Easier if you happen to be part of the IT department and understand precisely who can access what. A few more keystrokes happened before I could summon the will to stop.

I found myself on his PC. His desktop. Staring back at me from the wallpaper were him and his husband, arm in arm, wearing matching suits against a dazzling blue sky. A lake opened up around them, too—blue as far as the eye could see, cut only by the intrusion of beautiful columns.

Faces I'd never meet. A place I'd never go. What did the breeze feel like on their faces?

I wondered where it was, and then—as my senses came to me—I closed out of the remote session.

I heard the photographers before I saw them. The private lift left me toward the back of the building. In theory, that was where anyone except my father and I could make discreet exits or entrances if we wanted. That was true, mostly, as long as you timed things to arrive in the middle of the night. It was absolutely *not* true today. The chatter of the cameras was like the clatter of swords against shields. With every step you could feel it. Camera flashes rendered what little daylight there was into a dazzling dawn.

The lift let out into the green room for special guests. Just outside of it was the hallway that led to the secret entrance. My mother was there when I stepped out. Some last-minute adjustments to her makeup, it looked like.

"Are you ready?" she asked.

I flipped my hood up and drew the strings as close as I could. Between that, a pair of sunnies, and an N95, I was pretty sure no one could reasonably deduce that I was human at all, let alone the wealthy heir to an international conglomerate. I liked it that way—I didn't feel like a wealthy heir most of the time.

"Got my armor on," I said.

A small, sympathetic smile. She gave me a hug. "Do you want to come out with me, or with him?"

Her bodyguard, Aegisthus, touched a fingertip to the bud in his ear. Aegisthus was in all the family photos, pretty much. My mother never left the high-rise without him—and sometimes he even followed her around within it. With his cauliflower ears, buzz cut, and lumbering frame, he was a lot like an action movie goon in the wake of my mother's refined socialite. When he tried to smile at me, it always felt like he'd only learned how to do so by watching movies. This smile was no exception.

"He'll be there anyway. Might as well be the two of us," I said. Photos of me didn't sell very well. If I was walking with Mum, it might make the photos of her less valuable, too.

Together we went down the hall. Aegisthus led the way. He always stood in front of me, when he could, to block me from view. I'd asked him to do it once when I was a child and the cameras had scared me.

He'd never forgotten.

"Ready?" he asked at the threshold, as if my mother had not just asked me the same thing. She smiled whenever he did things like this.

Still, it felt good to be looked after. I nodded again. My sunnies slipped down my nose, and I frantically shoved them back into place.

The door swung open. Aegisthus blocked a lot of the light but not all of it—for a moment he was this blazing halo of a man. Then came the shouts from the crowd. Our names, mostly.

I should say *my mother's* name.

"Clytemnestra! You're up early!"

"Who are you wearing?"

Dozens of versions of that echoed against my skull. If it wasn't for the sunnies and the hoodie, I'd want to crawl into a pit somewhere to hide. Sort of still did. But I didn't want my mother to have to face all of this without some moral support, and—to be honest—I really was looking forward to seeing my uncle. His new wife had a kind face.

So, really, it was all bog standard stuff until I heard the question that started the slow collapse of my old life. The first arrow through the armor of who I used to be.

"Where's Agamemnon? What's he think of his brother's allegations?"

My head whipped around. Allegations? Uncle Menny got into his share of bar brawls, but it was never anything serious. And definitely not something the public found out about—my father usually buried all of that in the wee hours right after it happened. When he was asleep, that responsibility fell to me.

A weight that was beginning to feel heavy. What had he done this time? And *how had anyone else heard about it?* He was supposed to report that stuff the second it happened. The whole point of having an Heir of Pelops is so that the other members of the house don't have to worry about the curse; we take on the entire burden of the family. We serve. It's what we do.

So why the *fuck* had Menny left us out in the lurch?

I looked toward my mother. She ignored the question—kept right on walking to the curb, where she awaited my uncle's ride.

But I couldn't follow her there. The very border of the highrise was a few steps past the exit. A bronze horse inlaid within the marble marked it. If I stepped past its head, the curse would come for us all.

My mother and Aegisthus, though? They continued right ahead. And for the most part, the cameras followed them. Only a couple lingered behind to get photos of Pelops Corp.'s mysterious future CEO.

I stood, my foot on the horse's chest, and I swear to you that I tasted something on the air. That I felt something. Animals—I'm going to talk a lot about them, so I need you to brace for that—have better senses than we do. They can feel storms coming because they have a better understanding of air pressure; some snakes can perceive infrared.

I don't know what I felt then, watching my uncle's car pull up, but I can tell you that it was an animal feeling. That it lived somewhere in the deep forests of my chest. A cold ran through me, deeply at odds with the heat around me.

A flash went off right in my face just as the car pulled up.

"Miss Iphigenia Pelops, are you worried for the future of the company?"

My throat swelled. I swallowed. Whatever I said would be reported to the world within minutes, and I had no context for anything that had happened.

I glanced toward the car. Uncle Menny's driver was already

running to open the door for him. The second he got out, all the cameras would shift to his new wife. Could I hold out that long?

"N-no comment," I stammered.

"Your father is already in his fifties. Surely you've thought about how your Pelops Corp. would differ?"

No, not really. I tried not to think about the business side of things at all. Very little of our business was our own decision, anyway; the gods gave us direction on how to influence the human world, and we carried it out as best we could. But I couldn't say that. *Oh, yeah, all those pagan gods are real, and that's how we can get you the finest chocolate in the world while keeping it ethically sourced.*

Uncle Menny got out of the car. Small for a man, but broad, he always reminded me of one of those Bruce Timm superheroes. All width and angle until you got to his waist, and then everything got suspiciously tube shaped. His red beard was thick except for a slash across his cheek. I didn't have the full story on that scar. A bar fight injury probably.

For all his violence, I never feared my uncle. He had that boisterous charm about him. Often I would hear him across the halls before I knew he had come over for a visit: a loud *bwa-haha!* that seemed to echo through the whole high-rise. His ear-to-ear grin often swallowed up the scar. When I was little, before I had siblings, he would scoop me up and take me right to the very edge of the horse's head. He held me up there, my feet dangling above the bronze, perilously close to the real world.

"See? It's not so far," he said. And when my father inevitably came over to yell at him for doing this, Menny would scoff. "Let the girl have a handful of reality every now and again."

It meant so much to me. Not being able to attend his wedding *killed* me. I spent the whole day scowling. Though there was a whole company in the high-rise, it felt like it was only my father and me when it came down to it—the two heirs, trapped as usual.

But Uncle Menny took the time to FaceTime me. Not just my father. He took the time to say hi to me, personally, on the most important day of his life, and to tell me he wished I could be there to tell him all about whatever game I'd gotten into lately.

And now, as he got out of the car, he was dark as a storm cloud. My mother tried to greet him, and he gave her only a glare in return. The chorus of photographers became a horrible blaze of voices and lights; Aegisthus blocked them while my uncle and my mother walked the whole way back to the bronze horse.

"Uncle Menny—" I started.

But he walked past me. My heart sank into my stomach. Whatever was going on, I had to find some way to help. My uncle didn't deserve to suffer like this. That was my father's place, and it was mine.

Our siblings were supposed to have normal lives. That was always the deal.

As I walked back to the hallway and then to the green room, it was all that I could think about. We had crisis management.

Of course we did. If I told you how much we spent retaining two different agencies around the clock, you'd cry, and you'd be right to. It was more money than any company should ever rightly have. I could contact them and figure out what to do next—

But Uncle Menny had those numbers, too, and he hadn't used them. Ugh. Maybe it was something personal? Something private?

As the door closed behind us, a piece fell into place for me. It wasn't one I liked. Uncle Menny was *alone*. No bodyguard, no attendants, and, most worryingly, no wife.

"I'm going to kill him, Cly, I swear I will," he said. He didn't even wait until one of us asked him. "Who does he think he is?"

"Be careful what you swear upon, Menelaus. Our Guests are always listening," my mother answered. Despite my uncle's face going as red as his beard, she was cool and collected.

I had to back her up. "Besides, we don't need their help to solve our problems, right?" I said. "Tell me who we're arguing with, and I'll get it sorted, Uncle Menny."

He looked to me and set his jaw. "Iphy, doll, this isn't something we can fix with money."

I tilted my head. He couldn't be serious. You could fix everything with money. There had never, in the entire course of my life, been a problem that we did not solve with money. Whether we paid for expensive solutions or paid for the people who could come up with them, in the end it all came down to cash.

That's the thing about money, by the way—it doesn't really buy happiness. It buys peace of mind. It buys time. It buys *leisure.* All of those things, combined, make it a lot easier to be happy. But it all comes at the cost of letting yourself go as dull as worthlessly as an unused knife.

But back then—no, I couldn't think of anything that money could not solve. So I stood there and gawped at him a little when he said that, saved only by my mother knowing far more about the world than my gilded cage could ever teach me.

"It's her place to help," she said. "That's all she's trying to do."

My uncle rolled his shoulders. Normally he'd help himself to some of the sparkling water or the snacks in the green room. Today he made no such motion. "I'm glad to see you," he said to me without an ounce of gladnesss, "but this is something that needs to stay between your parents and me."

There was a lot I wanted to say to him. I mean, I had so many questions, just to start. What was it that had happened? Why was it so hard to solve? To be blunt: How fucked were we? Above all of these was the thing I really meant when I asked them: How can I help?

And there were the nonquestion items, too. *I have to be responsible for all this eventually. I should know. Whatever this is, everyone already knows, so it doesn't make sense to keep secrets.*

But looking at him, and looking at my mother, I could still hear the din of the crowd outside. They had the same questions I did. They hadn't gotten any answers. Why should I be any different? He wanted to handle this with my parents. Well, wasn't that helping, too? Wasn't it helping to get out of the way?

So I swallowed my own wants and needs, my own fears and concerns, and nodded. "All right," I said. "It was nice to see you."

He flinched, as if I had hurt him, and reached for my shoulder. Bruises stained his knuckles, and scars etched lines across his hands. "It was nice to see you, too. Really."

I couldn't think of anything to say. Ignoring what I wanted out of the conversation felt like the right thing to do—but what would I do then?

"I think Ellie and Ori are going to class soon," I said. "I'll make sure they're all right."

I didn't need to think about it. Even then.

My siblings, thankfully, were at the age where you could have an actual conversation with them that didn't involve dinosaurs. Not that dinosaurs aren't cool. Just that for a solid two years there, maybe more, it was all Ori could talk about.

He still liked dinosaurs. But these days he liked video games about them, and I could meet him there. I found him sneaking in a cheeky Minecraft session when I stopped to check in on him.

"Oi, Ori," I called, knocking on the door. "The driver will be here to take you to class in a half. How about you stop fighting the Ender Dragon and get ready?"

The groan that came from the other room probably would have frustrated most people. Maybe even me on another day. But that meant that he hadn't seen the news at all. Ori kept his phone on do not disturb more often than not. It made contacting him terribly annoying...but it also meant that he wasn't aware what was going on downstairs.

Good.

"Can't I just have my tutor stop by?" he said. "I'm so close!"

"You could," I said. We had the money to. "But then you'd lose out on seeing your friends, wouldn't you?"

He paused Minecraft and pouted at me. "I can see them on the internet. We can FaceTime. It's not that big a deal."

I wasn't about to tell him that FaceTime was the only way I ever saw most people outside of the family. He didn't mean any harm, after all; he was talking about *his* life.

And the reason I couldn't see people was so that *he* could. Of course it doesn't occur to him.

I hid my wince by rubbing my mouth on my sleeve. "Right, well, how about a bet? I bet I can beat that dragon by the time you finish getting ready."

He rolled his eyes. "All I have to do is put on trousers and a shirt, Iph."

"Yeah," I said. "Deal's a deal. If you win, you can stay in. If I win, you go to class and you bring me back something from a halal truck."

Halal truck food was a big temptation for me. Somehow it never tasted the same if you DoorDashed it. Lamb over rice with extra white sauce? Sign me up every time.

"Don't know why you're so obsessed with being a loser," he said. He set the controller down.

I moved over to pick it up. "Three, two, one..."

I unpaused the game and got to work.

Here's the thing: Orestes was right in that all he had to do was put on trousers and a shirt. But I knew that kid. Aside from my mother, I had practically raised him. And I knew that, like most teen boys, he kept his good clothes and his dirty clothes in the same pile. He actually insisted that the housekeeper not touch it, and he had certainly never lived the sort of life that forced him to clean up after himself. And I knew that despite this being his preferred way of keeping his clothes, he was very particular about wrinkles. So he had to find the shirt, pluck it from the pile, and try to tug the wrinkles out of it with the de-wrinkling spray.

The same went for his trousers.

That process added about five to ten minutes, which was all I needed. He might play a lot of Minecraft these days, but I had played twice as much for twice as long. With the dragon dead, I stood and ruffled his hair.

"Bring me something new this time," I said. "Something I haven't tried before."

His eyes went wide. "There's no way—" He looked at the screen. "Iph, how did you do that?!"

"Older sister secrets," I said. "Have a good day at class, yeah? And don't forget the food. I'll mess with your save files if you do."

Ellie, my younger sister, is a little younger than Ori. Old enough that she doesn't usually need me to remind her about anything.

Still, I stopped by her room anyway. She'd probably seen the news. Ellie was kind of obsessed with gossip.

My instincts served me well. When I knocked on her door, I could hear her sobbing on the other side of it. "El? Can I come in?"

"It's *awful*! I *hate* this family!"

Yeah, she'd definitely seen the news. Whatever it was. I still hadn't gotten up the courage to seek out the details. Well, I was going to have to figure it out. It's not like I could just leave her there.

I opened the door. Ellie was sitting on the edge of her bed, sobbing into her hands. I sat next to her and gave her a hug.

"It's hard, I know," I said.

"Everyone's going to *know*, Iph! How am I supposed to show my face? Every single question I'm going to hear is going to be about *her* and why she just…"

Helen, probably? She must have left for Uncle Menny to be so mad. And in a big showy way, or with someone no one liked? Hard to place it.

"If you want to stay in, I don't think anyone would hold it against you," I said. Except maybe Orestes. "I can have the tutors come over, or you could take the day all the way off if you wanted."

She sniffled. "Won't stop the texts. My mobile's *blowing up*," she said. As she did, the chirp of a new message played four times in succession.

"I could take it for a few hours. Let you recover," I said. "Sometimes it's good to put things down—"

"But they'll know! Everyone's asking me how Menny fumbled so bad and what we're going to do about it and-and—" She took a quick, snot-filled breath. "And Joey's already asking me about it, too, and what if he was just dating me because he wanted to get close to Aunt Helen and—"

"El, one thing at a time. Come on," I said. I put my hands on both her shoulders. "Look at me. That's good. Deep breaths now."

More sobbing, but we got there eventually. Class was definitely not in the cards for her today. "You're staying home. We're going to set your mobile to do not disturb, and I'll change the password on it. Just for the day, yeah? Just for today. It's Ellie day, now. I'm here."

Ellie nodded and collapsed against me. "I just… He's so mean about it. He said that we must have done something awful for her to just leave in the middle of the night and to show up with…"

That… admittedly did not sound great. What was going on?

"What if he's right? What if we did mess up?" said Ellie. "I just. What if it's… What if this is like, you know, whatever it is that keeps you in the stupid building all the time? The curse, you know?"

I had the same thought. Not that I wanted to voice it. The heir staying on this land was supposed to mean the others didn't have to deal with the curse. Had something gone wrong, or was my uncle just a dickhead?

"I'm going to find out," I said. "But I need time to get the details. Uncle Menny and Dad are talking right now. Once I figure out what's going on, I'll let you know what we're going to do about it. But I need some time, yeah?"

Sniffling, snot dripping from her nose, she nodded. "O-okay. You promise, Iph?"

"'Course I do. I've never let you down, right?" I said. And she nodded against my shoulder. "Let me get my work laptop. I'll bring it over here and hang out until you're feeling better. And when you are, I'll go see about the size of the mess we're in."

I stood to get my things, but Ellie called after me.

"Hey, Iph? I know you're kinda weird about romance or whatever—"

"I'm ace, Ellie. It's not that weird," I said. Although it was weird to a lot of people on dating apps. Go figure.

"Right," she said. "But, um. Well. How do you know when someone's right for you?"

I leaned against the wall. This wasn't something I had a ton of experience with. My circumstances made it hard enough to date to start with. Add in the whole ace thing and, well...I could get a lot of first dates from people who wanted a look into the mystical Pelops Corp. and its hermit heir, but nothing past that.

Not that any of that was going to stop me from helping my sister out. She knew who she was asking. I had to give the best advice I could.

"They make you better," I said. "And not like they're forcing their will on you or anything like that. It's more that having them around...It makes you feel like you could do anything. Someone who makes you braver."

A silence in the room. Then: "Joey doesn't make me feel brave."

"Yeah, 'cause he's a baby kangaroo," I said. "If he doesn't make you feel like you could take on the world, then he's not good enough for you, El."

"But he's nice..."

"Is he, though?" I said. Then I took a breath. "How about we chat more when I come back? And I'll get us breakfast, too."

When I picked up my work laptop I had five emails from my father.

All of them said versions of the same thing: Prepare for war. Four of them told me to go upstairs and report for duty. That he had things he needed to tell me.

But I had made a promise to my sister, and I wasn't about to break it. No matter how much the word *war* scared me.

So... I turned off my own notifications, too. At least for a while. And I went back to Ellie's room until she felt safe enough to be on her own.

Chapter Two

I'm going to tell you a little about my family now. I want you to understand the situation we were in now that you understand a little about who we are as people.

Centuries ago someone in my family fucked up. Who exactly wasn't relevant for most of my life; it wasn't the sort of thing people spoke about. I asked my father more than once, only for him to tell me that our Guests would hate to hear me looking into it.

What is relevant is that the fuck-up involved the gods. Either our ancestor had killed one of them or insulted them gravely, or something along those lines. Something unforgivable. For some reason beyond our understanding, the gods reacted to this not by killing our ancestor but by binding his children to their service. The firstborn child in every generation was to serve the gods in the human world.

Now, you know how this works. The gods have their worlds: lavish Courts that they create and embody, within which they can do whatever they like so long as they obey the Laws. They don't lie, they don't renege on a deal, that sort of thing. And sometimes they'll take a human into their world as an Oathsworn, a sort of spouse who has an elevated status. Often they'll have children with their Oathsworn—or with another human they're fond of—and those will be demigods. Most of the time, demigods stay in the Courts. Why wouldn't you, really? Access to that kind of wealth and luxury is hard to come by, even for someone from a background like mine. The gods are on another level.

A demigod can go between the two worlds no problem. But a god usually can't unless they're doing a specific task. Given that there aren't a ton of demigods and they tend to make themselves extremely obvious when they do show up, if the gods want to affect the human world directly, they don't have many options.

That's where my family comes in. We represent their interests in the human world. Most of the time this means that we do business for them, since in the current day and age that's the easiest way to nudge the world this way or that. All of the gods have their own little industries they come to us to manage—hence why the Pelops group is a conglomerate. We sell the Queen of Flame's personal beauty products, the King of Flame's work in engineering and manufacturing, the King of the Waves's maritime products. It's made us very, very wealthy.

But the downside to that is how we have to live. The firstborn in every generation of the House of Pelops must serve the gods fully. We must stay on the land allotted to us (though we are allowed to ask for a change of scenery every few generations), and we must never leave it. We are directly beholden to them. I can't tell you how many times my father has made a disastrous business decision because the whims of the gods dictated he do so.

A lot of this might be stuff you already know now that you've gotten your foot in the door. Maybe it isn't. I don't know where we're starting from, so I figured I might as well start from scratch. And even if you know the basics there's plenty more to learn, and plenty you don't know about my family.

See, there are other gods besides the ones that you and I know. You've heard stories about them. All of them exist, of course, with their own rules and their own Courts...but they can't manifest in our world without a great deal of effort, either. So they have their own human servants.

And, well, sometimes godly rivalries become business rivalries.

That's the context. It doesn't make what happened any better. But it is a strange situation, and I wanted you to know all this before I kept yapping about my own problems. I want you to understand the weight that was on my shoulders every day of my life. See, if anything happened to me, then the burden would go on to my brother. He'd be the one trapped inside. He'd be the one who couldn't feel the sun on his skin except through a window or within ten steps of a high-rise. The one who could never go to a market or hang out at a friend's place or go swimming in the ocean.

My father and I bore that burden. And I think it set us both a little out of our heads.

When I got back to my room that night, my father was waiting for me. I knew he was there before I saw him. Something in our blood has always made us aware of each other. Like all my blood curdling in my veins. I wondered if he felt the same way, but I never asked him. I had a good idea of the answer. For all that my father loved me and all the time that we spent together as a result of our curse, there was always something a little disgusted in his expression. Like he was holding back from vomiting.

I didn't hold it against him. It was like that for me, too. And as I stepped into my room, I felt my stomach start to bubble, and I covered my mouth with my hand and took a breath. My hackles rose at the back of my neck. Ignoring my notifications hadn't been smart. But I could defend myself and that decision. The heir was supposed to look after the family, after all, and that's precisely what I'd been doing.

Dad was studying a mounted bass on the wall. Like my uncle, he was tall; unlike Menny, he had always been reedy.

"Iphigenia," he said. "How is your sister?"

"She's solid now, but she was losing it earlier. There's a lot of chatter online," I said. I stood by a great big leather couch one of my ancestors had gotten. Bit of an aspiration. Even for all our wealth, the heir didn't get many guests aside from the godly ones. Not *personal* guests.

"Yes. People are talking," my father said. "But I've told you before—they will talk no matter what we do. It makes little sense to wait on their every word. They cannot know our lives."

He still hadn't turned around. I wasn't sure I wanted him to. There was something in the line of his shoulders that felt horrible, a violent tension.

"I get that, and I usually don't care," I said. "It's just that Ellie is in tears. She's got a right to know what's going on. We all do, don't we? It's our family. Menny said I couldn't help—"

"Menelaus is a shortsighted fool. And he is the reason that we are in this mess," said my father. Sharp and sudden.

I won't lie to you—I flinched. "Then let me help. Tell me what's going on. The two of us are supposed to deal with whatever goes on here, right?"

My father still did not turn toward me.

"It's war," he said. He had gone quiet again.

"But why? And what kind of war? Is this just a god thing, or—"

"The Great King has forbidden her children from interfering," my father cut in. "Our Courts will lend us no official aid. But it is a war, all the same, and we are the pieces they will use to fight it."

I pinched my nose. "Can you please just come out and say what's going on?"

He looked over his shoulder at me. The lights caught him weird; half his face remained in shadow. He had the face of a man carved from flint. "A rival Court has taken Helen."

I went to the minibar and picked out a beer. Felt like I was going to need it. My father made no move to stop me. To be honest, having the cold tin against my hand helped me think.

"But why?" I said. "I don't get it."

"Because a beautiful young man caught the eye of the Queen

of Flame, and she promised him an equally beautiful bride if he named her the fairest of all the gods," my father said. He looked to the fish again. "The only woman suitable was apparently your aunt Helen."

"How does Helen feel about all this?" I asked. "Did the Queen of Flame compel her to leave? I mean, you don't just grant someone a wife without consulting her. Kind of bullshit if you did."

"Watch your tongue when you speak of them," he said. I frowned, but he kept going. "We don't know what Helen thinks of it. We haven't been able to speak with her. But from the interviews, she seems perfectly happy with her new husband, Paris."

I winced and took a sip of my beer. Can't tell you how nice it was to have something fizzy and bitter to focus on instead of...well, everything. Helped me think. "So...why are we going to war? I mean, I get that Menny's upset, but if she's happy with this new guy, then that's her choice, yeah?"

"Because your uncle went to all of his mates and told them what had happened," said my father. He turned to face me—hands held behind his back. "All of them. Including the demigods."

"Oh."

You could not trust a demigod farther than you could throw them. Literally all they cared about in the world was glory. Every single one of them was somehow a bigger, more pompous arsehole than the last. And if Menny had gone and told them that his wife had been stolen away, well...

They'd want to fight.

"It happens that young Paris serves a Court just as we do. It also happens that your uncle's friends all swore Law-bound oaths that they would come to his aid should anything happen to Helen. They all wanted to marry her, so they swore to defend her to keep the peace between themselves. But the situation is more complicated now."

The pieces were starting to fall into place. I drank half the beer in one go. We were…real deep in it, weren't we?

"They're fighting the other Court's demigods, aren't they?" I said. "They're challenging them, so that brings all their godly parents into it, and…"

"A mess," my father said with a nod. "You see now why it was a problem money could not solve. Helen refuses all offers to return, and Paris will not even entertain them. The demigods seem to think that hauling her out of there bodily will solve matters…"

"But that's—"

"Impossibly stupid. I know," my father said. As he nodded, I could see the dark circles beneath his eyes. "I managed to convince them to keep their fighting in the Courts, at least. And given that Helen is a demigod herself—"

"Wait, really?" I said. I leaned forward on the sofa. "But she's never said as much. And they're so damn loud about what they are."

My father shrugged. "What's the saying these days? She's 'built different.'"

Despite the nausea and the awfulness of the moment, I couldn't help but laugh. I mean, really. He sounded so ridiculous!

He smiled a little in turn. "At any rate, if she's going to make a decision one way or another, they'll be able to reach her there. Wherever she is."

I looked down at the near-empty can in my hand. This was all so...dumb. Just some blokes arguing over a girl when it came down to it. One who seemed happier elsewhere. But it was going to get ugly if the demigods were getting into it, and that would make *everything* messy. Gods were as protective of their children as any good parent would be.

"Be on the lookout over the next few days," my father said. "We're anticipating some level of counterattack from the other Court's representatives. Trade deals..."

"Or a cyberattack," I finished. It was the only reason he would want me, in particular, to pay attention. I rolled my shoulders. "I'll keep an eye out."

My father walked to the door. "Iphigenia?"

"Yeah?"

He stood there for a while, studying me. I couldn't read his expression very well. Maybe it was the shadows that clung to him. Maybe it was the beard he'd clearly not trimmed masking what I knew of his features. Maybe...

Maybe it's just hindsight.

"I'll be by in the morning," he said. "We have a meeting with one of the gods about this."

I raised a brow. "Didn't you say they were staying out of it?"

"You know how they can be," he said. "Parents tend to defend their children. And there are plenty demigods looking for a little trouble."

He stood there, and he almost said something to me, but after a moment he closed his mouth again and left.

I have often wondered what it was he was going to tell me. Was he going to warn me? If he told me to run, would I have listened?

You might think to yourself that I went to bed. After all, we started this little tale with me being awake in the wee hours, and after speaking with my father, it was nearly midnight.

I did not. I wanted to. I can't tell you how badly I wanted to; how sluggish I felt, how heavy my limbs. My focus *craters* when I stay up this long.

But I couldn't sleep, and I knew it was useless to try. My mind was racing even as my body did its best to make my life difficult. At times like these I imagined that I was like a pilot in one of those giant robot anime. My mech was state of the art when it worked—but more often than not I was slapping the consoles of my mind, begging the damn thing to take a single step.

Coffee helped, though, so I stopped by the company café and got myself some more. They mostly keep things locked up except for a fridge at the back labeled for me. I've wandered down there enough that they leave me regular offerings of cold brew. I guess I'm as mystical to them as the gods are to most people.

The mug my mother had sent for sat already empty on my desk when I returned. Within a couple of hours this new mug of cold brew joined it, shoved to the side as I turned my attention to our security.

Most of the time my job is boring or frustrating or some combination of the two. I sit in my room listening to people play through my favorite video games while I answer emails, order supplies, and remote into people's workstations to restore deleted files or run support. I do it at all hours because it keeps me busy at all hours; it's good to have something to do when the night starts to stretch on and all your friends go to bed.

This night was different.

The requests poured in one after the other, so many and so quick that the notification pings blared in my ears like a war siren. I had to mute the thing for the first time in my life. *Everyone* was having trouble. Every single department. Dozens of sites for our products and businesses were down; contact forms flooded with AI slop; inboxes absolutely stuffed to the brim with bots. It was a *madhouse*. One request normally takes me anywhere from five minutes to an hour to sort, depending on how intense it was. Here I found myself ignoring the simplest ones entirely. How else could I keep up?

People locked out of their accounts were going to have to wait until I could make sure there was still a database of accounts to draw from.

There were plenty of nights, working that job, when I wanted to bang my head against my counter until I felt the sweet embrace of unconsciousness. People are stupid about technology. The number of times that I've patiently worked through a support call only to discover that someone hadn't plugged in their bloody mouse would boggle your mind.

But this night? Oh, this night I couldn't even focus on my stupid Twitch streams. There was just too much going on. I'd be in the middle of recovering a database only for someone to message me that the lighting system in their offices had been hacked. Whoever did it was making a rave of the building—flash flash flash, sirens blaring.

I mean—it was awful stuff.

I wasn't the only person who worked IT, of course, but I was the fastest to respond. My colleagues were drowning in their work, and I had to cover for them, too, as we tried to figure out which IPs we needed to block, which things to restore, which were now infected with whatever virus they'd snuck onto our system.

By the time a slice of light cut through my curtains and onto my dual monitors, we had a good idea where it was coming from. One of the hackers had left a .txt uploaded onto our servers even after we'd undone most of their wanton carnage.

Know that you will never again know the face of beauty so long as Priam of Troy lives.

Honestly, it was kind of cringe. Like, what kind of script kiddie leaves threats like that? It's just so stupid. But it was the kind of stupid that made you want to track them down and make every keystroke play ultra loud, ultra condensed duck quacks in response.

Not that I could do that. My talents didn't lie with offensive work: I spent all my time learning how to keep the company safe.

But I *really wanted* to do it. I even went and downloaded the duck quacks just in case I got the chance.

Still—when I saw that slice of light I knew my time was coming up short. It was the shock I needed to try to shower and get ready for whichever god it was we were going to meet. The text on the screen was little more than a bleary mess; the music I'd been listening to rang in my ears as I took off my headset. Flecks of fake leather clung to my hair from its worn headband. I needed to get a new one. Maybe when all of this was over.

I stood and went for the shower—but to my surprise, I found that I was not alone in my nerd chamber.

There, standing behind me like a fucking horror movie villain, was the Swift Lord. The golden light of the morning did nothing to hide the quicksilver nature of his skin; it only lent the gentle lines of his lithe muscles all the more emphasis. He was nude save for a wrap around his waist. Like most gods, he wore a mask to keep me from seeing his face. His was the most modern of them all: a projected grid of pixels that he used to display different emoji. He was hitting me with an old-school smiley this time.

"My lord," I stammered. When you don't know why they've shown up, you have to be careful with them. No mask can fully hide their sharp teeth or their alien nature. "I wasn't expecting to see you. My father mentioned a meeting, but I had no idea you'd be so... personal."

The pixels jumbled into a big grin. He spread his arms wide

toward my room. "You really live like this, don't you? How old are those cups, Iphy?"

He was the only God that called me that. Never quite sat right with me. Not that I could say as much. "If I had known your lordship was going to pay me a visit, I would have cleaned up."

He walked over to one of my video game statues and picked it up. The dragon, for which I'd paid a couple hundred dollars, looked shabby in his hands.

"Eh, I like it better that you didn't," he said. He poked the dragon's scales with his silver finger. "Your people have strange ideas about what a mythic beast should look like."

I gritted my teeth. Of all the gods, there were only two who were actively a pain to deal with. This was one of them. The other, the Lord of Merriment, was unfortunately one of our biggest money makers. "Is your lordship here for...sightseeing reasons?"

He set the dragon down and picked up another one of my figures—this time one of my favorite Crystal Dragon Knight XIV characters. Without a care for the hours I'd spent carefully posing her, he started moving her around all willy-nilly.

"You could say that. I wanted to visit you. Is that so strange?"

"Forgive me if I err, my lord, but I thought that the Courts were restricted to the top floor unless they were on official business."

The pixel eyes on his mask rolled, and the face huffed a big, dramatic sigh. "You're so tiresome when you talk about rules."

Rules were often the only thing that kept the gods from eating us or worse. I knew that better than most. Oh, sure, they wear human shapes. But if you forget for one second that they enjoy our flesh the way we enjoy a nice succulent leg of lamb, you'll be roasting on a spit before you know it.

"It's a burden to be tiresome, but someone has got to do it," I said. "And I wouldn't want your lordship to waste any of his precious time. I'm sure there are important messages you're carrying."

He set down my figure, now doing a painfully outdated dab, and looked at me. Two sharp angles appeared above the smiley face.

"I have a message for you from a very unusual client," he said.

When you're exhausted, people often assume that your heart can't race. It can. In fact, it races more than it rests. I was already on edge when this god showed up—and to hear that there was a message for *me* sent me into overdrive.

"What the *fuck* do you mean, there's a message for me?" I said. Then I pinched my nose. Shit. You aren't supposed to curse around them; they take it as an insult sometimes—

The Swift Lord laughed. It sounded like the clatter of a keyboard mixed with windchimes—eerie and discordant, but kind of pleasant in its own way. "See, you can be fun."

I looked at him. "I would really appreciate it if you told me. I've had a very long day and a half, my lord."

"I'm sure that you have," he said. "But it's only going to get longer, so I won't make you sweat."

You don't turn your back on a tiger, and you shouldn't turn your back on a god. But the way he was talking made me consider it. I crossed my arms.

"I can count on one hand the number of times the Queen of the Wild has depended on me to convey her wishes. Normally she'd let her brother do it. Well, perhaps better to say that he'd anticipate her needing to talk with someone other than a heaping husk of fur and muscle and communicate whatever it was she needed to that person. I mean, she's the worst."

He scoffed then, like he was a stand-up comedian in the middle of a story. It didn't matter to him that I was starting to sweat. What the hell did the Queen of the Wild have to do with me? I'd only met her once or twice when my father was otherwise occupied and she showed up with her furs. We hadn't spoken much—I got the impression that she hated talking and didn't press her.

"All of that to say, Iphy, that you should count yourself fortunate. At least for now."

I raised a brow. "What do you mean for now?"

"The Queen has a message for you so simple that I wonder why she's bothering to say it. Profound, though," he said, waving a finger in the air. Then he beat his chest and continued. "I have two questions for Iphigenia Pelops. The first is: Are you happy? And the second: Who do you trust?"

My mouth hung open. Was this some sort of joke? "That's it?"

"That is it. But I am to wait for the responses," he said. He mimed checking a watch; the pixels on his mask shifted to mimic a clock. "Tick-tock, Iphy."

I had a lot of questions about all of this, but I knew better than to keep a god waiting. Particularly the Queen of the Wild. Whenever we'd met, she had the aura of a woman who, any moment now, would decide I'd caused too much trouble for my own good. An animal pacing an enclosure.

"All of my family's fortune is bound to turn to misfortune if I set foot out of this place. Happiness was never meant for me—it was meant for my siblings," I said. Lying to the gods was generally unwise; they could sense when you did, and most of them took it as an insult. "And as for who I trust: My siblings. My parents. My family, I guess, that's the easy answer. Just say my family."

"I have to say it exactly as you said it. Stuttering and all."

"Do you really?"

"I do," he answered, his pixel face a wide grin. "Thank you for answering so promptly, though. And for what it's worth, you have my sympathies on your less-than-happy life. I hope it doesn't trouble you much longer."

"What do you mean—"

But as I took a step toward him, a flash of silver light filled the room. I was left to shield my eyes from the glare. By the time shapes and figures came back into view, he was gone.

I stared at my stupid, dabbing figure.

The Queen of the Wild wanted to know if I was happy.

But why...?

I showered and put on my favorite hoodie.

My father was probably going to tell me that I needed to be "presentable" when we were talking to the gods, and that was *going* to be true when I became the head of the company. Until that day, I figured I had a little leeway. It was my father who was making the deals, after all. Why should I have to crawl into a suit just to impress people who weren't sure of the current century's fashion?

So it was my favorite hoodie, comfortable slacks, and trainers that I wore. And when my father saw me, he said nothing.

Not a word. Only a stare that I couldn't quite read.

Down the hall we went. My father took me to the business elevator, the one that led to the levels only he and I should ever visit.

"Have I ever told you how much I've enjoyed being your father?"

"No, because no one talks that way," I said, rolling my eyes.

"It comes from our terrible socialization," he said. The smile changed, became more genuine, and he shook his head. "You don't talk like a normal person, either."

"Oh, because I know what a meme is? Sod off, old man," I said with a smirk. "The internet's free, you know."

"It isn't," he said. The elevator rang. The doors opened not to a plush corporate interior but to a swirling void of black. He stepped in without any hesitation. I followed, all of *my* hesitation politely bottled in my chest.

This elevator didn't go up or down—it went *elsewhere*. When the doors closed around you there was no weird gravity sensation, no vague mechanical humming. None of that. Even the buttons were different. Instead of flat things with numbers on them, they're little holes with bits of different Domains in them.

My father plucked moss from one of the buttons. He handed some to me and ate the rest. I stared at the silvery-green on my palm. The Court of the Wild? I didn't have a choice in the matter, so I ate it, but I had questions.

And it seemed she had questions for me, too. "The Queen of the Wild," I said. "That's... unusual."

He kept his eye trained on the slit between the doors. "I won't lie to you. Times are desperate."

"I got the feeling," I said.

Around us there was perfect silence.

The doors opened again. Gone were all the trappings of a Sydney high-rise, all signs of architecture. We were in the Wild now. A full moon hung overhead, illuminating a tangle of trees that seemed more at home in one of those goth movies than in real life. No leaves clung to the branches. Black against black, sharp against sharp, the strange forest loomed ahead of us.

"Keep pace with me," my father said. "If you get lost here, we won't be able to find you."

He didn't need to tell me twice.

"I've made some mistakes, Iphigenia," he said.

Just what I wanted to hear as a wolf howled in the distance. "A-are we lost?" I ventured.

"The company is," he answered. If the wildlife bothered him—the glowing eyes watching from the brambles, the scent of raw meat in the air—he gave no sign of it. "We're facing down a terrible time. An uncertain future."

Something huge and furred bumped against me. I bit down a yelp—you couldn't show weakness in the Courts—and jumped away. But as we walked, I felt the low rumble of its breathing. It was following us.

"I'm twenty-five next year," I said. "I can formally take on the title then. M-maybe I should start now?"

I didn't want to. Truth be told, I never did, but I knew I had to at some point. My father couldn't keep doing all that work on his own. The older you got, the easier it was to slip up on the intricate contracts the Courts demanded of us.

My father laid a hand on a blackberry bush as if it were a curtain. The thorns bit into the flesh of his palm. Blood trailed down the stems and coated the berries. He looked back at me with an awful, profound regret.

"I'm afraid that isn't possible," he said. He moved the branches aside, exposing a clearing beyond them. "This way."

By then the chill in the forest had frozen my blood, too. My throat felt tight. What was going on? This...this didn't feel like a normal meeting.

But I couldn't run away. Not then. I was too worried about what would happen to my siblings if something went wrong here. I'd always known my life wasn't going to be a normal one, but theirs could be, if I did my job right.

So I stepped through into the clearing.

And that was the first time I saw her in her element.

How do you describe her? How could you? It's like trying to describe the changing faces of the moon. The second I laid eyes on her, I knew something in my life was about to change. She wasn't even looking at me at the time, but I felt it all the same. A predator. A knife in the dark, an antler at my throat. I couldn't tell which parts of her were hers and which belonged to the landscape around us. That massive animal that had followed me along stood at her side.

She, for her part, was standing over the corpse of...something. Even with the moonlight I couldn't be sure what it was. Human shaped, yes, but not human. Too big for that. A god of some kind? No—they don't have organs, and this one clearly did. The animal by her side was gnawing at them. The victim's skin was molten silver, a scrap of fur tossed over their face. From the dark splatter beneath the fur I guessed there wasn't much face left. The being wore intricately woven clothes in dark geometric patterns; in one of its three arms was a bloodied, curved sword.

If this were a story, I'd have said something quippy about the whole thing. Some joke about a full moon, maybe, since her furs left that part of her uncovered. But I'll tell you the truth, Psy—I was too terrified to talk. I watched her drive a knife into that person's body and carve them up, and I could not move or talk or even think.

All I could do was watch her. This woman who wanted to know if I was happy.

Because she was beautiful in all her horrors. As beautiful as blood on snow.

"Great Queen of the Wild, Lord of Hunters, Arrow-Thrower—I have come as requested," my father said to her.

The Queen of the Wild did not stir. A gout of arterial blood painted her cheek as she cut into the victim's chest.

My father looked to me. "You remember the formalities."

Oh, like it was easy. I was watching a being from another

dimension carve into something I had never seen before, and he wanted me to offer her a beer.

But—I've never been one to shy away from familial duty. I took a breath to try to steady my nerves.

"Great Queen of the Wild, Lord of the Hunters," I began. But I couldn't just say exactly what my father had said, so I tried to pivot. "Most beautiful, it is an honor to make your acquaintance. My name is—"

"Iphigenia," the Queen rumbled, and at that moment she carved the soul from my body as easily as flesh from bone. When I was too stunned to continue, she hummed. "We've met. Do not pretend otherwise."

"I-I was just trying to be humble," I said.

"You *think* that humility suits you," said the Queen. She set the knife down beside her. "It does not."

It was then she stood. And it was not graceful. Vertebra by vertebra she lifted herself up, muscles shifting beneath the skin, until she loomed so high over me that I had to tilt my head to take her in. There was no hope of seeing the moon or the stars—she blocked them out just by standing.

Not that I had need of the moon with her eyes burning so bright.

"Agamemnon of the House of Pelops," she said—yet she kept her eyes on me. "Is this the dearest thing you possess?"

My father answered without hesitation. "She is. The apple of my eye."

I wasn't sure how much longer I could bear that woman staring down at me. My knees trembled.

"Are you...willing?" she asked me.

"W-what?" I said. "I-I, uh—"

Only then did she turn away. Her hand shot out like an arrow, her fingers closed around my father's throat. I screamed and jumped back.

"You haven't told her. Coward. *Coward!*" she roared.

Before I could protest, she flung him away as easily as a child flinging their phone across the room. He landed in the blackberry bush with a sickening crack.

"Y-you... What did you do? We didn't break any compacts, we haven't hurt you—" I started. No amount of training could have shut me up.

I was walking toward my father when she laid a hand on my shoulder. It was heavy—so heavy! Like wrought iron. I let out a terrified sound and froze up.

"Tell her, Agamemnon," she said.

And so my father did just that. Righting himself from among the thorns of the blackberry bush, he adjusted his tie and smoothed over his hair. Bruises stained his face. Already one of his cheekbones swelled like overripe fruit. But he was smiling. I'll always remember that. He was smiling as he said it.

"Iphy, dear," he said, "the family needs a sacrifice, and I'm afraid it's going to be you."

Chapter Three

Back in ancient times people used to train for a job their whole lives. In Greece they had these runners who could cover huge distances in a couple days at most. To find people who could not only run that long but do it over rocks and brambles and hills, they had to take them young. Any kid running around the agora ran a risk of being plucked away from his safe life to become one of these messengers. Sure, it was a lofty position, a holy one, but when they were climbing those mountains barefoot for the third time in a week—do you think those kids were happy?

I can tell you that I wasn't.

The first time my parents told me to think of my life as less of a life and more of a service I was fifteen. Orestes was maybe three, and Ellie just starting to speak in sentences. I found Ori slobbering all over my laptop. The two of us were having a bit of a tussle when my father pulled us apart.

"Iphigenia, you have to give your siblings your things when they ask for them," my mum said.

"But they're *my* things!" I said. "What's he going to do with it, anyway? Check his stock portfolio?"

My mother shook her head. "They're the family's things. You serve the family. That's why you're so important, sweetheart; we can only do what we do because of you and your father. Show him how to use it and we'll get him something more age appropriate for tomorrow."

I looked up at him then with his placid smile and his jet-black eyes, and I thought to myself, *I don't wanna be a freak when I grew up.* So I kicked him in the shins and cried about it.

But the rules never changed. The Law never changed. The Heir of the House of Pelops serves the house. Over and over I heard that line. If I do not, all our fortunes become misfortunes.

Serving wasn't so bad if I didn't think about it too much. My siblings got to live their normal lives, and I—well, I had the internet and more money than I knew what to do with, what was there to worry about? At some point I'd succeed my father and have to run this company, but until then it was smooth-ish sailing.

Until now.

Limp and weak-kneed I fell to the ground. The Queen hooked an arm beneath my shoulder to keep me from hurting myself.

My father walked to me. He was slow about it, careful like. He took my hands. Behind me, the Queen twitched.

"I know," he said. "I know. It's so much to bear. If there were any other way, Iph, I'd take it, but there's nothing to be done. We need a sacrifice."

Sometimes you don't notice you're crying until you try to speak. "Why?" I creaked.

"There was a prophecy from the King of Song. If we of the House of Pelops do not sacrifice that which is dearest to us, our patrons have no hope of victory. If you are not sacrificed, your aunt Helen will never return home, your uncle will lose his wife, and all our fortune will turn to misfortune." He gestured to the Queen. "The Queen has volunteered to take you."

I drew away, and she let me. Like a child I scrabbled backward across the dirt path, away from the both of them.

"Is that true?" I asked.

The Queen sank down onto her haunches. With her legs spread, darkness was her only concealment. The antlers, the burning eyes, the bow at her back, and the dog at her side—there was no mistaking who this woman was. A predator.

And I was the prey, wasn't I?

"It is not false," she answered. Like teeth around my throat, that voice. "I'm afraid so. For what it's worth, I'm sorry."

"But why me?" I said. I'm not too proud to admit I was whimpering. "Why does it have to be me?"

She loped forward on her knuckles. The beads and feathers tied to her antlers swayed, and I realized that most of the beads were really carved bones and teeth.

"Ask him," she said.

My attention shot to him. "Dad. Dad, why...?"

He stood and dusted himself off. "Like I said, there's nothing for it. It has to be what's dearest to me. And if it isn't you, it's your siblings."

The woman I had thought so beautiful was coming toward me like a wolf, and my father was threatening my siblings if I didn't sacrifice myself.

So I said the first thing that came to mind—the thing I'd heard over and over. It wasn't so much something I wanted as it was a reflex.

"The Heir of Pelops serves the House of Pelops."

The Queen rumbled. "Are you willing?"

Was I?

I glanced to my father. Already he had turned away. I saw what I thought was the flare of a lighter. He had mostly given up smoking. Seeing him revert to it now... it was an odd kind of comfort. Like an admission that he'd been putting on a brave face for me. I wondered if his hands shook.

"What will you do with me?" I asked. If I was about to die, then I might as well know how. Maybe that would make it less scary to confront my death.

But was I scared, really? What I felt then wasn't exactly fear. Something else. Something that changed when I looked at her, like clouds shifting over the face of the moon.

The Queen came to me as quick as an arrow. Then, to my surprise, she touched her forehead to mine. "Hunt."

A chase, then? At least it would be an interesting way to go. Part of me always assumed I'd die heaped over in the plush meeting chairs my father kept in the office. My office, by then, where I'd spend most of my life serving the duties thrust upon me. A chase with the Goddess of the Hunt was heroic in comparison.

Her mouth was still slick with gore. When her breath washed over me, I could smell the death clinging to her.

Death that would come for me before too long. Would it hurt, whatever she did to me? When she caught me and sank those teeth into my bare neck, when she tore my throat out—would it hurt?

Or would she put me out of my misery by then?

I had to admit there was a fair bit of misery already. In spite of all the things I had going for me—the money, the fame, the siblings who loved me—my days felt empty more often than not. What did I really have to look forward to except a job I never chose?

Dying was the easy thing. I hoped that she'd make it easy.

No, I wasn't afraid.

In the end there had never been hope of anything else for me. It was a life of boardroom meetings and simpering to the will of the Guests—or it was this.

"I'm willing," I said.

And then I was gone.

The Queen wrapped me in black. This wasn't the black of night, no—this was an absolute black. All I knew and all I could know came from my other senses. I was sure, for instance, that something was carrying me by the scruff of my hoodie. Every breath made pine and cedar grow on my tongue. Behind me the great beast's breath rumbled and growled.

Was I already dead?

When I fell out of the dark and felt my back slap against the trunk of a massive tree, I have to tell you, it was a relief. Pain made sense. Getting your bell rung, there's something noble to it in the right contexts. It gave me something to focus on.

But when I saw the Queen... What does an aging gazelle feel when it spots a lion?

She grabbed me around the waist, like a sack, and laid me out on a giant tree stump. Smooth, sharp bone sailed across my skin as the Queen cut through my hoodie and shirt. Gooseflesh rose wherever she touched. And yet, the whole time, staring up at the Queen... I wasn't scared. I wasn't excited.

I was grateful.

Yes, that's it. The gazelle knows it's got to die. Did you know that? A gazelle, when it gets old enough, will stay behind on purpose while the others graze. One day they wake up and that's it. They stay behind. The lion goes straight for them and ignores all of the rest.

It's just nature.

Her bone knife on my skin. Her eyes boring into mine. I was bare before her in every way that mattered. The Heir of Pelops doing her best and most final duty.

When she was done she laid the tip of the knife at my collarbone.

"I asked after your happiness."

As the knife pressed down and drew the first bead of red blood, I looked up at that feral, unknowable face, and I said, "You did."

Her expression went cloudy, her mouth twisting into a line. "You said that you were not."

She was so close to me. Every breath I took was full of her. "Why did you ask? Did you know?"

"Yes," she said. She made a sound somewhere between disgust and pity. "You said you trusted them."

"I do. Did." The drop of blood rolled down my chest.

"Iphigenia," she said. How heady my name sounded coming from her. "Will you trust me?"

What a thing to ask at a time like this. And yet I was so full of worry and revelation and fear that the answer was clear to me.

"Yeah. Why not? Sure. Just make it quick."

I closed my eyes. If I was going to die—well, I couldn't have asked for a better reason, or a better person to do it. Soon the knife would press through my heart and end all of this, and soon we'd share something only the Wild understood.

In the end, the knife never came for me.

Vines snapped. The world shifted. She hauled me up off the stump and set me down on my feet.

"You will hunt," she said.

And then—darkness.

Chapter Four

Waking up in the middle of a forest all on your lonesome is pretty shit.

Now, I know what you're thinking: There are plenty of days you'd *like* to wake up in a forest. You're thinking it's *scenic*. People *pay money* to do this. They traipse halfway or sometimes all the way across a country just to visit a particular forest they think will be the nicest to wake up in. It's a whole thing.

Well, there are a couple differences between what happened to me and what happens with most people. You see, most people are *camping*. They have their little cabins all set up with their portable generators if they're the pampered type. If they're more adventurous it's a tent and a sleeping bag. Only the most hardcore types go out with no gear at all, people who have trained their whole lives to learn how to do just that.

So the first difference is that when I woke up in the woods, I had only the cut-up clothes on my back and whatever was in the pockets of my hoodie. So I had to retie the thing just to get back to square one. Let me tell you, it's not easy to re-tie a shirt together in a way that doesn't look daft.

The second difference is that I'd never had any wilderness training at all. Not unless you count some survival horror games. I'm pretty good at those. *Dead by Daylight* especially—have you tried that one? Anyway, it's not relevant. This wasn't a game.

And the third difference between me and most folks? Before that day I'd never even seen the bare sky overhead.

For a little while the sky was the only thing I cared about. I couldn't even process the rest of it. I didn't care that I was lying on a "bed" of moss and branches and dirt, that my family had maybe left me for dead, that I didn't know how to cook things unless they came in microwave-safe containers. I didn't care about any of that. The shittiness of my shituation was but a distant thought somewhere buried deep in the folds of my brain.

Because the sky was that beautiful to me.

I'd seen the sky in the movies. I'd seen it on shows. When I played games, if I could mod them, I always made sure to track down the prettiest skybox I could find, so that my characters could look up and see what I couldn't. Oh, I got a bit of it sometimes. I loved opening the curtains at night and looking out over the city—wondering what it'd be like to be down there on the streets looking up into the dark. But there was always a layer of glass between me and the sky. We couldn't afford windows that opened, you see. Not for monetary reasons. Just, at some point some other Pelops firstborn had gotten too desperate for freedom and... Well, we can't have windows that open.

Can't say the thought hadn't crossed my mind once or twice. What would it mean to be swallowed up by all that blue? To feel wind, real wind, against my face? It wasn't like I had any friends who would miss me.

But then I thought how mad Ori would be at having to stay inside for the rest of his life, and I made my peace with the windows.

Lying there on all that loam, though...I didn't need to fall. The sky was right up ahead. A beautiful, shifting, scintillating blue. The longer I stared at it, the more my eyes hurt. Through the canopy of trees I watched the clouds drift overhead, fluffier than I could have imagined. The light shifted this way and that, and I *loved* it. I loved the way the sun felt on my face. You know how you can feel the sun even with your eyes closed? How your skin sort of tingles? I'd never felt that before.

And the sounds! Birds flapping their wings, rustling leaves, the wind. A high-rise is alive in its own way with the hum of conversation, ringing phones, and pacing, but the outside world was something totally new. I could *smell* things here—and not all of them nice! Sure, I loved the light, bright, piercing scent of the trees all around, the faint traces of fire. But turns out dried blood kind of stinks when you leave it out too long. And whatever it was that lived in that place had made its presence known already. The longer I lay there, the more I could pick out the unpleasant, the weird smells along with the nice ones.

But I was so giddy that it didn't matter to me.

I don't know how long I lay there. It felt like forever. But I can tell you what finally woke me to the shittiness of the situation.

I didn't notice it at first, clever little bugger that it was. Lying down with my eyes closed, how could I have known that there was something coming? I mean, obviously I could have heard it. But I didn't know that I had to listen. So it sauntered closer, taking its time, sniffing at the air... Maybe it thought I was dead. I was close enough, by most people's definition.

I didn't notice the fox until I felt its nose against my skin. Cool, soft, a little like leather. Wet leather.

"What the...?"

When I opened my eyes, there it was: a black fox, white fur like ash across its forehead, staring right back at me. As I stirred it drew back its lips and snarled.

Shit.

I did what anyone would do: I screamed and grabbed a stick I saw on the ground. Look big, right? I waved it around in front of me like a sword.

"Go on!" I shouted. "Get away from here!"

The fox stayed put. Growled louder, even.

"Don't make me hurt you, you little troublemaker. I will!"

My tongue stuck to the roof of my mouth... until it sprang alive all at once and spoke without my knowing.

"Queen of the Wild! You better be around here somewhere!"

The fox stepped down, onto the brush, its eyes still locked on mine. Its plush black fur was all a-bristle, its red tongue gnashing over its teeth.

"I know you can hear me!" I shouted, backing up. A twig snapped under my feet, and it occurred to me that maybe I should have picked better footwear for this journey. Wherever I was.

The fox didn't have any trouble. It kept right on sauntering forward. Mouth open, mouth closed. A low rumble in its throat, building, building.

"You didn't leave me alone here. I know you wouldn't do that."

I did not, in fact, know that—but unlike gods, I can lie as much as I want.

I swung the branch again, backed up again. Found myself up against the cool bark of a tree.

But then I spotted a second of the little guys loping out from the woods. And a third. And a fourth.

One fox I could maybe deal with. Four?

All I had was a stick!

And I know what you're thinking: you were so *resigned* the night before this, Iph. You were ready to die. Why the worry now, why the fear?

Here's the thing: I was ready to die when I knew death would be quick and easy.

These foxes? They'd tear me apart bit by bit. I'd feel every second of it. No matter how little I feared death, I *really* feared pain.

"Queen of the Wild, I, Iphigenia of the House of Pelops, beseech you!"

The words rang out in the cold air. The foxes closed in, a half circle of fang and fur around me, and I swung the branch again.

Only for her to catch it. She'd appeared in the falling of a leaf. Like a great wolf before a lap dog in comparison to me—the furs she wore made her seem larger than she already was, every inch of her corded with hard-earned muscle. The wind that blew through the clearing set the ornaments hanging from her antlers to drift. It also blew something of her feral scent straight toward me.

The Queen didn't say a word. All she did was grunt. The foxes scattered like terrified interns back into the comfortable embrace of the forest.

"Thank you," I started, but she didn't let me finish.

"Too quick," she said. The bright morning light couldn't hope to touch her veil. Impenetrable night hung over her face beneath the swaying bits of bone and feather she used to baffle her divine features.

"Foxes are pretty quick, I guess. Never really thought about it until now. Where are we?" I said.

"Not the foxes," she said. She slapped a hand against the bark behind me. Three heads taller than I was, she had to contort to bring us eye to eye. Most gods hate doing that—they know how seeing them affects us, and they try to avoid causing that harm. Not her. Two moons burned against the blazing blue sky. "You. Too quick."

I swallowed. "Can you try to speak in more than one syllable? Maybe?"

In the shifting of the dark, I thought I saw the flash of teeth. "I brought you here to learn."

"Learn what? How to run from foxes?"

"To be a handmaiden. To survive," said the Queen. "You need to learn."

"You can't be serious," I said. "A handmaiden? What does that even mean? I'm supposed to be dead. That's what my family wants and... that's what's best for them. They need me dead, right? So why bother with any of this?"

Death I had already accepted. I was ready for it! What was all that with the knife and the altar for if not for killing me? Had she just been putting on a show? Breaking the Law was a huge deal. Even gods will die if they go against their oaths; it goes against the core of their being. Forget me dying—wasn't the Queen putting herself at risk, too?

If I just died, this would be easier. If I just wasn't here, it'd be easier. No one would have to risk anything at all.

She put a hand over my mouth. "You will not die for them."

I wanted to speak. I wanted to say, "But if they need me to, then who am I to say no?"

But I couldn't. I couldn't speak, and even if I could, I didn't know if I could bring myself to say that. It hurt too much.

So I didn't say anything at all. I just looked at her—into the velvet dark around her face, the features I could barely see, the disks of her eyes.

She touched her forehead to mine. "You will find your way out here. In the woods. Life will find you."

The voice that had only minutes ago sounded harsh was now soft as the sea lapping at the sand. Fear's high tide ebbed away, leaving only a salt line to show it had been there at all.

"You will learn. But it will not be easy."

She lowered her hand.

"If I need you..."

"Call. I will come," she answered. "But only once a day. Any more and it is too easy."

"Too easy? I don't know what I'm doing at all. I've never even been outside, let alone wherever this is—"

"Somewhere safe," answered the Queen.

"I literally just got attacked by a pack of foxes. You'll forgive me if I don't exactly agree with your ladyship's threat assessment."

"Hrrm," answered the Queen. It was a low rumble, an animal sound, and one I was beginning to recognize meant she was thinking. "I...am trying to help. There is a lot on my mind. Much to deal with in the Courts."

How could she think any of this is normal? Gods above and below, I knew they could be a little detached from reality, but come on. I guess if you live and breathe hunting it doesn't sound so hard. My blood was pumping and my head spinning and I kept thinking of all the stories I'd seen where people died in the bush after only a couple of days but sure, fine. Let's stay out here with no training. That sounds reasonable.

"I don't know if this is...I mean, you're dumping me in the middle of nowhere out here."

"You're safe," she repeated. Then, after thinking about it for a moment, she flicked the tip of her nose and added: "From the others."

Oh, good. I hadn't even considered that rogue god attacks might end up being a problem. Good to know I was safe from that threat I had literally never had to consider before.

Why didn't she just let me die? Now I was going to have to struggle against...all of this.

"And from the animals?" I said. "You could protect me from them if you wanted. You could give me some kind of blessing so I don't have to worry about getting attacked, if it really is important to you that I stay out here for whatever reason. I can't believe I'm entertaining this. Maybe I'm already dead."

That grunt again. She grabbed my jaw and tilted it up toward her. She was so quick! I knew deep in the pit of my stomach that she could eat me whenever she wanted. But she held me like a bird she'd found wounded in the bush.

"Iphigenia," she said.

My heart skipped a beat.

"Please try. I will try, too. And I promise that I will explain when I have the time—but please, I would like if you tried. For a few days if nothing else."

And when she put it that way—when she was so gentle with me—how could I refuse? My arguments fell away like a winter coat of fur at the turn of seasons.

I could promise a few days.

"Okay," I said. "But only because you're asking nicely."

Standing alone in the forest as I was after she left, I wouldn't have believed that this was the easy part. What was easy about having to live in the woods? Maybe if you'd had training it could be.

I was just... some girl.

When she left me alone in the clearing, it was like something in me had been yanked away. A cord to which I'd been clinging. The world seemed bigger without her in it, but not in a way I liked. It was this awful sort of hollowness. If I lost focus for too long, I'd fall away into forever.

Couldn't think about my family. Couldn't wonder if Ori was getting briefed right this minute about his new duties. Couldn't wonder what my mum thought of any of this. Couldn't feel bad about leaving Ellie's promise unfulfilled.

If I started to think about it too much I would... Well, I wouldn't get anything done. And I had to keep going forward through this bullshit situation.

So I knelt down in the clearing and I tried to get my bearings. I grabbed a stick and started to write in the dirt.

First Order of Business:

I stared at the letters. The dirt already clinging to my hand was cold and wet and grimy. My stomach rumbled. How long had it been since I ate? I reached for my mobile. Maybe it still had some battery?

Fuck yeah it did. *8:49 a.m.* No signal, but that was all right. I didn't expect to have signal... wherever this was. I turned it off and stashed it in my pocket. Having a mobile was good—it meant I had a flashlight, whatever games I could get to load without service, a camera, and several gigs of bookmarked *Crystal Dragon Knight* fanfiction to pass the time.

Given that I didn't know how long I'd be out here.

"Stupid Queen," I mumbled. Then when good sense caught up to me: "I mean that in the nicest way possible."

I looked around the trees. When no foxes emerged, I got back to thinking of my list.

First Order of Business: Find Shelter.

Stabbing the stick into the ground to make the full stop, a little pride welled up in me, as if naming the goal was completing it. We were on a roll. What else did I need?

My stomach rumbled again.

Right.

Second Order of Business: Find Food.

Two nice, easy goals for the day. Couldn't be that hard, right?

I stood up and dusted my hands off. With the stick in hand I could *probably* chase off most small things if I tried, and if I saw anything big…well, I'd just run.

I promised I'd try, and that's what I set out to do.

All that was left was picking which way to go. There was the north, where the foxes had come from. Probably not a great idea to head *toward* carnivorous predators.

West? The trees that way thinned out, though I couldn't see more than five meters or so beyond where I was because there were thorny bushes. It was going to be a *massacre* without some way to cut through.

I liked my skin too much to sacrifice it here. South I saw heaps of rocks leading up to the biggest, heapingest rock of all: a mountain. My knees said no thank you.

East…?

That looked promising! There, the ground sloped away. Plenty of those big trees up ahead to give me cover from the sun, no bushes to be seen. Of course, the trees got denser that way, and if it got too dark in there I might get lost. Still, worth considering. But I couldn't make my decision without evaluating all my options. That would be *foolish*, and I wasn't a *fool*, just some girl lost alone in the woods without any survival implements or training who should maybe already be dead.

Nothing foolish about that.

East it was.

I picked two trees I liked the look of and walked between them. With every step I took, my feet almost bounced against the springy earth. Not that it made it any easier to walk when I was in so much pain from the hunt last night, but I did *like* the feeling. It was nothing like the plush carpets back home, nor the unyielding tiles of the kitchen and board rooms. Wind blew through the branches. The leaves and branches sang a whispering song, at once loud as the din of salesmen trying to close deals and as quiet as the whirr of the aircon. As time wore on, I had the thought that there were probably no people around for kilometers.

The thought stopped me in my tracks. Two followed in its wake.

The first: No one could help me if anything went wrong here. Well, the Queen could, but I'd already asked her for help once today. I couldn't ask again until tomorrow morning. If something happened between then and now, I'd have to deal with it on my own, be it a scrape or broken bone or who knows what else.

The second thought was the same thing in a different key: *I am alone out here.* I could do whatever I wanted, and there was no one to stop me. I could jump around as much as I wanted, tear off all my clothes and run naked through the woods, sing along as badly as I wanted to whatever song I wanted without my sister telling me I sounded like a strangled duck.

When people talk about the beauty of nature, this is part of what they mean. There are times when it hits you that you're all you have out there. Solitude's a frightening thing, sure. But having the chance to explore who you are when no one's looking is…incredible.

In the middle of the firs and the pines there was a giddy excitement brewing in my chest, a feeling as light as the fear along my spine was heavy.

"Hello?" I called.

I knew no one could hear me, but I shouted anyway. The hairs on the back of my neck stood on end. Part of me worried I would hear a voice or a growl or a roar.

But there was nothing. The syllables echoed over and over, the insects buzzed, and *no one gave a shit.*

"Hello!" I shouted.

Louder they echoed, louder they went. Birds took off from the branches overhead, and still no one gave a shit.

Laughter bubbled up inside me. "Hey! Is there anyone out there?!"

When I heard only the resonance of my own voice and the nittering of some small creatures, I broke down laughing.

Alone.

Really alone. And though I was aching and kind of cold and had just been threatened by foxes... I wasn't afraid. Not really. Hearing myself laugh like that my fear fell away, shed like old skin, and I stood in the comfort of my own company.

Who would have thought?

Chapter Five

Home turned out to be a cave.

See, I tried to figure other stuff out. On TV, in movies and games, everyone always makes a little lean-to and goes to bed beneath that. Leaves and moss for a blanket and pillow, and Bob's your uncle. Why not give that a go?

I'll tell you why: I didn't have a bloody knife. It's a lot harder to set those up when you can't chop away at the wood. For a while I picked up what sticks I could find and tried to make something out of those. I had maybe five or six good ones, and I thought that if I laid them against a tree the right way, then I could figure something out.

No dice.

I could hardly fit in the space I'd made. After I set the whole thing up, it was maybe half a meter tall, and narrower than that at the base. Like trying to fit yourself beneath a bunch of brooms that you'd leaned against a wall.

They didn't hold. Of course not. My shoulder brushed one as light as could be, and down came the whole thing.

A particularly knobby bit smacked me in the face. With my cheeks swelling and red, I swore, got up, and kicked the rest of the sticks.

I had to figure something else out.

The little clearing in which I'd made this home was nice enough—but it didn't offer much in the way of shelter except the trees themselves. Cold was already starting to nip at my cheeks and ears. What had been a pleasant enough morning was about to give away to a cruel cold night. It didn't take a genius or even a wilderness guide to see that.

I hugged my hoodie closer around me as the wind started to pick up. There's a keening sound to wind when it whistles through the woods at night. In the mornings you can't hear it—there are plenty of beasties about to drown it out. The light itself distracts you. But when night pulls her veil down over the world?

Oh, you hear it then.

I watched my breath fog.

"Shit," I said. "Well. Let's find cover."

Up ahead of me was a gray patch among the verdant greens of the forest. Ash gray, with the rich brown soil gone brittle and dry. The trees themselves seemed to step away from it; the proud pines offered this thing its proper space. And it was a thing. The open pit was darker even than the blackness I fended off with the mobile's light—it was the darkness of death itself. A darkness that pulled me closer the longer my eyes beheld it.

I took a step forward. The pit, which I had taken to be vertical, wasn't actually. There was a bit of give to it. Worse than that—there was a stair. No mistaking it, either; it was flat limestone polished bright as you like, inset just below the lip of the cave.

"What the hell...?" I asked.

I swung the light down into the dark. Nothing changed—I might as well have been shining a light on a black curtain. It just... didn't penetrate at all. But there were traces of it on the polished stone, just enough that I could see another step beneath it.

My tongue stuck to the roof of my mouth. I looked around the clearing. Nothing—well, not quite nothing. Trees and bush and a cold that chapped my fingers.

Back at the pit. The air around it was warm. Not hot—not like the breath of summer or fire. It was more like the heat that comes off a pot of almost-boiling water.

I could spend the night outside. Or I could try the murder pit.

Don't do it, you little shit.

What do you have to lose? The worst thing could happen is you could die down there.

I laughed.

And then I started descending.

Quiet, warm, hidden. *On paper* this was the perfect place to rest.

Lethargy lay on my shoulders like a blanket. My stomach was grumbling, my bones tired, my muscles exhausted from the hiking. I didn't have much in the way of thoughts. I couldn't.

You need calories to think, as it turns out, and I didn't have any of those, either. So I plopped onto the ground.

Tired, so tired. If I got a little rest... Nothing to sleep on, though. Hmm, not quite true. It was kind of hot, and I had my hoodie. I pulled it off and balled it under my head.

As I curled up on the ground, two things occurred to me.

The first thing happened when I turned off my light. In the fraction of a second that it was pointed down I realized that it wasn't *stone* I was seeing beneath me.

Who lined a cave—walls, ground, and ceiling—in solid gold?

It couldn't be. I had to test it. When I pressed my knuckle against it as hard as I could it left a bit of a dent beneath me. Overhead, hundreds, maybe even thousands of gems glittered—so many of them packed so dense that at first I thought the ceiling was open to the night sky overhead.

Seriously?

What the fuck?

Who in the hells kept any of this stuff in some cave somewhere? Where had the Queen left me? She said this place was safe. Was it her safety deposit box or something? More than once I'd wondered where the gods kept their wealth and their riches. My father used to say they all left that to the King of the Dark—he visited once every quarter. I wasn't allowed anywhere near the guy. You could always tell when he showed up, though, because all of the people who liked men in the company would line up to get a good look at him.

Couldn't be me. My tastes had always leaned more toward

women, and I was weird about that stuff anyway. I didn't like the idea of anyone touching me that way.

Alone in the dark I started to wonder: Was this the King of the Dark's Domain? It couldn't be. I didn't know *that* much about him, but I knew gods could be *very* territorial. The Queen of the Wild didn't get along with anyone from the Court of Earth for that reason—they thought she spent too much time encroaching on their territory. The woods I'd seen could either be part of the Earth Court, or part of the Queen's. The latter was way more likely.

But then...what was this place?

I was too tired for speculation. My mind was already dragging me to sleep whether I liked it or not. I reached out toward the glittering gems, and even that felt like too much effort.

As the haze took me, I had that second realization.

You see, in that moment before sleep sunk its fangs into me, the moment I felt the drowsiness spread through my veins like poison...

I thought I heard a scream.

In my dreams, I lay on a warm bed of sand. Waves rose and fell like the breath of a god. They were, in a way. I met the King of Waves once or twice through the years. But that was the incredible thing about this dream—I wasn't in his Domain.

I wasn't in anyone's.

No, as I lay there, Bluetooth speakers blared Top 40 hits to whoever would listen, mothers chided their children, teens had awkward flirty conversations. Cans cracked open, and bottlecaps hit the surf.

When someone came over to ask me if I had a smoke, I knew exactly where I was. I could see it on his shitty, salt-stained tourist T-shirt.

Bondi Beach.

"C'mon, mate, I'm dying over here," he said. "You've got to have something."

I stared at him. He had a mop of curly brown hair gone frizzy thanks to the ocean air, strips of sunscreen unblended beneath each eye, a ghost of stubble along his cheeks. A man who was normal in every way, from the bottoms of his flip-flops to the split ends of his hair. My father would never have hired him. Good money he'd never even heard of our company.

I reached into my pocket. My dream-self decided it was a great idea to wear cargo shorts to the beach, apparently. Not sure what she was thinking when she made that call—but it did mean that I had plenty of space for cigarettes.

So I handed him one.

He slipped it between his chapped lips, fished out a lighter from his pocket, and lit it.

I watched the cherry burn.

A normal girl, on a normal beach, without a care in the world.

They say there's no cure for insomnia like hiking twenty kilometers. Whatever the case had been, I slept the whole night through.

Now, that meant that when I woke up, I had no idea how to function. All my life I've dealt with this weight of drowsiness, a heady sort of thing that, when it got too bad, meant I occasionally heard phantoms calling my name.

But this? *Rest?*

My body didn't know what to do with it.

I started to pace as I considered my options. Stretching my legs helped distract from both how much they hurt and how hungry I was. The rusted gears of my brain started to turn—but always steered me back to the hunger.

I could try hunting?

No, no, that was out of the question. What was I supposed to use to hunt? I couldn't exactly chuck my mobile at a passing deer and hope for a killing blow. Can you imagine the angle I'd need to hit? And I didn't feel like killing anything, anyway. I wasn't worth something else's life.

Right. So. No hunting. Foraging? That was probably doable.

Gods. As I stopped to stretch I could swear I felt every single muscle in my body tearing at once. Could I even walk that far?

I could lie here all day.

It'd be the easier thing to do. I'd be safe and sound if I did. Conserve energy that way, too. All I had to do was survive, right? So I could just lie here, if I wanted, and fulfill...whatever this was. A challenge? A test?

Thinking about it too much only confused me. I'd get the

answer out of the Queen—but if I was going to make any headway, I needed to at least try.

She'd made that much clear.

Which meant I couldn't stay here and curl up beneath the hoodie as much as I wanted to.

I had to keep going.

Deep breaths, Iph.

I tugged my hoodie back on and walked to the stairs. Raising my leg to climb them kindled fresh waves of ache. Taking the second step made me grit my teeth.

By the third?

By the third, I was swearing.

"Fucking asshole stairs, fucking…"

Did I really need to do this?

Another step. My legs were lead. All the walking I'd done yesterday might have been a mistake. Gods. Useless, useless. What was I doing out here? Maybe the Queen was watching with a bowl of popcorn or something. Maybe that was the point of all of this.

Pathetic.

Why not just go back down? So I'd disappoint her, so what? Was it really that important? Whatever deal she'd made with my parents meant that I had to die one way or the other. You can't weasel your way out of a bargain like that—especially not if you're one of them. It's one of the only ways you can kill them.

The terms were clear. I was an offering.

So why not just…

I screwed my eyes shut. There, in the explosion of colors on the back of my eyes, I saw the shadows of her face. In the rush of blood against my eardrums I swore I could hear a foreign heartbeat. Did she even have a heart?

What a weird thing to wonder about.

Fine, fine. Up the shitting stairs I went. But I made a little deal with myself: I wouldn't walk more than a kilometer in any direction. I'd try to stay as close to the clearing as possible. No more wandering around without purpose; no more lollygagging. Nature was beautiful, but it was going to kick my ass right back to bed if I let it.

And I couldn't let it.

For some fucking reason she thought I could do it.

You don't have to do it quick. You don't have to do it perfectly. But you do have to do it.

Each step took me maybe five minutes. There was a little process to it. Raising my front leg, setting it down. Taking a bit to recover from the pain, letting my head recover from the sudden movement. Putting my hand against the wall to brace myself for the next part. Raising up my leg and taking the next step.

Realizing that I had to do it all over again.

I can't tell you how long it took me to climb those damned stairs. Forever and a half. Cresting the pit didn't even bring with it any of those storybook victories, oh no. I fucking tripped on the last one and stumbled forward. Smacked my face right against the ashy ground. Inhaled some of it, too, so I rolled around there sputtering like an idiot.

But there was something so ridiculous about it, about the

whole thing, that I laughed. Which only made the coughing worse, of course. You should have heard me. Like a backed up engine, I was, hacking and laughing and sputtering. At least on the ground I didn't have to move too much—but every time I laughed my ribs ached.

Honestly it's a wonder nothing ate me. Then again with the way I was shrieking, maybe they thought it was some kind of weird hyena there and not a shut-in Australian girl.

But... it felt good. The sun on my face, laughter in my belly, the giddiness you get when you haven't caught your breath in a while.

It hurt, sure.

But it was going to be okay. As I began the slow work of getting back up, I was sure of it.

"Queeeeen of the Wiiiiiiiild! If you don't show up soon, I'm going to eat *allllll* of these berries!"

Only the woods answered me—the leaves, the distant sound of a stream. Yet my cheeks were going hot, and I couldn't keep from smiling. All I could do was imagine her, that stiff posture of hers, the shadowed face. Probably hissing like a cat at the sound of me.

Well, I'd give her something else to hiss about.

"Ohh, Queen of the Wild, my throat's full of bile, and I'm thinking that I may just dieeee! I ate a mushroom and got real hiiiiiigh! Ohhh, Queen of the Wild, gimme a diaaaaaaal!"

I held that note as long as I could. Which turned out to be until she flicked me in the back of the head.

"You're a terrible singer," she said.

I laughed. "Got you to show, didn't it?"

She sniffed. Not one of the more aggressive ones, though. This one was more like a sigh she didn't let out, like a dog who isn't sure whether it likes its food or not. "Are you going to eat those?"

I patted the earth next to me, where I'd stacked up a collection of berries I was quite proud of. A whole day's work!

"I'd like to. But I don't want to die for having eaten them, either, which is why you're here."

The Queen stared at my hand. A certain tilt of the head, a set of the shoulders. You always know when a cat is figuring out if it can make a jump.

"How about we sit down together?" I said. "I'm too tired to stand, to be honest, and that way you get a better look."

"Oh." Without much protest she sat. The beads of her mask clinked against one another. Her leather-pine scent wafted over to me. Like being wrapped up in a blanket with her in front of a fire.

I cleared my throat. Huffing god fumes isn't exactly... polite. And she was taking time out of her day doing whatever it was she did to answer my dumb question. Best if I kept my eyes on the prize and not on the play of her powerful muscles beneath her skin.

"So! I think the berries have got to be okay, right? You don't often hear about deadly berries. At least I don't. Though, honestly, I'm more worried about shitting my brains out than I am about—"

"That's belladonna."

I blinked. "That name's familiar."

She plucked the berry—a fat blue one the color of the night sky—from the pile and tossed it away. Then another, and another. "Eat it and you'll hallucinate. This many... You'd be dead in an hour. A horrible death."

Oh, how I shrank—just like that cook presenting a peanut butter and jelly to the judges. Here I thought I'd done pretty well!

"Oh, uh. That one," I said. I laughed more to soothe my broken ego than because of any jokes. "Well... The others should be okay, right?"

She hummed. "Spindleberry. Poisonous. Spurge berries. Poisonous. Sumac. Poisonous."

As she named them she moved them off the hoodie and laid them out in a neat line, each clustered with its own kind.

But that wasn't the worst part. The worst part was that I could hear her smiling.

"Hm. Blackberries. Those are good, but... how long have you carried these together?"

I hung my head back. Already I could tell what she was about to say. "I dunno. A while?"

"Hold your hand up to the sun horizontally. Count how many hands are between the sun and the horizon."

"Let's see... Five?"

"Five hours to sunset," she said. "Hm. Maybe not too long. How's your stomach?"

"Empty," I said. "Wait, is it really that easy to tell the time? That means it's gotta be noon or something, right? Maybe two?"

There it was again when she next spoke: "Already learning."

"You don't have to sound so smug about it," I said.

"Am I smug?"

"You sound smug. I can't see your face to tell for sure."

"You'd die if you did."

"See?" I pointed at her. "Smug! That's smug!"

And then I heard it: a sound like the bray of wolves, like the whistle of an arrow, like the pant of a creature through the woods.

Her laughter.

She laughed and laughed, her hand rising up to the darkness that covered her face, and when the beads of her mask knocked against one another, it was like the gentle ring of a tambourine.

"No one," she said, "has ever called me smug."

My ears felt hot. If I thought too much about what to say, I was going to ruin the whole thing. Better to shoot from the hip. "Yeah, well, I bet you haven't abducted too many firstborns and told them to fend for themselves in the forest, either."

Too much? A moment of fear—but then the laugh again. "You are the first."

"That explains a lot!" I said. "See, usually when you drop people in the middle of the woods, you give them some kind of gear, at least."

The laughter died away, then, but only as summer dies into autumn. She leaned back and studied me. "You'd learn less that way."

"But you'd have to spend less time looking after me, too," I said. I waved my hands as I talked. "I'm sure you've got a bunch of other things to do. Real hunters to look after. Hikers lost on the trails of the world. Women giving birth. *The Moon.* You know, I always thought it was a little odd that your Domain was so big, with so many things that don't really relate."

She hummed. The Queen of the Wild—god to countless thousands—got up and knelt behind me. Her cheek brushed against my ear; her ornaments against my shoulder. The tips of her antlers caught a couple strands of my hair. If I didn't move, it wouldn't be a problem, right?

"They relate," she said. "And I will get to them. But first..."

She turned my hands over in hers, my palms facing up. Her calluses were rough against my skin. "Eyes closed."

What could I do but what she asked? It was as natural as breathing. I closed my eyes. Without my vision to worry about, my other senses picked up. The sweet smell of the berries, her musk, the distant songs of the birds, her ornaments a-sway, the cool evening breeze, the heat of her presence.

I swallowed. "A-are you. Is this an unmasking situation?"

"No. Don't fear me," she said, and the thrum of her voice was like the vibrating of a reed. "This is a gift."

My palms tingled. Something was skimming their surface. Vines? No, claws. No, too soft for that. Fur? No, it couldn't be. With each new possibility my heart beat faster, and a certain coolness washed over me. It was as if I'd dunked myself in a winter pond.

Then it came to me: These were her hands. Her fingertips.

"A bow, for hunting. A bag, for gathering. A knife, for all else. Three-in-one, like the strands of a braid. Let it be that which you need, when you need it. My gift to you."

In the wake of her touch: something solid and wooden. She closed my hands around it. Then I felt something on my forehead—a raindrop, perhaps? But with more pressure than I imagined a raindrop could have. Not that I knew anything about that.

Her hand on my head.

"Iphigenia. Open your eyes."

When I did, it was there: a beautiful knife, its grip made from the antler of some proud creature; a thin sheath of simple leather to keep it safe. What I could see of the blade gleamed silver in the light.

"This is…" I said. "I was just thinking of, you know, some kind of stuff from the market or whatever. Not a divine…is this really okay?"

"Yes" was the simple answer. "Don't squander it." She squeezed my shoulder. "Still time for gathering. The blackberries were a good find. Get more of them. Tomorrow, I'll show you more."

How many blackberries did I need to eat to hold me over? My stomach was rumbling so hard I would have eaten anything. I thought of all the people on the internet who go on and on about fasting and how good it is for you. Always struck me as a load of bullshit, but now that I really was that hungry,

I wanted to track them all down and beat them over the head with sticks.

"And if I'm still hungry?"

"Look for oak trees," she said. "At the base you'll find fungus—large, tan, pale underneath. Lots of stripes. Safe to eat."

Okay. Okay, I could do that. Oak trees! Shouldn't be too hard, should it? And now I had a knife and a bag to work with. Even if I didn't know how to switch between the two right now.

The Queen of the Wild grunted behind me, and a second later a clarion sounded. All across the woods birds took to the skies.

"They need me again," she said.

I had to laugh—something about the exhaustion in her voice. I'd groaned like that more times than I could count. "Can't figure things out themselves, can they?"

"They don't want to," the Queen said.

"Rather have you hand them everything on a silver platter, clean as could be."

"Yes," she said, with an appreciative rise to her voice, an ease. "But there is never ease in the Wild. You understand this?"

I shrugged. "Back home I'd get calls in the middle of the night to go fix this that or the other thing. Didn't matter if I was sleeping or busy or whatever; if it needed doing, I had to do it. So it was always 'Iphy, could you...'"

Another grunt from her—but this one was different from the last. Lighter? "Troublesome."

"You're telling me. I can't believe they're doing the same to you. I guess it never stops, does it?" I said with a laugh.

"No. It does not," said the Queen. There was a pause, then, and the hard set of her jaw shifted to something softer. "I owe you answers, Iphigenia."

I tilted my head. "Yeah?"

"You are within my Domain," she said. "Everything you see in this place, with one exception, is part of me. My family cannot find you here."

I had the feeling—but it was good to have her confirm it for me. I nodded. "Thank you," I said. "Seems like they can find you, though?"

"They can call for me. I am obliged to answer," she said. "Only my brother can visit whenever he likes. But he doesn't often."

"That's probably why he's the only one who can," I said. But I couldn't lie—it made me think of Ori, and thinking of Ori taking on my responsibilities made my shoulders slump. I frowned. "This whole handmaiden thing. Does it mean my family's safe? That my brother won't have to bear all the weight I did?"

There was silence for a while. Maybe she was trying to figure out the words. The longer it went on, the more I started to worry.

"Your family believes that you are dead," she said. "They have reacted accordingly."

My chest tightened. Like a string, I snapped. "But I'm not dead, right? I'm still here. So that means that the curse—"

"Iphigenia." Her voice was not sharp—but it was authoritative. I couldn't make myself keep speaking. But when I looked at her, the pressure in my chest grew stronger. "You and I spread ourselves too thin for our families. I created this place so that I could be free. That is what I want for you, too. Freedom."

A dozen things I wanted to say, but which to voice? I swallowed. "Promise me they're safe. Promise me our fortunes haven't turned yet."

After a slow, agonizing moment, she nodded. The beads clinked together. "Your sacrifice has safeguarded them for now," she says.

The pressure let up. Not a lot, mind—but a little. I found myself clapping her on the shoulder. Like she was one of my mates and not a living breathing embodiment of nature. "Shouldn't keep your family waiting too long, or they'll find some other shit to nitpick."

The shadows of her face shifted, the glow of her eyes went soft. She squeezed my hand. "Be well," she said. "When I see you next, I will have more news for you."

She pulled away and began to leave.

But over her shoulder she called to me:

"Stay away from the pit in the woods."

Chapter Six

I stared into the pit, and the pit stared back.

It was a little after sunset. Cold had kicked the morning warmth out of bed and now settled in its place. My breath was starting to mist. With the drop in temperature came the familiar ache of my muscles and joints as the day's exertions set in.

How many kilometers had I walked today? Too many, that was for sure. At least I had a bag full of berries and a chunk of mysterious fungus to show for it. The Queen had been right—it was easy to find the stuff once I knew what I was looking for. Two hundred hours of *Stardew Valley* during a depressive streak (a *bad* depressive streak) taught me what the leaves of an oak tree looked like. I spotted one not *too* far from the pit—and at its base?

That thing. A chunk of fungus twice as big as my head. Maybe even three times. Pretty, in a weird way. I don't think it'd be the first thing anyone thought of when they said the word *beauty*, you know? And the Queen of Flame definitely wouldn't want this thing anywhere near her Court. The Queen of Flowers would turn her nose up at it, twisted and brown as it was, its stripes nowhere near as colorful as a tulip's. But here it was anyway, never mind what they all thought, growing and growing strong, the sovereign of this particular oak tree.

I held it in my hand, this chunk, cool to the touch and springy where my fingers squeezed it. When I next looked on the knife it had already transformed into a bag in my hand. I threw the fungus in and...made my way back to the pit.

The pit that kept taunting me.

That hunger was still in my gut, you see. That was the trouble. Down in the pit of my stomach I felt that hunger; around my shoulders was exhaustion's awful cloak; each and every one of my muscles ached as if struck by a hammer.

The Queen of the Woods told me to stay away from it. You didn't go against a god's rules when they gave them to you.

Stay away from the pit.

But it was so cold.

Stay away from the pit.

But I hurt so much, and I just wanted to rest.

Stay away from the pit.

My feet kept going. With every step the air got warmer—heavier. As if the pit itself was throwing a blanket around my shoulders and shoving a hot cup of tea into my hands. Gods, what I wouldn't have done for a cup of tea. My lips were cracked and bleeding; my throat so dry that it hurt to speak.

A cup of tea. A warm place to sleep. Maybe I was even tired enough that I'd sleep the whole night through again; maybe my body would cooperate with my mind and I'd not spend five hours unable to let consciousness slip through my fingers.

By the time I reached the bottom I was giddy. The warmth alone would have been enough to bring a smile to my face—but what I found waiting for me there was even better.

Laid out on the ground where I'd tried to sleep yesterday were two bowls. One held an absolute bounty of fruits—I'm talking any fruit you could name stacked up as pretty as could be. Strawberries, pears, oranges, apples, and even some I'd only seen in photos, like durian and starfruit. All of it was glistening. A thin film of dew clung to their rinds; I watched a drop of water caress the curves of a peach.

I'd like to tell you that I ran to this fruit and fell on my knees and gobbled it all up in a desperate, but human, fashion.

That's not what really happened.

No—the truth is that I was *so* hungry and *so* weak that when I tried to run, I collapsed. I did not fall to my knees so much as collapse onto them. I didn't even notice the pain, if I'm being honest; I was already one big hurt. On my belly I wriggled until I got to the bowl. Pulling it close I saw the inscription written along the rim: FREELY GIVEN AND YOURS TO TAKE.

First came the apricot. Juices dribbled down my chin; my skin sopped them up. My teeth hit the pit, and rather than pull back to take another bite, I scraped them down. Strips of succulent flesh came off right into my mouth, and I mashed them up as well as I could. Sugar, water, a tiny bit of fiber—I had no idea how much I'd needed them until I had them before me.

I ate all of them like that. The whole bowl, right there, all at once. My hands were sticky and stained red. When I looked to the second bowl, I realized my face was just as slicked over.

See—the second bowl was full of water.

I picked that up, too. Only spent a second or so staring at myself before I did. Who wanted to look at someone so grimy and covered in dirt and fruit and despair? The salt trails of tears at the corners of my eyes didn't interest me. The water did.

I drank it all in one go and then rolled over in a happy little heap on the floor.

Food. Water. A warm place to sleep. What else would anyone need? Oh, I missed the internet like you wouldn't believe. I missed movies. I missed being able to turn on a game and drown out all of the questions that bounced around inside my head like projectiles in a bullet hell. Most of all I missed being able to do all of this with my family. But I was too exhausted for any of that.

Was this place suspicious? Sure. Was it weird that I found food and drink ready for me when I came downstairs? Yeah. Was it probably bad to be here, given that the Queen had told me to steer clear? You bet.

But I wasn't going to argue with any of it. All of those were problems for later Iph.

I closed my eyes and prayed that sleep would come to me.

In the absolute silence of the wherever this was, the darkest parts of me whispered in my ear: *They left you to die.*

Sleep was not coming to me.

They left you to die.

They kept you in a single building your whole life.

You never got to feel the sun on your skin before the Queen picked you up, never got to feel grass beneath your feet, and what do you have to show for it?

I gritted my teeth. It didn't stop the thoughts from coming.

If I was so important to them—if it meant something to be the Heir of Pelops—then why had they cast me aside so easily?

Why did they need me to die? Couldn't they have found some other way?

Did it matter? All my life I'd been... not even really a person. Just a debt that needed paying. A position that needed filling. Iphigenia only existed when I was gaming with my friends, or talking with my siblings late at night, or...

When I was lying on a warm marble floor somewhere the Queen of the Wild had told me not to go.

Curled up on the floor, I looked into the darkness around me and wondered whether my siblings were doing any better than I was.

The darkness didn't have any answers.

In a lot of stories, I would have gotten up the next morning, exhausted though I was, and put my nose to the grindstone again. I'd tell you that I really wanted to impress the Queen. You would see it all in your head, like you maybe already do—me sitting up, grunting with effort, as I have some of the food I gathered with my own two hands. I'd take my bag along and leave this place behind me.

It's a nice story. An inspiring one.

But it isn't my story.

So I'd like to tell you that I got up. That I crawled out of there and faced the day again filled with the hope that I would triumph.

I didn't. I lay there for hours, unable to sleep, with only my worst thoughts for company, until I heard the scream.

Like a pair of scissors gliding through the gift-wrapped silence—that was the scream. Piercing and cold. Hearing it, I touched my ears out of reflex, as if the sound itself were enough to slice me open.

I started up from my depression nest and looked around. Nothing but darkness to be seen—only the foot of the stairs offered any kind of respite. Best I could tell, the sound hadn't come from that way. Which was...concerning.

I swallowed. My heart started to pound in my chest. The twisting in my stomach could have been nausea from eating so much after a long fast—or it could have been dread. It felt more like the latter. Despite the warmth of the chamber, a coldness settled on me, unnatural and irrefutable. As if I'd wandered into a meat freezer.

As I looked into the dark, I heard it again: a horrible, wordless cry. Not one of sorrow. It would have been easier if it was. When someone's in pain, you go and help them—or at least you tell yourself that you will. But what do you do when someone's angry? *Furious?*

The right thing to do was to run. I knew that. I felt it in my marrow, that bone-deep part of me that was prey where the Queen was a predator. I wasn't cut out for a fight. Not that I could with how weak I was.

But there was this whisper in the back of my head: *What if this is the person who laid out the gifts for me?* I couldn't just leave them. They were probably a Guest. To turn away from them when they needed me was against everything I've ever been taught.

The Heir of Pelops serves the House of Pelops. And the House of Pelops serves the gods.

I reached for the knife the Queen had given me. "Do you need help?" I called.

My only answer was another scream.

Shit.

Dizzy but determined, I took another step into the dark. The cold nipped at the tips of my ears. People talked about that sort of thing on the telly, but I'd never experienced it—the tingle-pain of numbness. A small part of me was thrilled to feel something new.

But mostly I was afraid.

"I don't know how to fight or anything," I said, "but I'm a pretty good listener. And I've made some good mates. Maybe. I don't know."

Another scream. Closer? Yes, it had to be. As I walked into the dark, I kept expecting to see something ahead of me. Dreading it. A man strapped to the wall of a chasm with birds pecking out his liver. Something like that.

But nothing came. It was only dark down there. Cold, unyielding dark. And with every step I took the comforting light of the steps faded away. A disk, an orb, and finally a little pinprick of white. I stood in the dark and watched the little slip of it, no larger than my thumbnail, and I wondered if this was really the smart thing to do.

My hands shook. Exhaustion and cold. Keeping hold of the knife was starting to become difficult, so I shoved my hand into the pocket of my hoodie and balled it up against my stomach. Smaller than it had been. There was a sag to my trousers, too. I wondered how pathetic I was starting to look. When I found whoever it was that was screaming, would I even stand a chance?

Did I want to?

Ahead of me, I saw shapes in the dark—a sort of lighter black against the void. Night against the grave, that sort of thing. If I squinted my eyes, I could see a human silhouette—or at least something like a human. The second I took in the size of him, I knew he was more than just a human. If he wasn't a god himself, he certainly had some of their blood in him. Had to be at least two meters tall, maybe even two and a half. He was doubled over, though, curled like some grotesque, his long spindly arm reaching for something ahead of him. When he swayed forward, I heard the splash of water.

"H-hello?" I called.

The shadows played across his ear as his head turned toward me. In the absolute dark of the endless abyss, the burning green of his eyes was bright as the full moon itself. Their light froze something in me; all of my animal parts went cold and still. The light glinted off his teeth as he smiled at me. Or scowled. Hard to tell.

"Heir."

He might as well have reached for my throat.

"Heir. You will help me, won't you? You're hungry. I'm hungry. Why not feast together?"

His voice was rough and dry; hearing it made my throat sore and called up an awful thirst. As much as I wanted to move—toward him or away, anywhere—I couldn't. Not with his eyes looking at me like that. My jaws clamped tight and my knuckles went white around the grip of the knife.

"We're in this together, you and I. And will be so long as we live. They don't want us to die, you know. Not really. They'd rather we suffer."

The splash of water. The war drum of my heart. Run, run, run.

But my legs weren't listening to me. Everything was listening to that awful voice. To him.

"I have water. I have food. But when I reach for the water..."

A bubbling sound. Water, circling the drain.

"It ebbs away from me. And when I reach for the fruit..."

Breaking wood. Flesh, splintering. An awful groan of effort.

"It is always out of reach. Always. Is that any way to live?"

My whole body began to shake. I could see only the barest traces of his silhouette, and even that was too much to bear—the hollows of a rib cage, what might have been a stomach, twig-like legs.

I wanted to scream. I could feel it building inside me like a balloon of misery, ready to burst, but there was no space for it to go. My mouth wouldn't open.

"It has to be you. The one who left you food...he is forbidden from helping me. It has to be an heir."

What do you mean? What does any of this mean?

I tasted copper.

The shape turned now, all of it, toward me. He was talking like he was human—but he couldn't be. Not shaped like that. Not with his bones bending that way.

The scream in me built and built and built, and as he reached toward me I felt his clammy touch on my hand, and it was then that I felt something pull me back. Something thin. A rope?

It yanked me back with such force that I started to throw up. The horrible shape, whoever he was, began to fall away into the dark. Screaming.

And as I hurtled backward I slammed against a wall of warmth and muscle. She wrapped an arm around me and scooped me up and carried me from that place.

"Oh, little deer. You shouldn't have seen that."

I clung to her with everything I could muster.

Chapter Seven

She ran with me clinging to her shoulders. I knocked against the slope of her back a hundred times, maybe more.

We came to a stop at the grove from the other day—where I'd learned all sorts of things about which berries are poisonous and which aren't. I realized I'd been screaming only when she set me down and fixed me with her eyes.

"You're safe," she said. The bones hanging from her mask clinked together. Aside from the calls of the nightjars and the owls, the loudest sound in the grove was my own labored breathing.

"I—What was—"

"The reason your family is indebted," she answered. She had laid me on the smooth surface of an eons-old rock. As we spoke she circled it. Not in any particular hurry or anything like that, oh no. It was slow. Deliberate.

I was in trouble. Not that my adrenaline wanted to help me out at all with that. No matter that the Queen of the Wild herself was saying I was safe; I kept seeing him when I closed my eyes. The shape of him. The bones that shouldn't have looked like that, the sallow skin hanging off him. Maybe he wasn't human, but he was something like one, once, and now he was anything but.

"Th-that's the guy that fucked us over?" I stammered. "What the fuck did you all do to him? He's being *tortured*!"

A grunt from behind me. "If given the chance, he would swap places with you."

"That's no reason to..." My head was swimming; I felt awash in the moonlight. "What could he have possibly done?"

"He is a kinslayer of the highest degree," said the Queen behind me. Then, with barely hidden disgust: "Like the rest of your family."

My throat full of glass felt like it was going to close. Everything hurt. I shot to my feet, anger preferable to the pain. "My siblings have never done anything wrong."

The Queen stared down at me. Though I sensed she had no wish to attack me, I couldn't help but notice that she seemed to be more night than humanoid. There was a sheen to her limbs that made her melt into the dark. "Your siblings are not in question. The rest of them? The rest of them would kill you without a thought. The rest of them *did*."

"Because they had to—"

She leaned in, her forehead touching mine and her fingers below my chin. So quickly did she move that I saw only a blur of black and then the burning silver before me.

"They did not have to, Iphigenia. They could have fought the war on their own terms. They *chose* to kill you," she said.

"Maybe you shouldn't have asked for me, then," I snapped.

I knew I shouldn't have said it—but what else was I going to say? So little of this was my fault. So little of this was my own choice. Why was everyone ignoring that?

Deep, rattling breaths. My chest hurt; I couldn't feel my extremities. If she killed me now, she'd be within her rights.

But I hadn't expected the arrows that found my chest when she next spoke.

"That was not my decision," she said. "My family made that decision when considering yours."

Did she see how she had wounded me? And could I even call it a wound? She'd said aloud my own thoughts—and those were *her* thoughts, too. Was it a wound to be understood?

She let out a breath. "What *was* my decision was saving you."

My cheeks were hot. If I lingered on what I felt at the moment, I wasn't sure what I would find. I had to just keep going. If she hadn't killed me yet, would she ever? "But why? You said I had to be sacrificed. If I'm still alive, then you broke the Law, and if you broke the Law then why aren't you dead?"

In the night symphony of the forest I was little more than a clumsy bit of percussion. Especially next to her. She was night's own silence; she needed no justification. And for a long while she was simply that.

"I should be," she said. "My half sister wishes it so."

I wanted to touch her. I wasn't sure where it came from but there it was: this urge to hold her. Was it because I'd spent so much time fixing things for other people? No, this felt different. Like by holding her I could hold us both together for a while.

But did she want that?

The beads of her mask clinked together as she rolled her shoulders. "But tonight I am not dead. And so, tonight, I am yours."

"But I was just a dick to you," I said. "And I broke your rules. I was just so hungry, and there was food right there when I went down there, and it said it was free, so I ate it—"

A gentle, heavy hand on my forehead. The hum that left her then surprised me. There was none of the dolorous anger I expected, but none of the disappointed. Instead it was...understanding. As if I'd pointed out a wound she'd had, one that had been troubling her without her notice. One quite like mine.

"I did not provide enough for you," she said.

Something in my chest shifted.

"I...It's...I'm not a god," I said. Tears rolled down my cheeks and over my hands as I balled them against my cheeks. "I'm sorry. I'm so weak. I...I should have gotten out of bed, you gave me the tools, but I just..."

The great woman next to me made another sound, small as the flap of a robin's wings. Something wrapped around me, heavy and thick, and the scent of the woods came with it. After it came the weight of her arm. She slipped a finger beneath my chin and tried to lift it so that I was looking at her.

I ducked. I was weakness, and she was the Wild. What could she ever want to do with me?

But I felt her fingertips playing with the hair at the base of my neck, felt the other hand wiping away my tears. Not the hands that drew her massive bow, but the ones that could caress a hummingbird without disturbing it.

"This is not your failing," she said.

"How could it be anything else? I was the only other person in that fucking place. You were clear as could be!" My voice cracked. I was screaming, again, and my throat wasn't a fan. I took a breath to try and calm down. "You told me not to go in there, and I should have known—"

"Iphigenia."

She said my name so soft, so sweet, you'd think it was made of moonstuff. But there wasn't any arguing with it. A night song so beautiful you had to stop and listen to the whole thing in one go, and maybe let it echo through the woods after, too, for good measure.

"Yeah." I sniffled. I wiped my snot against my hoodie's sleeve. With all the dirt and snot already caked into it, it probably only made me dirtier. But I didn't care. "That's me."

"Look at me, Iphigenia," she said. Then, after a beat: "I am not asking."

A small voice in the back of my head wondered what I had to lose if I did, anyway. My sanity? That's what went, when you looked at them without their masks. My grip on that was already holding on by a hair.

But the reason I did was...well, I wanted to look at her. I wanted to see the shadows of her mouth move when she said my name. I wanted to be seen by her, even if I couldn't see her in turn.

And so when she tilted my chin this time, I didn't fight at all. There was more of her face visible tonight than there had been before. The swell and curve of her cheeks, the bow of her lips. Looking at her felt like being launched into the air, no parachute, no nothing. Just the thrill of the rise and the horrible dread of the fall.

"Iphigenia."

I was too dumbfounded to speak.

"I am the Queen of the Wild. Of survival."

She touched the spot between my brows. Coolness spread from her fingertips.

"You are my handmaiden. You will survive. You will thrive here. And I will help you."

She drew her hand back again. The silver bolts of her eyes struck me from within the shadow of her mask.

"But you have to want it."

Cold water in my throat. An unnatural—but all too welcome—ease to the pain from my screams. I watched her. I could do nothing else. As the tears continued to stream down my cheek, I realized that they weren't sadness. Not just that. There was something else in there, something so painful and fragile I worried it would hurt me if I spoke it.

But it was the only thing I could speak.

"My own father sacrificed me."

The night was soft, and wrapped around me again. "Yes."

"Why did he do that? I mean, he told me. My fucking uncle getting into trouble, my aunt going missing. The Heir of Pelops serves the... the House of Pelops. All I was ever meant to do was to serve. To die, I guess, if I needed to, and at least it was me and not someone else. At least it was me and not Ori or Ellie, and they don't need to know about all of this, and I can finally do something meaningful, but it's. It's so. Oh, gods, it's so scary."

My chest ached. I whimpered and slumped forward—but she was there to hold me up.

"I know," she said. "And it hurts. I know."

And I didn't want her to say anything more than that. She didn't need to. How did she know that? To this day I'll never understand it. Nothing could have been worse than having to explain the way I felt. To have someone tell me that my pain was like their pain—because it wasn't. Who else could say they'd been through what I had? I didn't want to get into the details of it. The years I'd spent building up to... to that moment. To being the sacrifice.

I didn't have to.

She held me. So long she held me. The night was cold and dark, but it was velvet soft and it was mine, all mine. The glorious light of the moon. It wasn't the cold of lack, but of clear water. I was sinking into her as if I'd fallen into a pool of silver.

At some point I must have come to my senses. When I did I found she was holding me tight, resting atop the stump. How long had it been? Long enough that the gentle rise and fall of her breath made me think she was asleep.

But that's a stupid thing to have guessed. Gods like her don't need to rest. The moment I stirred something rumbled deep in her chest. The bones and leaves that hung from her mask swayed over my head, and I smelled the forest.

"My lady—" I started.

She grunted. "Talk in the morning. Rest for now."

I wanted to say things. I wanted to thank her for saving me from whatever that place was, wanted to apologize for causing trouble...

But when you meet certain people, you know there's no arguing with them. And there was never any arguing with her.

"Okay," I said. "I'll go find some place to—"

As I started to clamber away from her, she caught me by the back of my hoodie and set me back down in her lap. My head was against her chest again. "I said rest."

What else was I meant to do? Exhausted as I was, it was a blessing *and* an order.

Chapter Eight

The Queen of the Wild likes to start her days earlier than anyone should.

It was a little after dawn when she picked me up and gave me a little shake, as if I was a cat she was trying to tease for an Insta reel. Much like that cat, I warble-garbled as my head lolled back into consciousness.

"Mortals need the sun. We're taking advantage of the light," she said.

I blinked. "Huh?"

"This is the first day of your training." She set me down on the stump. Then she took her bow from her back and unstrung it. She laid the bow—as big as I was, if not bigger—down across my lap. "If you are going to be my handmaiden, then you will need training."

"Do I get a say in this, or did I lose that with the whole sacrifice thing?" I asked. I was too scared of the bow to touch it. What if I broke it or something? Never mind that thing felt as heavy as could be.

Midway through taking off her cloak she stopped and studied me. "Hrm. You should have a say. You're right."

There was a pause, then, as neither of us knew what to say. I was beginning to understand as the usual morning sounds of the forest filled the air. Flapping wings, rustling leaves, the wind.

Then: "What is your say, Iphigenia?"

I was really hoping she'd have an idea where to start with this. "Well... I have questions about what happened last night. I'd like to get those sorted before we do anything else."

She knelt down, then sat cross-legged next to me. Unlike a lot of the others, the Queen of the Wild never bothers making herself small around humans. Even with her sitting down, we were almost eye to eye. Not that I could see hers outside the lunar crescents.

"Ask."

"What did I see down there?"

There was a moment of consideration. She took off her quiver and laid that, too, in my lap. I was beginning to realize that she was the sort of woman who never spoke suddenly, never said something out of turn. Everything about her was considered. Intuitive, sure; sometimes it would seem like she was speaking out of nowhere. But it was never without reason.

So while she thought things over, I looked over the clearing, the same one I'd been to before, with my shoddy attempts at a lean-to, my piles of berries I couldn't eat. Something else had eaten some of the berries, and I found myself hoping that it was all right. Maybe its digestive system was better developed than mine.

Cheers, whatever critter you are, I thought.

And that thought made me smile. So did the sight of the lean-to, if I'm being honest. There was something I'd failed at doing—but even in the failing I'd left behind something that lingered for a whole day. Something real, something physical. Something I'd failed to build, but failed with my own two hands.

I looked down at them. There, at the base of my fingers, the skin was starting to flake. Calluses.

Never had those before.

"Iphigenia."

Her hand rested between my shoulder blades, gentle and warm. Maybe she was trying not to startle me.

"Yeah? Sorry, I was just thinking…"

"I know. It gladdens me," she answered. "You want to hear it, still?"

I gathered the quiver and bow up to my chest. They weren't plushies or anything, but it was nice to have something to hold on to. "Go on."

She didn't look away from me when she told me. I appreciated it then, and I appreciate it now, in the telling of it.

"The man in the pit is your ancestor. Tantalus. I will tell you what he did, one day, to earn the ire of the gods. But for today, you will learn that we imprisoned him."

In the ground before her she drew twelve circles.

"These are all the Courts," she said. Then smaller circles followed inside the large ones—some with dozens, some with only two, and one left completely untouched. "Domains."

I nodded. My father had shown me charts like this before. Every god belonged to a Domain, and the Domain belonged to the god. A Domain was both a metaphysical place to which a god could retreat and the suite of things they were bound to look after.

Sometimes more things got added to Domains and they got bigger. When they got big enough, and if the King of Gods allowed it, a Domain could become a Court all its own.

I didn't tell her that I knew all that, though. I liked having her explain it.

Anyway—some of the Court circles overlapped. One Court, with three Domains, overlapped the untouched Court just barely.

She pointed to that spot. "That's the cave."

"So...three of you have control over him?" I asked.

The Queen hissed. "I hate that word. Control."

How to rephrase it? Honestly, I couldn't think of another approach for it. I knew the basics of the situation now, and I could guess at the rest: They probably put him in three overlapping Courts so no one God could have any claim over him. If he disappeared, the other two would know immediately. Which meant whatever he had done had been terrible enough to warrant surveillance.

My ancestor.

No, I didn't like that.

"The half sister you mentioned last night..." I said.

A grunt from her. She didn't like this, either. "What about her? You said she was trying to get you killed."

"She is fond of weaving," said the Queen. And she said this as if it was the harshest indictment on the Earth; as if the very act of weaving was heretical.

Honestly, it was hard not to laugh. Weaving, of all things! But this was the one who wanted her dead, so I bit back.

"Do you mean weaving schemes, or...?"

There was a nod in response. She leaned back, surveying the circles she'd laid out. She pointed to one of them—it overlapped with the highest of the twelve circles. "The Queen of War. Wisdom. She has many names, as we all do. But if you speak the name Father gave her, she will hear us."

Ah. That one. She visited my father often. One of those meetings I was never allowed to attend. He said she was too exact for me to be there throwing him off in the middle of negotiations.

Which meant she and the Queen of the Wild...didn't get along. "And she wants you dead?"

"It is her place to enforce the Law. Father is too busy to bother with it," said the Queen. When she spoke of this, her voice lost a little of its edge. "She thinks that your sacrifice means your death."

"Oh." I, too, stared at the circle overlap. That little patch of dirt wanted me dead, then? Or maybe wanted the Queen dead. I was just collateral, then, as I'd always been.

"I have told her otherwise. When you emerge from this place, you will be my handmaiden, and you will have killed the old self who came into my care."

I blinked. Then I turned to look at the woman who, until just now, had seemed so wise to me. Because there was something about the way she phrased this, something about the very slight touch of desperation, that piqued my interest.

"You didn't have a plan when you took me, did you?" I said.

And she laughed, then, an exhausted sound. "No. No, I did not."

It hung in the air for a minute: There had been no plan. That night when she had taken me, she had done so knowing it might kill her. And in the aftermath, while I'd been screaming or asleep or trying to gather berries that wouldn't kill me, she was arguing with Wisdom to keep the two of us alive.

The Queen stood. "She will offer a test, one day, to prove that you are worthy of the title. And you will pass it. I know that you will."

She offered me a hand. "But we do have to begin training."

The sky was clear above, a brilliant, beautiful blue. Wind tousled my hair. When I took a breath I could smell her, yes, but I could smell the rest of the woods, too—the berries I'd left out going a little sour, the animals nearby, the trees themselves.

This place was just as much an expression of who she was as the form she chose to wear. It was her.

And it had welcomed me, even if I didn't understand it.

The least I could do was help her.

"Fine," I said.

Being a handmaiden means a lot of different things to different people.

The Queen herself wasn't *entirely* sure what the parameters were. Wisdom would decide that. But until we had in hand the exact things I needed to be able to do to qualify, the Queen figured it was good to get the basics out of the way.

Cooking, hunting, and woodcraft. Without a working knowledge of these things, no one could ever call themselves a survivalist. And if I was going to be the Queen of the Wild's handmaiden, I needed to be sure I could survive in those Wilds on my own.

For the next few days, that was all we did.

Cooking is hard.

The first thing she had me do was set up a fire.

When I started by making a great big pile of sticks and trying to get them to stand up against each other like a cone of shame, she actually laughed. And I don't mean a rude laugh, one at my expense. It was more of a guffaw of disbelief.

"Iphigenia."

"What?" I said. I turned to her and waved my hands in the air. "I'm trying here!"

"Are you?" If I didn't miss my guess, she was smiling.

But she didn't tease me for long. No—she came right over and taught me how to set the thing up. Turned out the cone-shaped one was just for staying warm. For a cooking fire, you want a square, all built up like a little log cabin. I put one log down, and she the next, and we stacked them up turn by turn. A game in the middle of these woods.

The Queen took my hands. She put the flint in one and the stone in the other. Then she struck one against the other.

"Ah," I said.

She stood up and reached for the bow she'd given me earlier. I heard the wood creak, saw it bend. She was stringing it. No matter how huge the thing was, it bent pretty easily. "Get it right."

"Or what?" I couldn't help but say. I repeated the gesture, imagining a set of crosshairs over the center of my vision. Maybe if I pointed the stone that way? Strike, strike, strike…

"If you manage it, you'll earn something special," she said. "I'm going to get breakfast. Have the fire going by the time I return."

I struck the flint and steel. I struck it again. I struck it a third time.

"Piece of shit rock!" I said. Survival games never made you struggle this many times with doing stuff.

But I knew this wasn't a game. If I wanted to make her proud of me, I needed to get the fire ready.

Or did I?

Wouldn't it be fun to find out what that something else was?

I struck the flint and steel again. Sparks flew and landed right in the center of the cabin. Though I was willing them to catch, they just sort of meandered into the ground.

Huh. The ground. Maybe...

I really was an idiot, wasn't I? Tinder. A flame needs tinder.

Bark seemed like a good bet. I shaved some off one of the trees with the knife the Queen had given me, then broke it into teeny-tiny little pieces. Some dead leaves mixed in made it look almost like the world's worst potpourri. At least it didn't smell.

I piled that up in the center of the cabin. Then I took the flint and steel in my hands. Cold and smooth, they were nothing at all like the woman who had handed them to me or the place I now found myself.

Twenty hits, thirty hits, forty hits. I don't know how many it took. The whole time I thought it would be so easy to give up. Why bother trying to do anything else?

But I tried anyway. Even though I didn't want to. Even though by the end of it I was gritting my teeth.

Because when the fire finally got going? When the sparks caught, and I doubled over to blow on it like a bellows, to stoke it into being?

The flickering orange light and the heat against my hands were almost as warm as the smile I saw on her face when she returned.

What she brought back to camp that morning was a single rabbit. It hung by the ears from her hand as she walked. So fresh was the kill that when she laid it out in front of me, its fur still bloodied from where the arrow had hit it, I thought it was still breathing.

"Breakfast," she said.

"You're going to skin that, right?" I said. My throat was already a little tight looking at the poor thing, and there was this tingling at the back of my head that told me she was going to say—

"No." She instead produced a small, flat piece of metal from her cloak. She set that down on the ground.

"But I don't know what I'm doing," I said. "And that—I mean, that's an awful lot of blood, isn't it? For a meal? Surely we could have had more mushrooms?"

She sat down with her knife at the ready. When she looked at me, my heart leaped with a moment's small hope. I should have known better. I could see the shadows of her features shift into a smile.

"You need to learn to clean an animal," she said. "A handmaiden attends their god in all tasks related to their Domain. This is the simplest of mine."

I stared at the once-living being in front of me. All of a sudden I felt clammy. I ran my fingers through my hair, trying to figure out where I'd even begin. *Take out the knife, Iph. The magical god-knife she gave you for just this reason.*

Why did it feel so heavy in my hands now? I laid the tip against the soft, bloodstained fur, and I thought I was going to throw up. How could I hurt something that had been alive not too long ago?

"You are touched by it," said the Queen. I glanced up at her. She was setting up a spit above the fire I'd made.

When I looked back down, the rabbit was there, waiting for me. "It's…hard to cut into something when it feels alive…"

In two great strides she knelt at my side. The knife that had carved the spit now rested in her hand, the tip of it resting against the rabbit's fur.

"That is because you think you are the rabbit," she said.

The rabbit's eye was starting to go glassy in the midday sun.

"When your family offered you to me, they thought I was going to kill you," she said. Her voice was level and cool—but not without its attachments. "I asked for what was dearest to them. They chose you. Offered you. To them you are dead."

The fire flickered. I smelled char and smoke, and to my shame, my stomach rumbled.

"The rabbit is alive to you because you are still alive. Still fighting."

I was sitting there having my third crisis of conscience in as many hours. I was a mess. How could anyone think of that as fighting?

Yet the Queen did not falter. She reached out and took the rabbit in one hand. With the other she began to cut.

"This time, you will watch," she said. "When you have learned that you are not a thing to be eaten, you are that which eats—you will do this yourself. You are not the rabbit."

A rank smell filled the air. Death, I guessed—though I was wrong about that. It was more like offal. I covered my mouth with my ratty hoodie.

"Breathe through your mouth," she said. "It is horrible. But you will get through it. It will pass. With every breath you're closer to its end."

She set the knife down and the rabbit to her side, where her body blocked it from my view. "Iphigenia."

I stared at the place where the rabbit had been until she spoke my name. Then, when I turned, there were those two crescent moons staring back at me. "The fire burns well. You're learning already. You're already living."

She smiled at me, a proud smile, and I forgot the rabbit was there at all.

When you think of hunting, you think of sprinting across fields with a bow in hand after a stag, or something equally grand. If you're a bit more practical you might think of chasing down rabbits. If you actually know what you're talking about, you know that an awful lot of hunting is staying the fuck put in a spot until something happens to cross your field of view.

I didn't know that when all of this started. That was the next lesson the Queen tried to teach me. Breakfast, delicious and morally dubious, filled my belly so much that I could *feel* the energy coursing through me. It was like every cell in my body immediately shouted "Finally, thank fuck!" at the same time. Pumped up as I was, I figured that I could do just about anything she asked of me.

So when she said in that grandiose rumble of hers, "We're hunting now," I picked up the bow she'd given me and hightailed it toward the woods.

She stood there with her arms crossed in the clearing. I didn't notice, since I was so excited; I kept right on running without a care in the world. Forests are a bad place to run like that, though. Common sense. But not when you're that full of energy.

Thump, thump, *twist*. My footsteps against the undergrowth, and my ankle getting caught on a root.

I beefed it. No other way to put it. Sure, I managed to get my hands up in time to break the fall, but it sucked. I could feel the bruises already beginning to form. Worse than that were the tears I was starting to see in my hoodie.

I rolled over onto my back and whined. "Eugh...That'll... teach me..."

When next I opened my eyes, she was stooped over me. I couldn't see much of her face—but I did get an eyeful of her muscles. Which *almost* made up for beefing it.

"Are you that excited to hunt with me?" she said. She studied the cuts on my forearm, each in turn. "There will be more death."

I groaned. "I know, but..."

"But...?" She leaned closer to the cuts.

"I wanted to see the woods, I guess. To do something new. I...sorta forgot about the—"

Whatever I was going to say died in my throat. The Queen of the Wild—one of the twelve strong enough to have her very own Court—was licking my wounds. And not lightly. This wasn't a "the food might be too hot, let me try it with the tip of my tongue" situation. Oh no. This was knee-deep in the passenger seat, ice cream cone in hand, going to town sort of situation. The heat of her tongue against my skin and the shock together made my heart thunder in my chest. All I could do was stare at her and whimper as she worked. It was such a feral thing for her to do—but she was so gentle about it, turning my arm this way and that to get better angles. The dirt and grime made no difference to her.

I lay there blinking at her for what felt like forever. This time, when I started to tremble, it had nothing to do with the pain or the hunger or the thirst.

Well—maybe the thirst.

Like I mentioned earlier, I didn't really like the idea of people touching me *that* way. Had never really thought about it. If I wanted to get off, I did it myself. Sure, there were fantasies, and some of them got filthy. Plenty of other people in those. But they never touched me.

She'd done it without thinking. Done it so casually. And...although it felt a little weird, it was the weirdness of a new sensation. Not a bad one.

"You're staring," she said.

"I. Um."

But while I was trying to figure out the words, she let out a small laugh. I felt her help me up. She even put the bow back in my hand. Closed my fingers around the grip of it, too.

"I need to keep you safe, so that you can pay attention," she said. Then she tilted her head. I could see it, again, the way she was smirking at me. "Can you pay attention, Iphigenia?"

"Sure," I said. Before I knew it I was rambling like an idiot. "Love paying attention. Love staring. Love…hunting…being in the woods…"

"We will work on it," said the Queen. She tilted her head. "Follow me. I will show you where we'll hunt. And watch your step."

I followed where she led. And with what had just happened—well, my eyes were on anything except my wounds. They didn't even seem to hurt all that much anymore, to be honest.

After a few days in the woods I'd thought I was starting to know them. Watching her move through them, though, I realized how foolish it was to think the woods and I had even gotten acquainted. The turns she took and the branches she moved to get there were hidden to me. There were whole ecosystems here I hadn't known to expect. We brushed away a curtain of moss and leaves to find not a pine forest but a rolling savanna up ahead.

"How is this possible?" I asked her.

She stalked through the grass ahead, low to the ground, so that not even the tips of her antler headdress were visible.

"I like a little variety," she answered.

The grass was a welcome reprieve from the roots and the brambles and the burrs and the branches. Here the ground was softer, had more give to it. The whole sky stretched on overhead into forever, the horizon a blur of distant mountains and clouds and yet more of this beautiful brush.

I couldn't stop grinning. Everything here was so alive. Up ahead there was a small watering pool, clear and rippling, with a whole menagerie gathered around. Two giraffes were leaning over to get sips of the water, next to a group of what I assumed had to be wildebeests. Two little antelopes were lazing about in the afternoon sun.

I wanted to run up to the giraffes and touch their flanks, wanted to run circles around the watering hole, wanted to lie there for a while among the animals.

The Queen stopped a little ahead of me. When she did, some of the antelopes came up to her and started to sniff at her hands. She pulled something from a pouch of hers, some kind of food or treat, and offered it to them as she petted their heads.

I had never in my life been so jealous of anyone. And it was weird to be! What did it mean that I wanted her to pet me like that? My cheeks felt hot. The thought of her touching the top of my head, telling me she was proud of me, calling me by name...

"My lady..." I started.

Again I heard her smiling. "We aren't hunting here."

"I wouldn't even if you told me to," I answered. "Sorry, I—"

"I am glad you would have refused," she said. She looked toward me as the second antelope came toward her. It laid its big head on her chest. There was a soft laugh from her as she gestured for me to come over with a flick of her antlers. "Come. Get to know them."

The antelopes didn't move at all, didn't acknowledge me, and I was fine with that. They were as fascinated by her as I had been back in the woods. "Pet them as you like. And remember always that you can refuse."

You have to understand, I'd never done anything like this before. Dogs, sure. Cats. We had our fair share of pets in the high-rise to make up for the fact that my father and I couldn't leave it. But before I left, before I came to this Domain, I'd never touched anything other than people and man-made things. Plants, too, sometimes.

This was different. I thought the fur would be soft, but it wasn't. There was a bit of roughness to it—*bristle*. And while I had expected them to be warm, I hadn't expected them to be *hot*, almost uncomfortably so. The heartbeats that I could feel only faintly in myself or in others *resounded* in the great chamber of this creature's torso. The only thing I could think to compare it to was touching a machine while it was still in motion; you could feel the shifting beneath, the rhythmic thumping of its internal workings. But this was no machine.

It was a living, breathing creature with a mind of its own.

And as I laid my hand against its flank, it turned to look at me with big brown eyes. Not a thought within them. This was not a being who had ever in its life heard the words *taxes* or *synergy* or *raid mechanics*, and it led a happy little existence all the same. In this moment it was as happy as I was without any further knowledge of the world.

My mouth opened. "G'day?" I said to the antelope.

It stuck its tongue out and started to pant.

"Yeah, guess it is a little hot," I said. "Thanks for letting me do this."

"It's beautiful, isn't it?" she said.

I bit my lip and nodded. It was.

She gave the antelopes a pat each. Maybe they understood it as some sort of dismissal, because they started to leave. She watched them go.

"You should see it at night," she said. And she began to walk.

I walked with her. "Yeah? What happens then?"

"My favorites glow silver," she said. "And the whole world is sacred."

I didn't need to know where the animals came from, or why the Queen of the Wild allowed there to be daylight in her Domain when she ruled over the nights. This place existed in this way because it was her, and she was it.

And it was beautiful here.

The hunting lesson. That's the thing that was the worst. And we didn't wait for very long before getting into it. The Queen doesn't run from things that frighten her. Guess she thought I should be the same.

It started wrapped in that same ease and comfort. We were simply walking through the savanna. There I was rambling when she put out a hand to shush me.

"So that's what we call a raid. You and your friends all getting together to beat up a really big enemy. I guess it's not that different from hunting when it—"

The gesture was a sharp one, so I shut up quick. When I followed her pointing hand I saw them: a pair of pigs snorting at the ground up ahead. They weren't particularly big, maybe the size of a large dog, but even so I couldn't help but see mounds of pork instead of cute creatures.

Part of me felt ashamed at that. When I blinked I saw the poor rabbit from earlier, the dead thing staring back at me, and the space between my shoulder blades tingled.

But my stomach? My stomach rumbled.

She waved to snap me out of my reverie. The next second she had drawn an arrow from her quiver. She slid the quiver over to me and stared at me with frightening intensity. I knew, without her having to say it, that I needed to hand her arrows as she needed them.

She took a slow step forward. Her feet made no sound as they moved through the grass. I tried to mimic the steps as best I could, lifting my leg with purpose and landing on the ball of my foot. The grass crunched.

I winced. Worried I had ruined everything already, I peeked at the pigs again.

They were still there. Still unaware of what was about to happen.

The Queen drew back her bow. The arrow whistled through the air, a bolt of impossible silver headed straight for the pigs. I wondered if she was going to do something godly here, if she was going to use her powers—but she didn't.

All she needed to do was aim. The bow did the rest.

The pig turned to face its doom. The poor thing was a little too late: The arrow crashed into its eye. A spurt of blood followed; he whined and thrashed, but there was nothing he could do. The arrow was in all the way to the fletching.

The Queen's eyes fell on mine again, silver as the arrows, and she spoke. "You are not the prey, Iphigenia. Grant it a swift death."

And it was true—somehow the pig was still writhing, still in pain. The other one had already taken off. A cloud of dust was all that remained of it. I wondered, in the back of my head, if the dying pig knew it was being abandoned.

I slung the quiver across my shoulders and pulled the knife from my pocket. I couldn't tell you what compelled me to keep walking toward the pig, but I did, each step heavier than the last. As it squirmed and writhed, I knelt down next to it—and she knelt down next to me.

"Hold it here," she said, and I did, too shocked to argue otherwise. "Tilt the head back. One cut, that's all. This is the best way to thank it for the meals it is going to give you: mercy."

It was still wriggling in my hands—but weaker with every passing second. Suffering. I knew it.

Could I really do it? Could I really kill this pig myself?

I screwed my eyes shut. I wasn't the one who had killed him, really. The Queen had. I was here to...to make the suffering stop.

So I did. I sucked in a breath and I drew the knife across its throat and its blood ran over me, like a wave, and in a few seconds it didn't struggle anymore—it was dead. Somewhere in the pool of blood that soaked into my sweats was the last of its life.

I dropped the pig.

She wrapped her arms around me.

And that's the other thing about her. This place is beautiful, and it is her—but it is brutal, too. And that brutality is also her.

"You did well," she said. "Cry if you need. I'll be here."

I did.

And she was.

Chapter Nine

She was there for me.

In the mornings she woke me, always a little too early, and told me what it was we'd be doing that day. Some days it was hunting—but not always. Lessons in shelter building, trap making, fishing, and a whole lot of things she called woodcraft with a shrug were all on the lesson plan.

We didn't eat first thing in the morning. Not usually. It meant you had to wait longer to go check on the traps—you don't want to get moving right after you eat or you'll get horrific cramps, as she let me find out the second day we went out. I insisted on having myself a bit of pork before we got going and spent half the day lying around, clutching my stomach.

But she was there for me then, too. She sat at my side with a pan of water she kept boiling for my sake. Every now and again she'd dribble some of it onto my lips. Her heavy, callused hand lay on my belly. To pass the time she tried to tell me stories about her family—but she's not very good at telling stories.

Way too direct, no buildup to anything. Just "This happened. Then that."

I teased her about it.

Her eyes fell on me, and I saw that half smile again. To be honest, I caught her smiling at me a *lot*. Inevitably it would come when she was teaching me something and I cocked it up.

The traps, for instance. They're delicate work. Have you ever tried to set up a figure 4 trap? I swear, they're the most finicky things in the world. So many things can go wrong! There's the rock not being the right shape or not heavy enough, there's each individual stick and all the ways you can fuck up carving them, there's the tension they have to rest in in order to spring properly... I could go on, but I think you're getting the point.

The first time she was teaching me to make figure 4 traps, it took me from noon to sunset to get a single one working. There I was, after so many hours of work, confident as could be, grinning like a cat with her fill of cream.

The Queen knelt down next to me. I had called her over from her very important work (feeding deer in the forest) to take a look at what I'd set up.

"Have you ever seen a trap so pretty?" I asked her, hands on my hips. "Look at that. It took me a couple tries, but I think you'll find that's the perfect rock. Flat on one side, heavy, kinda pointed on the bottom, too. And here's the little dugout by the trigger. Sort of forces the animal to hit it, see? The angle's set up so the fall is quick. Won't be any struggle involved—"

The Queen touched the trap's spring stick.

"Not sensitive enough," she pronounced. Sure enough,

though she was flicking the damn thing now, it wasn't going off at all.

I stared and stared and stared.

"I hate you," I said.

She smirked. "Liar. Brave liar."

She left it at that—stood back up and walked away, leaving me to my work. I watched her go. No matter how upset I was at the godsforsaken figure 4 trap—the nemesis of reason and all things useful—it couldn't match how thrilled I'd been to hear that quiet laugh or the small pride in her voice.

I got to hear more of that sound.

While the mornings we spent planning and the days themselves we spent doing, the time after the sun went down was reserved for talking. I cooked more often than not, because I was the one who needed to learn and she didn't need to eat at all, but she sat by the fire with me and took in the fumes for politeness's sake.

"You know, my father always told me to watch out for you," I said. It had been in the back of my mind for a while now. "He told me that you hated talking with humans. That you'd locked yourself away from them."

She sat there, propped up on an elbow, watching me cook.

"I don't like talking," she said. "More of my brother's specialty."

"From what I've heard, he isn't a very serious bloke, is he?" I said. "Saunters around all over with no real home."

She grunted—but it was one of those positive, affirming grunts I'd come to know from her.

"Can't imagine the two of you get along all that well. You

want to be left alone, and all he wants is to chat with whoever's around. Must have talked your ear off when you were younger. Wait. Do you have childhoods?"

"Not like yours," she answered. "We are young. We grow. We change. All things change. But no—not like you do."

To my surprise, she was the one who spoke up next.

"Are you afraid of me, Iphigenia?"

I shook my head as I turned the meat again. "At first, sure. I was terrified when I first saw you. With what my dad told me, I thought you'd turn into some kind of wild animal and eat me."

She laughed that low, rumbly laugh. "I can, if you like."

"See, that's why I'm not afraid of you anymore. Because I know that under that mask, in the middle of all that shadow, you're a little shit."

"Little?" she said, tilting her head.

I flicked a twig in her direction. She didn't even bother dodging it.

"Maybe I'll still get you some day," she said. "You don't know my other form. I could surprise you."

I narrowed my eyes. She was right—I didn't know her other form, and she *could* get me one day. A lot of gods could change shape when they wanted to. Some took advantage of it more than others. It made sense that, without a human around, the Queen would shift hers to something more animalistic. But I had the feeling she liked having a human around to tease too much to go through with it.

"Who's going to beef it for your amusement if not me?" I said. "You'd never."

"Who knows. You may walk into a trap someday," she answered. There, the smirk again. "I might leave you there."

"If it's a figure 4, I'll see it a kilometer away. Don't you go fucking testing me, I swear I will."

I knew the second I said it that I'd made a mistake—not because I'd upset her but because she would take that as a challenge.

She hummed a little tune, and I thought to myself, *This is going to be how I die, isn't it?*

"You swear. Hm," she said. "Well. Another night, perhaps."

My cheeks went hot. To try to distract from what was going on, I asked her about the other Courts and what she thought of them. The answers were short and to the point: Earth gives her trouble; they're too similar. Fire is straight out. The King of Waves repulses her. And so on. It didn't last too long.

But it was enough to give us a little more space to talk— and she took the hint to change subjects. The hours passed. I had too-charred pork and water I hauled from a river that very morning for dinner. I'll tell you now that it tasted at least as good as anything I ever had catered to us from a fancy restaurant.

As I lay there staring up at the moon, hoping I could sleep, she sat next to me. "Do you miss any of it?"

I held up my hand. If I tried, I could pretend I held the moon in my palm. "Yeah. People more than things, I guess. Wasn't expecting that. I spent my whole life wanting to get out into the world, see the sky, touch grass, and all. So that part of things has been great. But I keep thinking about my family..."

Ori loved camping. Mum was always taking him off to this or that wilderness camp out in the bush. He's in Scouts, too. I can't tell you the number of times he'd come up to me with a length of rope to show me a knot he learned how to tie. The day my dad gave him a fancy Swiss Army knife might just have been the best day of his life. When it came down to it, I was kind of living his dream right now, running around with the embodiment of the Wild, learning how to live out here.

Ellie wasn't so big on all that—but she really loved animals. She begged Mum for a dog, and always begged to go walk it. She covered her planners and other things in cute stickers: cats big and small, otters, rabbits. While I wasn't sure what she'd think of us hunting some of those things, I knew that if she were here she'd have a blast just looking at all the animals. Being near them.

They deserved to have this experience, the good parts of it. But no one should have to know their parents are all right with killing them.

My mouth felt dry. When I asked my question, I looked up at the moon—not at her.

"Do you think my siblings could visit sometime?" I asked. "I know you don't like people, but they're nice, I promise, and they listen to me pretty well when it comes down to it. They wouldn't bother you. In fact, they might actually be helpful. More useful than me, anyway. Orestes already knows more than I do. Do you remember when I was trying to start that fire? He can do it with just two sticks. Isn't that incredible? Doesn't even need the flint and steel."

The weight of her hand on my shoulder. "Iphigenia…"

"If Mum and Dad were fine with giving me away, maybe you could work something out for the rest of us. It isn't fair that my brother has to stay there. Sometimes I think about that. I mean, there's always got to be an heir to the House of Pelops, right? It's part of our arrangement. So that means it's got to be him. And I…"

She was picking me up and pulling me close, and I let her. With my head in her lap I looked from the silver moon to the shadow of her face. I reached up for her cheek. Her skin was cool, like she'd just come out of the water, but rough with dirt.

"Can you bring them here? Please?"

Her hand around my wrist—soft and gentle. I thought for a moment she might have been offended by my touching her, but she ran her thumb in slow circles along my wrist. Maybe she was taking my pulse. Maybe she just wanted to feel it beat. There was no hiding from her that my heart was starting to race.

"I cannot. Until they are free of their curse, I cannot. I wish I had a happier answer for you."

My heart was paper, the truth an arrow punching straight through it. I crumpled in her lap. She ran her fingers through my hair. I was aware, in a distant way, that she'd begun to braid it. When had my hair gotten long enough to braid?

"It isn't fair," I said. "Why do they have to stay?"

"Nothing my family ever does is fair," she said. "Once my half sister has made her decision, you will be free to do as you like when you are not needed. And you can visit them, as you please."

I was starting to sob into her lap. She had not much to soak up the tears—a fur loincloth, and that was all. Lying there felt more like cuddling a lion than a person. But it was her, and she let me cry as much as I liked.

I appreciated that. I appreciated so much about what she'd done for me. This Domain, this position as her handmaiden. The food and the skills she'd given me. I was safer here in this untamed wilderness than I had ever been. When she had no need of my services to help her in the hunt, I could go wherever I liked, except for the cave. And I often did go. Not once since the cave had she chided me for it. If I needed her, all I had to do was call for her. She'd show up. Sometimes it took her a little while, but she'd show up, and she'd never be annoyed that I needed help.

But why couldn't she just...

I screwed my eyes shut. "News would be great, if you can get it."

She hummed in agreement. Something touched my forehead, cool and soft. It was only when I heard the rattle of her headdress that I realized she'd kissed me there.

"What would make you happy, Iphigenia?" she asked. "If I can grant it to you, I will."

In the dark of night I fell into a storm of emotion. Bitterness toward my father, regret that I could not see my siblings, a longing to return home...and a lightness that came with the unexpected tenderness she'd shown me.

"You are my handmaiden," she said. "Not my servant. Not my sacrifice. I asked for you to save you, not to torment you. Let me make you happy however I can."

"Can I...Can I think about it?" I said. "It's hard to answer right now. For tonight, all I want is..."

She was close. I knew she was—I could smell her, feel the bones tied to her headdress against my skin. The coolness I felt was her—I knew that now.

"Say it. Name the mercy of the night."

"All I want is..."

Hands against my skin, the scent of the wild, to be treasured not for what I was but for who I was, to be...

"Iphigenia."

Her voice saying my name. In all the dark and the loneliness, to be found and to be held and wanted by someone. To be known.

"Say it."

I reached for her again. And I reached for the name I'd seen written on old pottery and reliefs, the name I'd known but never dared to speak.

"Artemis. When I can't sleep, I want you to hold me."

I opened my eyes. There, in the shifting dark, I saw the crescent of her smile. She pulled me close against her chest, wrapped her legs around me, and her arms around my waist.

"Then I will hold you every night, if that is what it takes," she said.

Artemis says precisely what she means.

I was getting to the point where she could leave me to my own devices for a day and not have to worry about me. My traps weren't *amazing*, but they worked. I could make a shelter and a couple of different kinds of fires. If I got hungry, I knew well enough what the safe plants looked like, and if it really came down to it, she'd left me a (much smaller) bow I could use to hunt. Most important of all, she knew I wouldn't lie there in a lump if she left.

I'd get up and I'd do what I needed to do. Some days that was only because I wanted to keep up my end of the bargain. I didn't want her to worry about me; I wanted her to be able to go off and do whatever it was she needed or wanted to do. Some days it was because I had a good feeling that I'd caught something in a trap; some mornings I found myself wanting to feel the river water around my feet; some afternoons I wanted to see if I could climb even higher among the trees.

I was finding reasons to try.

But no matter how long she was away—she'd find her way back when night fell in the Domain. Whenever I started to get tired, whenever I lay in the dirt or the grass or atop leaves and mud, she'd appear next to me. I'd hear her before I saw her. Without a word she'd pull me toward her.

I don't sleep for very long. I never have. I don't want to make it seem like this *fixed* my insomnia. The problem hasn't really gone away. I get drowsy at a certain time, and it's a roll of the dice if I'm actually going to be able to stay asleep. It's better, but not gone.

The best nights of rest I've ever gotten, though... I've always been with her.

I started to wander more.

Artemis encouraged it. If she had to leave in the mornings, she'd tell me to go find something new so I could tell her about it later. The forest was becoming home; as soon as I saw the deciduous trees I could usually find my way back to the clearing we usually used for camp. You'd be surprised the things you can use to navigate the woods. A few weeks ago everything had looked the same to me—I couldn't imagine that anymore. There were plenty of unique trees to go by. Carving symbols into some of them helped, too, and sometimes I would leave little piles of rocks here and there to note where the borders were with the other biomes.

Besides the jungle, where I tried my best to spend the least amount of time, there was also a mountain. It bled into the forest; you'd think they were the same from the outside. The trick to it was that the mountain was always colder, and its trees were all evergreens. Though it never got to be winter there—maybe she didn't like the winter?—you could always see your breath. And it was always cold enough that I wished I had more clothes than I did. What I wouldn't have given for a puffer jacket! And it only got colder the higher up you went on the mountain.

The first time I saw it, I didn't bother trying to climb it. Just seeing the craggy peak jutting out against the sky was already something new—and it took half a day just to get there if you walked. I cut my losses and headed back to camp. The second time, though, I set out with a purpose.

That morning I woke up without her. Naturally I went off to go check my traps—that way I'd know if breakfast had come to me, or if I had to go find it myself. There was a rabbit waiting for me. After thanking it for its trouble, I'd taken it back to camp to clean.

She was there, then, sitting with her head perched on her palm. "Family," she said, "is a difficult thing."

I sat next to her and started cleaning up. Despite having done this a couple times myself, I really didn't like looking. I was learning to do it by feel, instead, which was still a little gross but somehow felt less bad to me on a moral level.

"Your family is a lot more fucked-up than most people's," I said.

She grunted in agreement. "Too much trouble. Always a fight."

I was so used to her knapping or carving or cleaning when we spoke that her empty hands were an oddity.

"Best to keep out of that," I told her. "I mean, I know you try. You're here with me most of the time, and when you're not, I bet it's only because you're needed."

Another grunt.

"I'm guessing you were needed," I said.

The clink of her headdress as she nodded. "The war has taken a turn. The Queen of Flame's son has been harmed on the field. That now means it is everyone's problem. Despite Father telling us all to stay out of it."

"And you long for peace and quiet," I said. It was sort of funny—but I didn't laugh. It didn't feel right when she was so down. "How bad is the fighting?"

It took another couple minutes of the food cooking before she answered. The whole while she was staring at the fire. I wondered what she saw in it—or if she was seeing anything at all. Sometimes when you stare at something, it's more about you.

"Bad."

One word. Not one you pick on a lark, either. Not someone like her. I let it have the space it needed.

The next part came as I was putting my catch on a spit. I hated this part most of all. As if sensing that, she moved over to where I was sitting. Her great hands took the kill and spitted it as easily as if she was preparing a marshmallow to roast.

"Your family is safe," Artemis said. "Not happy, for the most part. But they are safe. Your uncle yet lives, as does your aunt; your mother and father are unharmed. Their champions fare well against those of the other Courts."

"They aren't happy?" I asked.

She turned to study me. "Iphigenia. You are no longer the heir. Your only job is to be my handmaiden. They have no hold on you."

"But shouldn't I be helping?" I started.

She took my hand in hers and laid it on her cheek again. I couldn't see my own fingertips—they disappeared into the magical darkness that kept her face from hurting me. But I could feel her. I was beginning to like that, the feel of her skin against mine.

"Please understand: Not all problems are there for you to solve. You cannot save everyone at the cost of your own happiness." She cleared a shock of hair from my face. "You have already helped me more than you know. Training you and looking after you gives me reason to avoid the machinations of my siblings. You've saved me from that."

The wild. Roast meat. Sweat. I could smell all sorts of things in that clearing, hear all sorts of things.

But all that mattered was her.

You saved me.

"Artemis..."

She touched the tip of my ear, my nose, her thumb lingering on my lips.

"My father is summoning us all. Please believe I will be back as soon as I can," she said. "And Iphigenia?"

The food might as well have burned for all I cared. It wasn't what I wanted to take a bite of, I'll tell you that.

"Y-yeah?"

"I treasure you too much to see you spend yourself on those who do not appreciate you," she said. She stood, and her hand lingered on top of my head. "I care about your happiness. Not theirs."

That was the last thing she said to me. Before I could answer her, she was gone. Just like that.

My eyes fell on the mountain. As much as I enjoyed her company, the Queen's bluntness sometimes left me with a lot to mull over and nothing to mull it with. I'd been putting off the climb this whole time because I hadn't felt ready. I still didn't. But climbing felt a lot better than thinking.

Time to give it a shot. Who knew? Maybe there'd be happiness up at the peak.

I didn't have much in the way of gear, but I brought what I could: cordage, pork jerky, and some nuts I'd gathered, my knife, a pelt I was using for extra warmth, flint, and steel. Nothing too major and nothing too heavy. This time, when I laid eyes on the mountain, I saw it as a challenge.

And there was this thought in the back of my head, like a whisper: *Take a photo for Ori.*

Whenever I got to see him again, he'd never believe me about all the things I'd gotten up to. Wouldn't it be cool to have things to show him?

And...well, there was this other thought.

"Until they are cleansed of their curse."

That was what she'd said about my siblings.

Looking at that mountain I had the thought for the first time: *If she can't free them, maybe I will.*

The mountain was less about my upper body and more about the lower. I was not even a third of the way up when my legs started to burn worse than they had in weeks. What looked to me like a gentle slope was anything but.

All right, I told myself. *That's fine. I'll take a little rest.*

So I stopped there and I sat on the cool gray stone, so unlike the dirt of the hills I'd come to know.

There's a springiness to dirt. Pile some leaves or straw down, and it's honestly not the worst thing in the world—as long as it doesn't rain.

But a mountain? A mountain is never going to yield to you. Even when you find yourself at its peak, I'll tell you now: The mountain hasn't yielded. You can think what you like, take photos for your friends, brag about conquering it all you want; none of it is going to change the truth of the matter.

And the truth is that mountain hates you.

Of course, I didn't know any of that back then. So I sat down on the rock and I thought I would be fine if I kept pressing forward. All I needed was to catch my breath. I had a little canteen of water, so I took a bit of it, had some of my food, and got back to my feet.

The second I did, my worn-down shoes slipped along the rock. I didn't have any time to react. I tumbled to the ground and knocked my knee against the rock. Stars shot across my vision; the pain hurt so bad I felt it in my teeth. But it wasn't over for me—oh no. I could never be that lucky. While I was trying to get my balance, my other foot also failed to find any purchase; I started to roll down the slope.

It was all I could do to curl in a little. I'd taken enough falls to know I needed to protect my head.

You'll be happy to know that I didn't give myself a concussion. Just a sore back and side and front and top and bottom. Lying in a heap at the bottom of the slope, I felt about as big as an ant. Then my pack smacked me in the face and I thought, *Maybe an ant is bigger, actually.*

Two thoughts came to me. The first, *fuck mountains*, needs

no elaboration. The second was that I couldn't let this thing beat me. Only depression and insomnia could beat my ass that bad. I had to get back up and try again.

But I was going to need better gear if I was going to give it a try.

When it no longer hurt to breathe *that much*, I pushed myself back up. Cursed up a blue streak. It still hurt to breathe when I was upright. Worse, it turned out that putting weight on the leg was a mistake the likes of which aren't often seen outside of YouTube fall compilations. I beefed it *again*, crumpling the second I tried to get any momentum.

"Shit," I said.

I needed to get a look at the state of matters. Taking off my hoodie caused another fresh wave of pain, though none so bad as the knee. My arms were horribly scraped. I'd gotten used to that. There were a couple of scars here and there from some of the tumbles I'd taken; these would just add to the number. I wasn't worried about those.

But when I pulled up my shirt? Now there was something to worry about. A big old bruise was starting to form on my ribs.

Okay, okay. So I'd fucked up. I could still make this work, right? I didn't need to worry Artemis with a little bruise. I was tougher than that! What was all this training for if I couldn't deal with pain?

Seeing what had happened to my knee changed my tune. I didn't bother pulling my sweats down; I just tore the damn things off right above the injury.

What I saw hardly looked like a knee at all. It was a swollen lump of purple-red flesh. Only it was swelling further, too. When I tried to wriggle this way or that I could feel it pulse with blood.

Maybe this wasn't the sort of thing I could figure out on my own after all.

I gritted my teeth. Fear's cold finger ran down my spine. Could I wait long enough for her to show up? What if it took all day? She had no way of knowing I was hurt. I held up my hand to the sun to try to get an idea of the time. A little past noon. Shit. It would be *hours* before she came back for her nightly visit.

I could lie here that long; I knew I could. I was the world champion of lying around doing nothing. But could *my knee*?

Looking at it only made me more nauseous. I covered it with my hoodie and tried to get myself to take some deep breaths.

"Artemis!" I shouted. "Artemis, if you can hear me, I could really use a lift! I'm in pain!"

Nothing. Birds and wind, that was all. I took another sharp breath.

"Kind of scared, to be honest! Got a little ambitious, and I don't want to lose my leg over it. Please, if you can hear me, help!"

Nothing.

And then—the sky overhead flickered; the light flared so bright I had to hide my face in the crook of my elbow to keep my eyes from burning. For the first time in months I heard something unnatural: an unseen hand plucking at harp strings.

"Now this is interesting. I know what *I'm* doing in my sister's Domain. But what are you doing here, little human?"

Shit. Shit shit shit. The light plucking of a harp could mean only one thing.

The King of Song.

I kept my face right where it was. Without an oath to protect me, I was probably fucked no matter what I did, but I didn't want to go out by staring at him. I hardly knew him. My mind raced as I tried to remember how to talk to gods who weren't Artemis. There were things I was supposed to say; they all had their own epithets. If you got them wrong, they were liable to turn you into a plant or an animal, curse you, or who knows what else.

Hard enough to try to remember them after so long without considering that sort of thing—worse when my knee felt like someone was bouncing on it with a jackhammer.

"Glory to you and to your many-splendored crown, Lord of Music, King of the Light, Winner of Hearts, and Fairest of Men," I said. Then I sucked in a breath and hoped that I'd buttered him up right.

"Fairest of Men is Father's cupbearer, actually," he said. He continued strumming his harp. "Father's womanizing is far better known, so I'll forgive your ignorance. But I appreciate the flattery; it's bought you a little time."

An almost overwhelming warmth near me—not heat, but warmth. As if I'd stepped into a stuffy room in the middle of the summer. I kept my head bowed.

"Thank you, my lord. To answer your question..." Shit, this hurt. "I'm here as a guest of the Queen's. I'm her..."

"Oh. The new handmaiden in training. I've heard about

you. Old Gray Eyes simply won't stop her diatribes about you. Don't suppose *you* know where sister dearest has gone off to, then?" he said.

"Believe me, if I did, I would have crawled my way over there already," I said.

He hummed. The tune was so beautiful that, I swear to you, for a moment there I felt no pain at all.

"You've gotten yourself into a bit of a situation, haven't you?" he said. "The knee, I mean. I'd wager you were trying to climb the mountain when you hurt it. Then you tried to walk it off, which put more weight onto it, and now it's... rather the color of a plum, isn't it? And about the size of a mortal's head. It must pain you terribly."

I did not like the cadence in his voice. No, I didn't like it at all. When a god spoke to you like that, it meant they were going to ask you for something. But what choice did I have? The deals weren't always bad. I braced myself.

"It does," I said. "I was hoping I could speak to your sister, the Queen, and she might help me with it."

I heard him tut. He was standing next to me, if I didn't miss my guess. "That's not *her* thing. That's *my* thing. The best she could do is lick the wound like some sort of wild animal. From the look on your face, I see she's already tried that on you at some point. It's all psychosomatic, you know. It isn't *real* healing. She can't do that, no matter how much she'd like to pretend that she can. Why do you think she has to bother with bandages and stitches and the like? She has no hand in medicine, unless it's birthing. And you've never given birth."

"My lord, that's a very personal thing to say to someone with a uterus," I said through gritted teeth. No wonder Artemis didn't like him much. "But I would be thankful for any help that you could offer, if you were so inclined to offer it."

"I might be," he said. "How about you and I forge a little deal, then? Whatever your name is. Pelops girl. I'm sure you'd love to treat with me. I'm far more charming than she is."

Uh-huh. Sure you are, buddy. Couldn't say that, though. "What are the terms, my lord?"

"Very simple," he said. "I want you to deliver a message to her when you see her. It'll save me the indignity of having to track her down, and I won't have to smell her. If you do, I will heal your injuries. Your bodily ones, at any rate; the mental ones I'm sensing will take more work than I care to do."

Now what the *fuck* was that supposed to mean? Oh, man. I had to fix my face after hearing that. I had to remember, no matter how much anger boiled in my stomach, that I was at this man's mercy. If I was too mean when I responded to him, if I looked too ungrateful, he could kill me. He could do far worse. My swollen, misshapen knee...With a snap of his fingers he could turn my whole body into an equally twisted mess.

But I really, really wanted to clock him. My fist ached to hit him. Could you imagine? Oh, I'd probably die right after. Maybe in the middle of it! One good hit, though—just enough to remind him he couldn't talk to people that way...Artemis would forgive me, right?

It was a daydream I couldn't afford to indulge when the absolute bastard was right there in front of me.

"That's all? A message?" I asked.

Instead of a normal response, I got a flourish from his harp. People would probably kill to have heard the tune and, admittedly, it was so beautiful it hurt—but I really wanted a yes or no.

"It's an important message. And you have to find her shortly."

Great. I had to track down a woman who hated being tracked down—a woman who could hide from the eyes of the other gods when she liked.

Another pulse of pain from my aching knee. I took a deep breath.

"How shortly? We have to set some terms, don't we?"

"Oh, you'd be right to," he answered. "I should have known you'd want specifics. You and your clan have dealt with us more than enough for one lifetime, haven't you?"

"My lord, I'm only trying to make a good and fair bargain. I hope you don't...*shit*...begrudge me that."

"Of course not," he answered. I heard a sound around us—some sort of animal I hadn't gotten used to yet. Sounded big. As if we didn't have enough to worry about. "Hmm. Shall we say before the night falls here? That seems reasonable enough to me. What I have to tell her is important."

Think, think. Agreeing to the very first thing you were offered was a stupid thing to do. There was always room to negotiate—until there wasn't. But you would know very quickly when there wasn't any more room.

Think of the terms here. Before nightfall? How could I possibly track her down before then? She'd only show up when she wanted to. I couldn't compel her—and, to be honest, I didn't want to.

Part of what I liked about her was that she was so much herself. Artemis didn't care what people thought about her. Sometimes that meant that I didn't enter her mind until she was done cleaning a kill, or setting up a fire, or whatever it was that had her attention.

We could share the quiet because we both knew we'd find each other again. We had that trust.

Could I violate it by going after her? She'd said she liked it when I challenged her. They weren't just words, either; if I pointed out something she'd missed, she'd always give me a little grin. Maybe she'd like being tracked down by a human.

But how would she feel if I'd done it for her brother's sake? I knew how she felt about him.

The king played another tune as I considered my options. He let out a sigh. A dramatic one, the shithead. "It isn't often I'm made to wait like this. I'm being so kind to you, and you're hardly giving me the same attention."

How had no one decked him yet? "My lord, please forgive me. I was thinking. You wouldn't want me to agree thoughtlessly, would you?"

Only music for an answer. So that's how it was.

I couldn't waste any more time, or he might withdraw the offer. With a sharp draw of breath to get me through the pain, I answered him.

"Please give me until the next dawn. I'm sure you know how tricky she can be to find, or else you wouldn't be asking me. I'll deliver your message and whatever else you like—so long as it doesn't bring her harm."

The music stopped. The hairs on the back of my neck stood on end, anticipating a transformation into who knows what. But it never came. Instead, there was just his stupid voice again.

"Hmmm. Very well. You will tell her that Wisdom has devised her final exam for the handmaiden. You are to assist her in felling a beast. If you perform well and survive, you will be permitted to continue on in your service, and she will not be found in violation of the Law. If you fail to gird her, to arm her, and to clean what she has killed, the two of you will be found in violation."

What the...? That sounded more like a message for *me* than for her. He could have just come out and said this! Ugh, the song-and-dance with him.

"As for what else to bring her... I will give you a note. It's easier that way. If I give you a poem to recite, it might burn your mouth on the way out. Can't have that."

Uuuuugggggghhhhh.

Maybe I could recite godly poetry if I wanted! He didn't even want to try. What a pompous...

"I agree," I said. "My lord, I agree to your terms. And I ask kindly that you heal me, because I have no hope of finding her as I am."

"You certainly don't," he said. "Not to worry. This won't hurt at all. Keep your eyes closed until I say you may open them—my countenance is too great to mask."

Like *hell* it was. Artemis could do it! The King of Gods could even do it! This... Oh, I had so many words for him.

But I had to admit, he held up his end of the bargain.

The king played a song the likes of which I'll never hear again. Quiet fell upon the mountain; no one else wanted to interfere. Not the large animal I'd heard stalking the camp, not the wind, not the trees, not the dozens of little things that lived and breathed among the grass and the brush.

The world itself went quiet.

Even I held my breath. I didn't like the man at all—but that didn't mean I was immune to his magic or blind to his craft.

The song he played was a loved one smiling at you after a long while away; it was an outstretched hand to the falling; it was warmth and light and love. My heart brimmed with it until even my hatred of him was like a distant memory. All that was left was this feeling of rosy pink, of a lover's bedroom, of the radiant adulation of a crowd.

The bastard was good at what he did. So unbelievably, undeniably good. Not that it gave him the right to act like that. Still, having heard him play, I understood why he'd be so obsessed with himself.

I might be, too, if I could do that.

By the time the music came to its end, I was too focused on the beauty of it to even remember that my leg had been in pain. I tried to hold on to the melody so that I could share it with Artemis, but the second the king spoke the music left.

"You're healed now. You're welcome," he said. "Try not to be too disappointed when you hear your human songs after this. You're all doing your best. You can't help that the divine is out of your reach."

"Thank you, my lord, I'll keep that in mind," I said.

He hummed. I heard the shifting of his clothes as he stood; the blaring light against my eyelids began to shift. "Count to ten out loud. Open your eyes only when you get to ten."

"Of course, I understand. Thank you for making a deal with me."

"Tell my sister it was nice to meet her plaything," he answered. "Even if you are horribly cursed. Now, start counting."

I did as I was told. To be honest, I rushed the numbers just a bit. I couldn't wait to be free of him. But I counted, all the same, loud and clear and with some semblance of propriety.

When I opened my eyes he was gone. In his place, resting next to my now-healed leg, was a bundle of parchment tied with a glittering gold seal.

The letter, I assumed.

I admit I was a little curious. Who wouldn't be? A letter from one god to another could hold all sorts of unknown secrets. I wouldn't blame anyone who took a peek.

But the thing is, I know all too well what happens when someone takes a peek at the gods.

So I picked up the letter, shoved it into my pants pocket, and started searching.

Chapter Ten

This place was her, and she was this place. But her brother couldn't find her within the Wilds, which meant she either wasn't paying attention, or she was off elsewhere. If she wanted alone time there was little anyone could do but track her down. To find her, I had to figure out where she went when she wanted no one else to find her.

Where had I gone at times like those?

It was easier in the high-rise. One of the benefits of an office building designed to contain everything someone might need for their existence was a complex series of shortcuts to get from one side of the place to the other. If I wanted to, I could move about that place without anyone ever seeing me. People rarely did. The most they'd notice was a missing burrito off the food counter, or someone's workstation now having new, funny wallpaper.

I hiked back toward the forest.

I walked and walked and walked. Thought about running, to be honest. As much as I had hated it at the start of things, running did get the blood pumping in a way that helped you think. But it wasn't wise to run here. I mean, I'd already beefed it once. Had to have the grand dickhead himself help me out of that jam.

And the last time I'd gone running through the forest—

Wait.

The last time I'd gone running through the forest I'd *also* beefed it. And that had been the day Artemis showed me the watering hole.

It was beautiful at night, she'd said.

I grinned. That's where she'd be. That had to be it!

All I had to do was find my way there without her. Not that that was an easy thing to do... but it would be easier now. I knew the forest. I'd left marks and signs.

The Iphigenia that Artemis had carried here in her arms could never have found her way to the savanna.

But this one?

I had a fair shot.

My gut told me to head north. I did, for a little while, and managed to ford one of the nonsense rivers—those that had no rhyme or reason to their route—with only a little bit of trouble. I knew we hadn't done that when we visited the first time... but we'd also been near a cliff. And I thought I'd seen one of those on the other side of the river. If I just walked to the edge of the tree line, I should be able to find it.

One step, then another. My feet ached and my shoulders, too. I'd never spent the whole day walking like this. Trying to climb a mountain was tough enough—to hike several kilometers afterward was bordering on insane.

Most people would rest.

I couldn't. I had a promise to keep.

So even when I heard the low growl of a bear up ahead, I knew I had to keep going. Even if it was dangerous.

This time, this one time, I was going to get through on my own power.

I sank down into a crouch. The first order of business was to figure out where the bear was, and the second was to figure out what kind. I'd heard the growl from a little to the northwest. Not far, which wasn't great news. A bear is faster than you think.

Now, the amateur logic would have it that you should bolt as quick as you can for your intended destination. Most of the time that was true. Especially if you had a clear field of view, the thing to do was to shout as loud as you could, make yourself threatening, and bolt after the bear turned tail.

But the thing is, you really had to make them turn tail first. And you could only do that to smaller bears. There was no intimidating a grizzly. And it wasn't out of the question that I would find one here.

A black bear, though?

A black bear I could scream at.

Maybe two minutes after I first heard him, I saw him loping through the woods ahead of me. Big guy—fuzzy, too. And unluckily for me, he was as brown as brown can be.

That left a few options. Either he was a grizzly, or he was one of two kinds of brown bear.

Artemis was very particular about me knowing the differences between these guys. When she told me there were no less than four different kinds of bears in her Domain, I stared at her as if she'd grown a second head.

"But you don't hunt them. Why do you need so many?" I asked.

She smirked. "I like them," she said. "They're cute. And powerful."

Crouched in the middle of the woods, I watched two hundred kilos of pure ferocity moving in front of me. You could see his power with every step he took. Branches as thick as my wrist snapped when he put his weight on them.

No matter what he was, I knew for sure he wasn't a black bear. No use fighting back. I could still intimidate him a bit—but he wouldn't be the one running away from this. That would be me. Slowly, backward, and after I'd already let him know I was around.

I stashed my knife and put my bow in its carrier over my shoulder. Then I knelt down and covered my hands in the dry topsoil. Claps would sound louder with a little dirt to help.

Staring at the bear, I drew myself up to my full height and took a big, deep breath. The sort that makes your belly swell wider than you thought was possible. Then I clapped my hands together so hard that they were already tingling on the first hit.

"Hey, bear!" I shouted. "Mate, I need to get through here! Will you let me pass? Bear! Hey, bear!"

The bear turned its big, fuzzy, adorable, extremely deadly head toward me.

Let's get one thing straight: Whoever designed bears did not have humans in mind. Not in the slightest. If they did, they would have made bears horribly intimidating. Big sharp shapes, all tooth and nail, maybe piercing eyes like those giant river otters have. But instead, aside from the pure size of them and their massive muscle, they're adorable. Uniformly adorable. Show me a bear that is not adorable. I'll sit here and wait. You can't.

The trouble is, though, that no matter how cute a bear may seem, they're probably the worst thing you can encounter when you're alone in the woods. Or maybe I should say that a *hungry* bear is the worst thing you can find. When they've got full or mostly full bellies, they generally keep to roots and berries and fish and such. They don't go looking for fights, and they don't go out of their way to interact with humans at all. Most days, a bear's just trying to get by.

But when he's hungry?

When he's hungry, he's a different beast. Did you know a bear can run as fast as a horse? They sure can. Through difficult terrain, too. Granted, they can't keep it up as long as our equine friends, but if you think you can outrun a bear, mate, you're cooked. And don't think you can get out of his way by climbing, either. That'll work against most wolves—but it's no use against a bear. Either they'll climb up there with you or they'll just knock over the bloody tree.

Unless you've got bear spray on you—and I really hope you do, if you're going into the woods—and then your best bets are trying to let it know you're there to start with and praying it doesn't bother you, or playing dead and praying to the deity of your choice.

But all of that's just to say that even though they're cute, and even though I'm calling them cute, you should never under any circumstances underestimate a bear.

So.

This fella was staring at me. Eyes locked on mine. I noticed with some relief that there wasn't any blood on his muzzle, but that quickly turned to fear. No blood on his muzzle. Did that mean he'd eaten and wouldn't bother me...or that he hadn't eaten, and he would?

I didn't have time to split hairs over it.

"Hey, bear!" I said. I took a quiet little step back. Even as I did, I waved my hands in the air like an absolute maniac. "Hey, bear! I'm telling you, it's better for both of us if you just let me pass!"

The bear stirred. He put one of his big old paws in front of him, and his mouth opened. I could see each and every one of his teeth. Not that it's the teeth you have to worry about so much as the jaw itself and the tremendous amount of power it can generate.

Oh, let me tell you, I thought about it. It was so easy to picture my arm snapping like a twig when his jaw clamped those teeth shut.

As he took a step forward, I let out another shout. This one was wordless. If I stepped back when he stepped forward, he'd *know* he had the advantage. I had to hide that as best I could.

And the best way I knew to do that?

The same way I had hidden how trash garbage I was at most MOBA games: being *super* toxic.

"Hey, bear! You absolute bastard! What kind of a scrub do you have to be to come after me, huh?" I said. I took to jumping up and down to emphasize the point, smacking my hands against my bare knees to try to get some more sound into it. "Have a go at someone your own size! Haven't you read the tier lists? Humans are apex predators, mate!"

I jumped and shouted and screamed and called that bear a bunch of things that, frankly, would ruin our friendship if I repeated them. I got about as toxic as it was possible to get without getting canceled.

And you know what? After a little while…

The bear started to move away from me. Turned his head around, showed off his cute little stubby tail, and started to disappear into the woods. One step after the other.

I kept shouting for a few minutes after he left. You've got to. Otherwise they think you're gone and double back. But when it was done—I stood there huffing and puffing and doubled over, proud as I'd ever been.

I'd scared off a bear.

There was nothing in the world that could have intimidated me except maybe the King of Gods herself.

I took to the woods again.

I remembered that I should sing when I traveled. I'd forgotten to, earlier, which might explain why I crossed paths with the bear. If you sing as you go, they're less likely to come anywhere near you.

Artemis had told me that. But of course she'd followed it up with "Since you're human, you may need to know that," like a total shitter.

After I gave her the message, I was going to tell her all about what had just happened.

What was her singing voice like, anyway?

You may notice I'm not talking much any more about my trip to the savanna. That's because I've forgotten a lot about it. You see, I was traipsing through the woods absolutely high on life without a care in the world other than getting to her. Granted that's a big care. I took it very seriously!

But when I think back on the minutes before I found her, I don't remember the path I took or the animals I saw or what I heard. I remember a little of the soreness, and I remember the river making my clothes all wet. There was a bit of chill because of that even as I made my way to the warmer parts of the forest, the ones that gave way to my destination.

What I most remember is how excited I was to tell her what had happened.

And I imagined what she would say to me when I told her.

My head was in the clouds when I made it to the savanna.

Which is why I didn't notice the trap until it was already sprung.

Chapter Eleven

So here's the thing about snare traps. Yes, we're going to talk more about them. It's important you know these things. If I'm spending all this time talking to you, then you're gonna learn some bloody survival skills, at the very least. You've learned about bears—now let's have a quick chat about this.

A snare is one of the most flexible kinds of trap you can set. They're not the simplest—that's probably going to be a deadfall—but what they consume in time they more than make up for in adaptability.

Here's how they work: There's the snare itself, a trigger it's tied to that the animal knocks over when it runs through, and a base that holds the snare in place. That's it. That's the whole principle.

For small game you don't even need to set a trigger. Just tie a rope in a noose, loosen that up so it's big enough for them to run through, and then post it somewhere they *will* run through it. I don't like doing it that way—it's less ethical, since it takes longer to work—but if you're in a situation where you've got no energy, it's easy enough to do.

Or you can take the same principles and scale them up. It'll take you a while to make the cordage, sure, but it's doable. If you're just sitting around camp anyway, you might as well make yourself useful with a little weaving. It's kind of soothing. Make enough of it and find a solid enough base, and you can, in theory, catch things as big as a deer.

So. Now you understand the basics of a snare trap. Snare, trigger, base.

Here's where I start telling you what an idiot I am.

I didn't notice the snare. It was down by my feet, a loop about the size of a rabbit, and with bright white cordage. I wasn't watching where I was going. No matter how many times I'd beefed it, my head was too full of schoolgirl fluff to watch my step.

I didn't notice the trigger. The bright white cordage I'd mentioned was strung up high, drawn tight over one of the lower branches of an oak tree. The branch was young enough that it still hadn't developed that famous oaken sturdiness; it had enough spring to it to snap up when the snare got knocked off it by my big, clodding, idiot foot.

And I didn't notice the base, either. *That* was not anything someone would have spotted, though. I feel confident and reasonable in saying that this part was not too much my fault. See, this particular snare, which was built to hold the not inconsiderable weight of a single shut-in Australian, used an entire boulder as its base. The cordage wasn't tied around it as you might expect, either. Oh no.

The cordage for this base was held in place not with any earthly force, but with the tip of a brilliant silver arrow pincering it in place.

You might be starting to see where this is going.

I didn't. I didn't see a thing! There I was, strolling my way along the lanes of the forest, not a thought in my head that wasn't of a homosexual nature, my eyes firmly on the canopy and the light playing through the trees.

My foot skated through the snare, and I *still* didn't notice it. That's how light this cordage was, how finely woven!

I got maybe two steps out before the snare pulled itself off the trigger. It wasn't until that moment that I realized I'd fucked up.

Fuck? I thought, and then I was upside down. There wasn't even enough time for me to process that as a real swear. It was a question, a bit of wonder, an abrupt curse of confusion as my world literally went upside down.

My ankle was held high enough in the air that I could reach my hands out below me and still not touch the ground. Flailing as I tried to get a sense for what had gone on wasn't helping matters.

But it turned out that I didn't have to wait very long to find out what was going on, or who had trapped me.

The second the trap was sprung, that silver arrow whistled. And not long after that, when I was swaying in the air, a flash of silver light made the blur a little less miserable for a second. And after that?

After that, her hand landed on my calf, and I heard her soft little laugh, the one that always made me want to call her a too-smug git.

"Iphigenia," she said. "I've got you, little deer."

As the blood pooled in my head and she trailed her hand down toward my knee, I blurted out what I could.

"I'm really sorry but I met your brother in the woods and he fixed my knee, which was broken something awful, and in exchange he made me promise to tell you that Wisdom made up her mind about a test for me and it's some kind of weird hunt for a beast and if I help gird and arm you and clean what we catch, I can live. Also, he left a note for you—that's in my hoodie pocket, I think—and he said that I should tell you that it was nice for him to meet me, except he called me your plaything—"

"Is that all he told you to say?" she said. I was braced for her to sound angry—but instead there was a sort of... acceptance to her tone. Like something that couldn't be helped.

My tongue stuck to the roof of my mouth. My temples started to pound as I tried to think of what else that absolute bag of dicks had said to me.

Which was really hard to do when Artemis was touching the back of my thighs, beneath the sagging hem of my new sweatshorts, as if it was the most natural thing in the world. My blood flow was already weird!

"I, um. Yeah?" I said. "I think so. It was—"

"Your message is delivered and you are safe from the Law," she said. She kept touching me. The roughness of her hands against my skin was sending shivers up my spine.

"Um. You don't seem troubled," I said.

"I'm not," she said. Her hand withdrew. I was spinning too much to get a good look at her.

But you know what did work? My ears.

And you know what has a very distinctive sound?

Rope being let out.

For a second there I thought she was going to set me down. I expected the sound to come with a lowering of my current weird landscape. But the sound kept coming and, what do you know, I didn't get any lower.

"Artemis...?"

Her hands on my arms. Gentle, but insistent. She bent them so that they were behind my back and close together. I felt her adjust here and there to lessen the tension and strain.

"Iphigenia."

And that's when I felt the rope against my wrist.

"I would like to watch you squirm against this rope. To see you bound," she said. There was a lowness, a roughness to her voice that I hadn't heard from her. "I want you to surrender to me. But only if you want to."

I must have misheard her. Was she...serious? A god like her? The sort of thing she was asking me to do was...well, it was *kinky*. And I hadn't done anything like this before, either. Wasn't exactly easy to find yourself in a situation like this back at the high-rise.

Did I want this? Did I want her to tie me up and...What did she even mean to do?

I was breathing heavier. Completely and totally at her mercy, I felt small and defenseless and...

And yes, I felt *hot*. Hearing that tone in her voice, feeling her hands against my skin, knowing that *she'd* been the one to ask *me* permission for this.

I could hardly think. My heart wanted to say yes, and from the heat I was starting to feel, my body did too.

"I...um. What do you want...to do? When I'm all...I've never..."

Her hand was gentle, resting now against my ankle. I think she was trying to reassure me that she'd cut me down if I wanted.

"Are you asking if I will ravage you?"

Did she have to put it that way? I bit my lip. My cheeks were getting hotter. "I...guess so. I, um, I don't—I've never really done anything with anyone else, and..."

A hum. "I will not," she said. "I have no wish to. If that is what you want, then you must know I will never provide it for you."

My breath still caught in my chest. Was it weird that that was sort of a relief? As much as my mind was fogging up with need, it wasn't necessarily a need for *her* to touch me. Oh, sure, I got horny now and again. But I usually took care of that myself. Letting someone else get me off felt weird.

But with her, I wanted...

I wanted to show her how I felt.

How my heart was racing at the thought of her tying me up. How badly I wanted her to see me like that. How much I wanted to make her happy, and how the thought of doing that made *me* happy.

"Is it okay if I...If you won't, then is it okay if I...?"

I heard that soft laugh again behind me. "You'll have to work for it. I won't help you," she said.

"But if I do, it's okay with you?" I said. I couldn't believe what I was saying—or how everything in me was tingling at the thought of her watching me. "It won't...be weird...?"

She trailed the rough rope against my forearm. I couldn't keep myself from shivering, wriggling at the feel of it. "It wouldn't," she said. "I told you how much I love seeing you happy."

"Happy is...I mean..." That was *one* word for it. "Artemis..."

"I meant what I said. Pleasure or joy, it makes no difference to me. I want to spoil you. And torment you. *How* did you not see the snare?" she said.

"Because it was so low to the bloody ground and I was *distracted*—" I started. And I broke off into a laugh, because I realized then that the finer points of it didn't matter. I didn't want to sway here and watch the opportunity pass me by.

I wanted to do this. I wanted to be...I wanted to be her prey. Just for a little while.

"I was too busy thinking about being near you," I said. I took a breath. "Please show me the error of my ways. I'm your handmaiden in training, and I want you to do with me what you like."

I didn't see her smile—but I heard the soft sound of her approval, and I felt the rope around my wrists, and I knew how happy I'd made her.

"Iphigenia," she said. I was never going to be able to hear my name the same way again. It would always be this. Iphigenia, each syllable its own prayer, soft and needy in the fading light of dusk.

"Let me get you upright. I want to look at you."

She looped the rope around my wrists with attention and care. When she drew them tight, it was not as a single line around me, cutting off my circulation, but a careful lattice. There were five or six rounds of my wrists involved.

Each one felt like a promise. My heart was beating so quickly, and she'd barely even touched me. But the thought of her taking all that time, all that care, to tie me up... It was such a heady thing.

Midway up the loops of the rope she tied another knot, and this she looped around the tree branch above.

She wrapped her hand around my throat. Didn't squeeze, didn't press—it was like she was holding me more than anything else. My pulse beat wild against her thumb. She caressed my skin with a light possessiveness—as if she was surveying what now belonged to her. The hands that fired unerring arrows and cleaned what they killed... the hands that nurtured the wounded, that called to the soft.

I was at their mercy now. Her mercy.

"Iphigenia," she said. "Listen to me. Are you listening?"

My throat was stopped up with excitement. Breathing alone brought a rush to my head, and between my legs. Hanging upside down still with Artemis's lithe, cool body against mine...

A tug of my hair—not sharp, but enough to keep me from falling too deep into the pit of pleasure.

"Are you listening?" she repeated.

I bit my lip. The little spike of pain helped me focus, but only barely; it melted into the pressure of the ropes and the touch of her hand at my throat.

"I, uh, yeah," I said. My voice came out wavery and nervous, and I felt like some kind of idiot.

But she made a soft, pleased sound, and then I didn't feel like an idiot at all. "Good deer," she said. "What I'm about to say is important. I need you to pay attention."

I nodded. As I did, she let go of my hair, and I heard the rasp of the rope against the tree. Hanging now from two places, I was pulled upright. Or closer to it. In reality I was now parallel with the ground, staring down at it. Most of the weight was off my ankle and on the lattice binding my arms together. It was a far gentler pull...and one that made me feel far more like there was no getting away.

Artemis came around to the front of me. I was eye to eye with her waist, and the rich smell of her filled my senses. My mouth opened. When she knelt down, she must have found me staring like a dog.

But she cupped my face as tender as could be.

"If anything starts to hurt, you will tell me. If you have trouble breathing, you will tell me. If you tire of this, if your mind changes—you will tell me."

She was looking straight at me, straight into my eyes, and I was trying to look straight at her too. Much harder for me. Her face was hidden, sure—but more than that it was hard to focus on anything except the way my blood was flowing. How could it be so intense when we'd barely begun? Was I this much of a mark for being tied up?

"Do you understand?"

I nodded. She touched my cheek.

"Good. If you want me to stop altogether, you will say 'Crescent.' If you want me to slow down, or if you need me to change something for you, you will say 'Wane.'"

She let her hand sink below my cheek, down to my jaw, where she tilted my head to make sure I was looking at her. My whole jaw fit in the palm of her hand.

"What will you say if you want me to stop?" she said.

What did it mean to be held this way? For her to look at me like this? There was no one else in the world, so far as I was concerned. Nothing else mattered but her. And I so desperately wanted her to be proud of me.

"Crescent," I said.

She dug her nail in and trailed it along the line of my jaw, not enough to break skin but enough that it tingled.

"Good deer," she said. "And if you want me to change something, or check in on you?"

"Artemis..." It came out without my trying to say it. I took a breath. *Come on, Iph, focus.* "I-I'll say Wane."

"That's right," she said.

And then—with a sharp pull of the rope—I was higher up. She leaned forward and pressed her lips to my forehead, and I thought to myself that if I died right then it would probably have been worth it.

But there was more to come. She moved behind me. I heard her unwind more rope. Every beat of my heart was like a hammer against my rib cage. Almost better than the touch of the rope against my skin itself was not knowing when and where it would come next.

It was my legs.

I can't tell you the thrill I felt with her behind me like that—a perfect predator so near to prey, powerful and unseen. Yet I knew she would not hurt me. I wondered what would come next: She had tied my arms together behind my back. Would it be the same for my legs? Would she bind them together, or...?

I got my answer when she started to tie the rope around my other ankle.

"A trophy as pretty as you are needs to be properly displayed," she said. I felt one loop, then another, and another. The pressure against my skin built and built. "When I am done with you, I think I'll leave you up here for a while."

I couldn't follow the knots she was tying if I tried. They were complicated. It wasn't just trussing me up like a chicken waiting to be roasted, oh no. It was more like being trapped in a spider's web. Every single knot was careful and considered, every one of them shifting the weight just so. Her rough cool skin; the unyielding rope. Every sensation against my skin felt heightened.

"You'd like that, wouldn't you?"

I couldn't argue the point. I was so far gone that I wasn't even wondering *why* it was me she wanted to see this way. No—the thought was so erotic on its own that I could feel everything with perfect acuity.

My nipples, already so hard, against the inside of my worn sweatshirt.

My pussy starting to throb with heat. I'd had to do away with my only set of underwear very early into my time in Artemis's Domain. I was thankful for that now. Not just because the lack of anything except a pair of torn-up shorts was thrilling on its own—but because if I *had* been wearing underwear, I would have already soaked through.

"You want to be admired. You want to be adored. That's what you've always wanted, isn't it?"

She was right.

The Heir of Pelops doesn't get to do much for their own sake. Everything's got to be for the family. But this? There was no one here but the two of us. Her eyes were mine, all mine, and her hands were on my skin and only mine.

The Queen of the Wild was focused only on *me*.

"Admit it," she said, her hand on my thigh. "Tell me how much you love this, and I'll reward you."

Oh, but it was so hard to talk. Everything was this fuzzy block of pleasure as the network of ropes across my body grew and grew. My legs were suspended behind me now, the both of them, each slightly bent and held apart. The pressure was so evenly distributed through my body that I couldn't escape from it; every inch of me felt the weight of the rope, the suspension.

"Artemis...I-I'm so lucky to be your handmaiden," I whimpered. There was no other word for it. I sounded pathetic and small, and there was something so *exciting* about that, about being that person for her now that I knew I didn't *have* to be. "Whenever you look at me, I feel..."

Her nails gliding across my thigh, beneath the ragged cloth. "How do you feel, Iphigenia?"

Gods above and below. The nails and the pressure and her asking me to pay attention when everything was so heady—

Again she tugged at my hair, her whole hand grabbing hold of me and tilting my head back. She was still behind me, but I could feel her.

"I feel like I can do anything," I said.

The pleased hum again. I heard something shift—not rope this time, but her fetching something. The soft whisper of leather.

I shivered. Gods. I couldn't wait to see what she'd do to me next.

"Good deer," she said. I felt the flat of something against my thigh—something hard and flat and cold. It took me a moment to realize it was the grip of my knife. "Top, or bottom?"

What was... What did she mean with the knife? She wasn't going to hurt me, I knew she wasn't, but what did she mean...

Oh, it didn't matter. I wanted more of it.

"Bottom," I said. It was the first thing that came out of my mouth; I didn't think about it at all.

"Predictable," she said. I could hear her smiling. And the next thing I heard?

The tearing of fabric. My shorts, torn apart in one long cut, the ropes binding them to my body undisturbed. But that didn't last long. She tugged them off through the gaps in the knotwork, and they fell to the ground.

From the waist down I was bare to her.

Oh, I was writhing. Wriggling. I couldn't help it. Nothing this hot had ever happened to me before. Suspended from a tree in front of someone else with my legs spread and my pussy bare to the cool evening air. Let alone having this happen in front of a god.

She wouldn't touch me there. I knew she wouldn't, and I didn't want her to, but I was so desperate for release, and the pressure was starting to build up behind my eyes.

"You want release," she said. Her hand in my hair again, pulling, owning. "Don't you?"

"A-Artemis—"

"What a sight you are. So needy," she said. "The sounds you're making just for me. What fortune that you will be *my* handmaiden."

I took another gasping breath. She was standing at my side, one hand in my hair and the knife lying flat against my ass.

"I could tie a knot for you. It would make it easier," she said. "You wouldn't need me to touch you."

"P-please," I whimpered. Because even the thought of it was making me so hot I couldn't think of anything else. I needed *something*.

She smirked. "But I won't," she said. "I told you. I want to torment you."

"You b-b-bitch," I said. Good sense had long flown from me, and I had never wanted anything more than I wanted a thick knot of rope against my clit right at that moment. "Oh you b-b-bitch—"

She laughed, rich and deep, and drew back from me. I heard

the crunch of her feet against the underbrush as she made her rounds, standing in front of me.

I had never seen her so smug as this. It was in every sinew of her body: the confidence of knowing she'd left me in this shape.

She knelt down. We were eye to eye again.

"I'm going to leave you here, and I'm going to make dinner," she said. "Relieve yourself. If you can."

Another wave rolled through me. It was a challenge. I knew it was. And I knew, more than that, it was an *invitation*.

So, as she stepped away from me and started to set a fire, I thought of nothing but how badly I wanted to get off. What I would do if I could move my hands. Just the thought made me struggle more against the ropes, and that made me sway in the air.

There was no friction to speak of—the only thing I had going for me was that I was so sensitive even the air itself against my pussy was like a finger buried deep. And the more I wriggled, the more I got of that air.

The pressure was mounting. I watched her as she sat down across from me. Though her hands worked at setting the fire, her eyes never left mine.

She was watching me. And she wanted to see it as much as I wanted to show her.

Every swing of my body, every desperate rock of my hips, brought me closer and closer. And as I started to get close I couldn't stop trembling.

"A-Artemis…"

The fire crackled to life. She set one hand on each of her thighs, and watched me.

"Go on," she said. "You have my permission."

It was too much to bear. The rope holding me up and spreading me wide, the goddess's eyes on my bare skin, the way she watched me even sitting all the way over there. The air itself against me and the unbelievable knowledge that this was really happening, that she'd chosen me for this when she could have had anyone—

Me, it was *me*—

"A-Artemis!"

I came. I came harder than I ever had sitting spread-legged in front of my computer in the wee hours of the night, harder than I ever had on my own. And I couldn't touch myself at all. I came for her and for me and for us, a great wave of pleasure, and a gush that hit the ground beneath me like a burst water balloon.

"There's a good deer," she said. Just the way she said *good* alone made me a little lightheaded again—but as I gasped for breath, I think part of me knew I needed a break. And the smile I saw on her face across the way was a reward all its own.

She got up. As I hung there quivering and trying to breathe, she walked over to me and laid a hand on the bonds tying my arms together. With her other hand she tilted my chin up to look at her. I wondered, in the headiness that comes post-orgasm, if she'd ever let me see her face. I decided it was all right if she never did, as long as I could still see that smug little expression.

"Iphigenia," she said. "You've done so well. How are you feeling?"

My tongue was still a little numb. "Pretty... pretty great."

A hum of agreement from her. She smoothed my hair, moving the sweaty parts away from my face. To my surprise she even started to braid the rest of it.

"I'm happy you enjoyed yourself," she said. Her fingers moved so quickly that I could hardly feel them, only the weight of the braid against my back as it was shaped. "Would you like me to cut you down?"

My breathing was starting to slow down. The heat I'd felt earlier was fading to a kind of warm fuzziness. "Hmm... what do you want?"

I heard her tut as she came around to the front of me again. "Your happiness and comfort. You must answer first."

Probably not worth arguing. But... I was starting to know her pretty well. And earlier she'd said that she wanted to look at me. If tying me up like this wasn't about orgasm for her, if it wasn't something she did for sexual gratification, then maybe she wanted a little more out of it.

And I wanted to give it to her. I wanted her to be able to enjoy herself as much as I had, even if she didn't enjoy it the exact same way I did.

"I think I want to stay up a little longer," I said.

She had started checking over the knots she'd tied as I considered my answer—but when I spoke her hands stopped midmotion. She spoke more softly than I'd ever heard her before.

"Really?"

I nodded. I had that much movement left to me, at least. To be honest, it would have been nice if she tied my braid to the tree, too. When your whole body is suspended from rope you start to notice how heavy your noggin is.

"You want to hang here for my amusement, knowing I won't do anything more to you than this?" she said.

I leaned my head against her palm. I don't know if I'd ever think of those hands as rough again. Not after what they'd done for me. "Yeah. I'm happy like this. It's kind of comfortable, honestly. And I like you watching me about as much as you like to watch."

A small silence followed. It wasn't a showy one. I wouldn't call it dramatic, either. But it meant something to her and to me—that little silence, that space of understanding.

She started to check the ropes again. Her lips brushed the top of my head as she did, a little kiss on the part of my hair.

"Well. Do you like this position, or should I move you?" she said. "I can tilt you vertical if you want. Make you more stable."

I found myself grinning. Here she was fussing over my every worry and care. What a big softie she could be beneath all that wilderness.

"Stability's probably for the best. I think if I keep moving, it's gonna be like I'm on one of those roller coaster rides or something," I said.

"I don't know what those are," she answered.

I had to laugh. "You know, I barely do. They didn't have them on the high-rise. A roller coaster is like a tram a bunch of people get on that moves really fast, lots of hills and loops and stuff like that. They ride it for fun."

"What's a tram?" she asked.

I had my work cut out for me when it came to stuff like this—but I didn't mind. It gave us something to chat about as she fixed the ropes.

The thing about being tied up like this, by the way, is that it doesn't happen quickly. It can take quite a while to get everything set up properly. And that's before you factor in that you have to rotate the person who's tied up every so often so their blood doesn't pool in the wrong places.

In the movies and the books and things like that, it's always all so quick. But that's not what I like about it.

What I like about it is how long it takes. It's how long we share the experience together—this space where I'm trusting her with my body and my safety, and she was trusting me with a part of herself she found delicate. She was the one in charge—but that was because we were working through this together.

I liked chattering about roller coasters and video games while she spent an hour adjusting the way I hung in the air. Later, when she made us dinner, she came over and spoon-fed it to me. I loved that, too—being spoiled. Knowing she could make me beg for it if she wanted.

And she did, a little. She made me ask very, very nicely.

All told I stayed up there for a couple more hours. When I started to get tired of not being able to move, I told her I wanted her to cut me down.

"Crescent," I said.

And it was as simple as that. She came over with her knife, and she balanced my body against hers, and when she cut me down I slumped against her. She cut free my arms and my legs, and I wrapped them around her, somehow exhausted though I hadn't done anything at all.

"Good deer," she said. "So good. I'm glad you're practicing."

I was too tired to do anything but hum happily in response. She smoothed over my hair again and carried me to the fireside. When she sat us down, she set me in her lap.

"I was worried you wouldn't tell me to stop," she said.

"Knew you'd never forgive me," I mumbled in response. "It's trust, right? Goes both ways. I trust you not to hurt me. You trust me to tell you to stop."

She kissed the top of my head again. "Iphigenia."

"Artemis."

"I will always protect you," she said. "You will always be safe with me."

I hummed and laid my head against her shoulder. For once in my life, I felt sleep right around the corner.

"I know," I said.

Chapter Twelve

I dreamed I was back in the high-rise. I dreamed that my siblings and I were in the game room playing *Super Stomp Sisters*, talking all kinds of trash, giggling and shouting.

I set down the controller after a match, and I looked at them, and I said: "How about we get out of here and you guys show me all your favorite places in the city?"

And they looked at me for a little while like I'd grown a second head...but then they leaned forward. Each took one of my arms. Together, we all got to the window. We were on the ground floor, somehow, which isn't right for the layout of the high-rise. Not that I was complaining. One by one, we helped each other through the window and to freedom, and when I felt the sun on my skin it was not Artemis's sun but the real one.

I woke up to the sun staring down at me. This one wasn't Artemis's, either, but her brother's. Where Artemis masked her face with the dark of night, this pompous asshole did it with a halo only slightly less painful than if he'd left it uncovered.

He was standing over us, wearing not the flowing robes in which I'd seen him before but a practical hunting chiton. It left a lot of his bronzed legs exposed. I imagined he took a lot of pride in the graceful lines of their shape. He struck me as the sort of man who bragged about the thickness of his leg hair.

I was still in Artemis's arms; she hadn't broken her oath to me. Before I could tell her brother what I really thought of him showing up in our camp like this when I was hardly dressed, she had already thrown a cloak over my lower half, and pressed a kind (if insistent) hand over my mouth.

"You shouldn't have woken us," she said.

"The Law does not prohibit me from waking my sister, nor her..." Did I imagine the derision I heard in this pause? "Prospective handmaiden. You should have known I was coming."

"You've never been excited to hunt," she answered. "I thought I would have more time."

He crossed his arms over his chest. Though he'd opted for a hunter's dress, he wore thick gold bracers on each forearm. There's no accounting for taste. "You know how our half sister can be once she has set her mind to something. And, it must be said, the quarry this year is magnificent."

"What have you found?" she asked him.

I wished she hadn't—his chest swelled up with pride as he chuckled. He walked around our camp like it was something beneath him, like he was a kaiju in a model city. "A twenty-headed hydra," he said. "Mythic, by all accounts. We may well die in the pursuit of it. Isn't that exciting?"

Very few things could kill one of the gods. Mythic beasts and their products were among them. A chill ran down my spine. I looked up at Artemis. This was my test hunt?

"Brother. You must pick something you have some chance of killing. Otherwise I will have to save you."

"I didn't pick it. Wisdom did. Said she wanted to give your little plaything a test."

He picked something up at the edge of the camp. I realized with some small horror that it was my phone. But it was fine, right? He had no idea how to use that thing. Gods didn't bother with that—

This time, the bright flash of light was him taking a photo of me and Artemis all huddled up beneath the blanket.

Anger got the better of me. I yanked Artemis's hand off my mouth. "What the fuck do you think you're doing taking photos of women like that, you dickhead?"

"Oh, feisty, isn't she?" he said. "I can take a photo of whatever I like. You're the one who left this phone unattended here. Don't you think that's an unwise thing to have done?"

My cheeks burned hot. I wanted to stand and walk over there—but I couldn't, not in the state I was in. So I tied the cloak over my shoulder and stood anyway.

Artemis stood after I did. To my surprise, she didn't try to stop me; she leaned close and asked if I needed help.

I didn't. I knew what I was about.

While the King of Music scrolled through my phone, using

up what little remained of my battery, he hummed a tune. I picked up a small rock. Not big enough to do any damage, but big enough for what I needed. While he was distracted, I flung the rock right at his hand.

He drew back, because he was too vain to take a small bruise; when he did, the rock hit my phone and knocked it out of his hand. I lunged for it before he could get to it.

Was it over the line? Probably. In telling the story, I'm a little shocked I made it through.

"Must you always taunt the mortals?" Artemis asked behind me. She had come to stand behind me, her hand on my shoulder, as I glared up at him.

Well, maybe it wasn't so heroic as that. I couldn't look at him, radiant as he was, so I had to look at his hands instead. I wasn't exactly staring him down. Shocking, I know.

But I could tell from the tension across the backs of his palms that he wasn't happy. "You allow her too many freedoms."

"She has what freedoms she has taken for herself," Artemis answered.

The light shifted—he must have been shaking his head. "I don't have time for dealing with you and your favorite. Wisdom has found us the hydra; War and Passion are both eager to join. We shall not keep them waiting, hm?"

Artemis hummed behind me. "Let me prepare. Play a song you have never played before, and we will be done before it is through."

Now that didn't sound like a reasonable time frame to me. How were we supposed to get ready in four minutes? And that's if he didn't decide to chase trends and play for two minutes, tops. I glanced at Artemis to ask if she was sure. She gave me a wink.

"Only if you admit you like my music," he said.

"I have never said I hate it," said Artemis.

He took from his cloak a lyre that could not have fit there, and he began to play.

I'll admit that without Artemis to guide me, I would have stood there listening the whole while. As much as I hated him, whenever he got out that lyre he became a different person. The music wasn't simply something you heard—it was something that seeped into you, something that sank its hooks into you and pulled.

Artemis wouldn't let me fall prey to it. She covered my ears and led me away. Only when she'd found a tree wide enough to conceal me did she stop. By then we were far enough that the music was hardly audible at all.

"How will we know how much time we've got left?" I asked her.

"He's not going to stop," she said. She knelt down to the ground and started to dig with her bare hands. "Likes hearing himself too much. And discovering new music. He'll stand there playing for years if you let him."

"Years...?"

I couldn't imagine what that was like. How could anyone play that long? But if anyone was going to be that obnoxious, it was him. I shook my head and knelt down next to Artemis. I wasn't quite so good at digging—but I wanted to help where I could.

"Father used to make him play horrible songs as punishments," Artemis said. "But he liked it too much. And he kept playing long after the skin wore off. Kept healing, so he kept playing. Now Father punishes him by taking the lyre away altogether."

I couldn't imagine what it was like to play with peeled fingers; nor did I want to. Sinking mine into the wet and cool earth was a balm to my imagination.

Before long we found what Artemis must have been looking for: a bit of hide wrapped into a package. How it had made it this long without rotting away was beyond me, but I was learning not to ask too many questions when it came to all this god stuff.

She hauled it out of the hole we'd dug and balanced it on her thigh.

"Gray Eyes and I, despite our quarrels, have some measure of respect for each other," she said. "I asked her to make this for you. You have to be given a fighting chance, after all."

A hunting chiton. But not one made of simple linen, oh no. This one was as dark as a new moon night, and wherever the light fell upon it, there were clouds and stars to be seen. Not embellishments, mind you. Actual clouds and stars. It was as if the fabric was a glimpse into the night sky itself.

My jaw fell open.

"Artemis, I can't…"

"I knew you'd need it one day," she said. "When we introduced you to the others, I wanted you to be ready."

I reached out with a blasphemous hand to touch this incredible work. It was so soft that my fingers didn't register the fabric there at all.

"It is woven with threads of my own divinity," she said. "While you are hunting, you will always be safe."

Her own divinity? But that—

"You gave some of that up for me?" I asked.

She laid the delicate fabric around my shoulders and pulled me close. The beads and fangs of her headdress hung all round me. I thought of the first time we'd been this close—of the blood on her mouth, the death that clung to her. How I hadn't known what I was feeling at the time. I did now.

I loved her. And she loved me. The Huntress, the ever-changing Moon, had chosen me for her own even then.

As she was choosing me now. "Yes. And I would give up more, if needed. I will keep my promises to you, Iphigenia."

There was nothing for it. This gift, this impossible thing, was all my own. I took it in hand. Artemis helped me change—her touch was light and comforting as she pulled my hoodie over my head. It was her who helped me buckle the chiton in place; it was her who tied it around my waist.

Who was the handmaiden and who was the god?

For a moment she stood there with her hands on my shoulders, beholding me. Then she tapped my forearms with a smile.

"The rope marks are there," she said.

And so they were—ghosts of the time we'd shared together. I treasured them more than any golden armbands.

"I want them to be," I said. I drew a breath. "Artemis. Am I really ready for this? A hydra? It could kill any of you. What if I don't know what to do? What if I fuck it up and everyone dies?"

She pressed a kiss to my forehead. "You are ready," she said.

"And you will see. With so many of us there, the hydra will be busy. You don't have to fight. All you have to do is ready me, mind the camp, and clean the kill."

"But what if something happens to you?"

There it was—her confident little laugh. "Nothing will," she said. "The others scheme against each other. They do not scheme against me."

"It isn't the others I'm worried about," I said. But I had the feeling that I wasn't going to be able to sway her. Artemis, though she may hold the moon in her Court, is a constant. Her mind was already made up.

She ran a hand along the curve of my cheek. When she pressed her thumb against my skin, I wondered if it would leave a silver mark in its wake—if it would mark me like so much of her already had.

"When we are through with this, Iphigenia, you will be shocked at the things you have accomplished," she said. "You will look back on it with pride. And I will be there with you."

The trouble with her is that she always knows when I've fallen into her trap.

So, you've played about as many games as I have. You know how it goes. After you beat a super tough enemy, you get the really cool gear they drop. Always super overpowered compared to everything else you can find. I mean, you spend hours crafting something, and it's not as good as whatever the big bad had on him. You equip your character with stuff, and then the important part happens: You make them stand there for a while so you can look at how cool they look.

It's a vital part of the gaming process.

Turns out it's a vital part of the handmaiden process, too.

The King of Song was waiting for us when we got back. The first thing he did was conjure up a portal to one of the other Domains. Sang a song that made the world itself ripple, then reached out and opened it up in front of us, easy as that. But as the portal between worlds opened up I saw myself reflected in it for a second.

I thought it must have been someone else. The woman I saw in front of me was straight-backed, not a slouch to be seen, built lithe as a big cat. Her skin was a rich bronze. The only marks I saw on her were rope or scar. The look in her eyes wasn't flat at all, but rich and...happy.

It was the eye bags that gave me away. Even with everything else so glittering and perfect, I still wasn't sleeping the way other people did. I saw them staring back at me, and I thought, *I guess it must really be me.*

I turned this way and that. With the ornate silver quiver hanging at my hip and the chiton Artemis had given me, I looked like I'd just walked out of a story somewhere. Not to mention the bow. Artemis said it was my job to carry it for her when she wasn't using it, at least in front of other people. The thing was at least as big as I was. I had no idea how she could draw it as easily as she did.

I stared at myself in the mirrored surface of the magic, and when Artemis put her hand on my shoulder, I felt almost ready for the hydra.

On the other side of the portal was a world I could hardly understand. I'd been gone so long from the niceties of the "civilized" world that when I stepped onto the cool marble floor on the other side, the stiffness of it felt horrible to my feet. No give at all. The sandals Artemis had given me didn't have much cushion, either.

Then came the light. While Artemis's Domain had day and night so that the animals within it could lead natural lives, it didn't have anything *artificial*. Everything came from the sun, the moon, or what fires you could make with your own two hands. It was different in this place. For a second I couldn't see any of the details of it—the place was so brightly flooded that I saw only white, and my eyes hurt. I stood there with my face buried in the crook of my elbow just to get used to it.

The next thing that came to me was the scent. Saltwater, or at least I thought it must be. It's not like I got to smell very much of it in the high-rise. Still, I'd tried to expand my horizons where I could, and I'd sniffed at enough aquariums and boiling pots to know briny water when I smelled it. But it wasn't just that—there was a delicate floral scent, too, one that made the insides of my nostrils tingle when I caught wind of it. Breathing it in lent me a sort of lightness. I wondered if the gods ever got high, and if whatever I was smelling was what they used to do it.

Sound next. The crashing waves were no surprise with the smell hanging in the air. I'd heard it in movies and stuff plenty of times, but nothing prepared me for the sheer concussive *force* of the sound. When the waves hit the rocks, it sounded so violent, so insistent, that I worried I would be carried away, too.

In the static din that followed the waves I heard a fire crackling and the murmur of voices. But they didn't stay murmurs long.

"Hahahaha! So that's the *mortal*?"

It sounded like a man's voice—and a loud one, at that. The sort of bloke you can hear from two rooms away even when he's trying to be quiet. A man who has never in his life sneezed without hearing an echo. But also the sort of guy who's always shouting that the drinks are on him.

"I don't see why we have to turn this into a test," came the next voice. A woman's, rich and warm and low. This one I knew—the Prince of Passion, eldest daughter of the Queen of Flame. You might be familiar. She'd stopped by the high-rise a couple times before. You're probably not shocked to hear this, but my mother contracted her to bless an absolutely absurd number of chocolates every year. Obviously I'd never seen the woman smile from behind that mask of hers—but I'd never even heard her *sound* like she was smiling. Learning that Passion had lost a lot of her namesake over the years was one of the first times I remember feeling sorry for a god.

Anyway—she's better now, of course. But she was as down as she usually was that day.

Another new voice chimed in: cool and even, a sword being drawn from its sheath not in anger but for righteous justice.

"Because our good friend Moon has hidden her favorite mortal away, and we must ensure there is no trickery afoot," she said. "See to it that your faces are covered."

"Covered! Can you imagine such a thing?" said the man. "Children of Leto, your schemes always surprise. I hardly remember how to mask at all."

"You remember," said the other woman. The Gray-Eyed Queen. I shivered when the realization hit me. "Do not make a fool of yourself and a mockery of our family."

"Anything like fun is a mockery to you," said the man. "It's a wonder you're coming out to deal with this yourself. I would have thought you were too busy with your machinations in the mortal world, or that demigod favorite of yours."

I got the feeling that they were going to keep going—and also that my reflexes had probably saved my life. With my eyes hidden away, they couldn't dazzle me into nonexistence.

Artemis grunted like a boar skewering its prey. "Shut up."

"What my sister means to say, despite her regrettable lack of eloquence, is that you're all going to scare the poor mortal away," said her brother. "Though it might take some doing to scare this one. She's a Pelops girl. The former heir, it seems."

"Pelops?" said Passion.

There was no getting away from it. Despite blinding myself, I could feel their eyes on me, each one the sharp tip of a spear. Could they sense the rot in my blood if they tried? Could they see it with their eyes, so keen?

Bowing felt like the right thing to do in this case, so I did my best to. Let me tell you—it's harder than you think to bow when you can't see what's going on in front of you. Case in point here: My forehead smacked not into Artemis but into her brother. I knew it was him because he immediately darted away like a startled deer—and because Artemis's hand quickly pointed my head in the right direction.

"Yes, your grace," I said. "My name's Iphigenia, of the House of Pelops. You've worked with my father, Agamemnon."

I didn't hear her coming toward me so much as felt it: There's this deformity in the air that sometimes happens around the stronger gods. Like gravity itself tries to bow to them. It was like that with her.

"Athena," said Passion. "What's the meaning of this? Her blood is as cursed as the hydra's."

Words welled up within me. I knew how dumb it would be to say something here. Catastrophically, life-endingly dumb. And not just dumb for my sake but for Artemis's, too. If I made matters worse here, it would only reflect badly on her. Running my hands across my forearms, I felt the ligature marks, and I remembered what she'd said to me. She wanted me safe and happy.

For that to happen here, I really needed to keep my mouth shut.

"Is there a problem, Eros?" said Artemis. The answer was cool and collected. Artemis was the moon overhead, unbothered by the goings on of the earth. She may as well have been asking if there was a delay on the trains that morning.

"You've brought a mortal—"

"Aren't they only *mostly* mortal, the Pelops clan?" countered the King of War. "If she was fully mortal, she'd be dead by now. All of us in a room together alone would have killed her, eyes closed or not."

A silence followed, which, I imagine, was full of glares. I couldn't see them or hear them, though. All I had going for me was my own hammering heartbeat and the crash of the waves around us. And how much I could block out the truth of what War had said.

Well, that and Artemis's hand on the belt of my chiton behind my back. A single hand keeping me from drifting off into the ether of my nerves.

But it was not Artemis who spoke next—it was the Gray-Eyed Queen. She, too, was cool—but hers was the cold of a spear. "Our uncle speaks true. She is only mostly mortal. Calm thy blood's heat, Eros, and let the girl attempt her test in peace."

Passion huffed. "Don't understand why you brought the rest of us if you aren't even going to listen."

"There are many things you do not understand. That is why it falls to me to do the understanding," said the Gray-Eyed Queen. Her voice was as much a spear as the one she held in her hands; her status as the king's favorite as much armor as her famous glittering mail. "The mortal is here as an alleged handmaiden. To prove that she is worth the title, she must assist her lady in all matters relevant to her Domain. That means hunting, including hunting in a party. This way we may all observe her and witness her...aptitude."

I did not like the pause there. Did she want me to fail? Would she have made me this raiment if she did? I couldn't figure out the relationship between her and Artemis. She was arguing that Artemis had broken the Law—but they respected each other?

Maybe she respected the Law more than she did people?

"Though I have to admit that Artemis has argued for the girl with a passion unbecoming of her. I don't suppose you've broken your vow of chastity?"

Yeah, that was the sort of thing you asked only if you weren't so good at the social part of things.

"Thank you, dear sister, but my vows are intact," said Artemis. "Including the one I made to her family. She is my handmaiden now—"

"And a handmaiden must fulfill her duties, wouldn't you say?" her brother cut in as smooth as could be. "Why delay giving her the opportunity? Otherwise sister dearest will have gone back on the terms of her arrangement. Can't go breaking the Law, can we? I'm sure a tactical mind like your own can see the sense in that, dear old Gray Eyes."

I hadn't expected them to complete each other's sentences like that, but I suppose I shouldn't have been surprised. They were twins, after all. Even if they didn't have very much in common.

"If you ask me, there's been too much talk about things other than fighting," said War. I think it was him I heard rattling his shield. "Come down off it and let's get to work. If we tarry too long, my stepdaughter will start brooding again."

Passion groaned. It occurred to me that War was, indeed, her stepfather. I hadn't put that together until that very moment. You'd never link the two up with how they acted. More to do with the Queen of Flame's proclivities than anything to do with the two of them as people.

"Yes, let's keep the brooding at bay, shall we?" said the King of Song. A bright strum of the lyre somehow cut through the sound of the waves. "Passion, I've been working on this new song lately. I think you might even like it."

"Cover your faces," Artemis said. With that boom in her voice it was a command, pure and simple.

Whatever the Gray-Eyed Queen thought of me she kept to herself. There weren't any further arguments. For a little while, all I heard were the waves and the King of Song's harp. Then came Artemis's hand at the nape of my neck. She tugged me upright.

"Safe now," she said.

I opened my eyes and beheld them—the gods, and the monster.

Hydras are pretty popular in games. Kind of a stock enemy, really. Most don't even bother to attach any intense lore to them. It's just "hey, here's this big tough thing someone put here to guard sick loot!" That's enough. You don't think about them. In fact, you get so used to seeing them as a lazy plot device that you shrug them off. They don't impress you anymore.

I'm telling you now: Seeing one in person is a different story.

We were up on the edge of the cliff. Even so, surrounded by some of the biggest hitters in the pantheon, the first thing I saw was the hydra. I couldn't look away from it. For one thing it was too big—the thing was kaiju-sized, as tall as a building, and its undulating necks spread out like a fireworks display to make it all the larger. When the sunlight played on its scales, they became great mirrors of light; to look on it, you had to squint, or else you'd get a few of the scintillating rays searing into your irises. Its body was thick, like a croc's. When I finally followed its shape down to see its surroundings, I realized that it was standing on a little island of its own, hardly much bigger than it was. Statues dotted the earth. Its claws rested on one—a man with a massive spear standing at a regal sort of rest. It wasn't attacking anyone, not yet, but its heads all gnashed their teeth in our direction.

I *hated* seeing those heads. Growing up in Australia, you end up seeing more than your fair share of spiders. In person, of course, but also in all the PSAs and material about what to do when you see them, what the venomous ones look like, and all that. Same for snakes. Though they didn't get into the high-rise very often, it was an assumption on my part that the outside world was *crawling* with them. And I used to dread the day I'd ever see one.

See, I don't like things that skitter. Don't like things that twist. Something about the way snakes and spiders move just does my teeth in. My whole spine tingles, and my body cries out in an old, ancestral voice: *Get the* fuck *away from whatever that is!*

The hydra was all of that made gigantic. A whole nest of snakes, a ball of them together, wriggling and twisting and doing all sorts of things a living body should not be able to do. Each serpentine neck was topped off with a wicked, glow-eyed head. All these heads were moving independently of one another, too—there was no coordination to them, no rhyme or reason. You were watching this awful symphony of writhing from the start.

I covered my mouth so that the others wouldn't hear me retching. I think they did anyway. The Gray-Eyed Queen certainly did. If the height didn't give her away—she was tallest one there, and none of them were short—the scale mail and spear did. In place of a mask, she'd pulled her plumed helm tighter over her face. If it weren't for the gray suns of her eyes, you'd think the helmet was empty, it was so dark within.

"She will need to tame her stomach to dress you," she said. To Artemis, of course. Not to me.

Passion was kinder. I hardly need to describe her to you. She was wearing her armor then, though, and she doesn't usually get the excuse to do that. I had the thought that when she was happy she must have made quite the dashing entrances—flaming wings, golden armor, her bow of fire. It was everything you could want from a savior. And, despite her dour manner, she was the one who tossed me the fruit.

"Eat this. It'll keep you from getting sick for a while," she said.

I caught the fruit, but I didn't bite into it immediately. Being a handmaiden is a vague thing; there were rules, but I wasn't always sure of them. So I glanced to Artemis and asked, with my eyes, if it would be safe to eat. She nodded.

I crunched into my delicious meal. It was sweet as a mouthful of honey and just as thick, sticking to my chin as the juices ran down. The flesh itself was so tender it melted away the second I sensed it against my tongue. A warm tingling sensation ran through my body—and the nausea began to fade with it.

"Thank you, my lady—"

"Don't," she said, shaking her head. "I'm here to hunt, that's all. Surprised your lady hasn't given you any of these already."

Unlike the others, who mostly hid their faces with shadows or helmets, Passion wore a mask that covered most of her face outright. It was hard to read her expression. With Artemis, you could see the shadows shift sometimes. There was none of that here.

But her eyes were uncovered—and there was something flaring in them when she looked over to Artemis. Not that I was sure what it was.

But it was definitely reciprocated. Artemis stepped ahead of me, her hand laid flat between my shoulder blades.

"She didn't need them before," Artemis said.

A moment of their glares passed before War spoke up, banging his shield and spear together. He had taken the shape of a rugby-built man, thick around the neck, chest, and thighs. The cloak of pure flame he wore billowed over his bare shoulders. Took me a second to realize he was shirtless, though—his skin was partly burnished metal. It was as if there was a camouflage pattern across it, but with interlocking patches of bronze, steel, and flesh. Low around his waist he wore a thick, gladiator style belt, with golden straps hanging around his considerably honed thighs.

I don't mean to judge the man, but it was all a *little* smutty for a god of war. But maybe that's why he'd won the heart of Love herself. I got what she must have liked about him—even if I didn't much like men.

He let out a bellowing laugh. "So! Are we ready, then? How many heads will you claim today, O Wisdom? I tell you that my daughter—"

"Stepdaughter," said Passion.

He continued unabated. "—and I will take at least twice that number. There won't be enough heads left for you, that's how many we'll take."

The Gray-Eyed Queen turned her head in his direction but, ultimately, decided not to dignify him with a direct response. Instead she gestured that we should all gather around her shield, which she turned over to serve as a table.

"I won't have any of you forgetting the plan—human or not. We'll discuss it one last time before we launch our attack," she said. Where her fingers touched the surface of the shield, they conjured threads—and the threads then bound themselves together into tightly woven dolls. There was one for each of us, and a large one in the center of the shield to stand for the hydra.

"We don't have any hope of killing it by severing its heads. My half uncle taught us that at no small cost. Therefore, we must turn our attention to more effective means."

"But shouldn't we take at least *some* of its heads?" said War. "What's the point if we don't?"

"The point is to exercise our talents and stay sharp in the case of a coming war, and for the girl to prove she has overcome her mortal failings," answered the Gray-Eyed Queen.

"And to write ourselves a few new stories. There are plenty of songs waiting to be born," said Artemis's brother.

Artemis grunted—but she didn't contribute anything to the discussion just yet. The Queen continued.

"Poison is one method of dealing with the issue of replication, but there is another option open to us. One that may sate the bloodthirsty hearts of our beloved War and Passion."

"I'm not bloodthirsty," said Passion.

"The trail of hearts and bodies in your wake would beg to differ. You've caused more wars than your father and I put together," said the Gray-Eyed Queen.

Passion said something then, but the hydra drowned it out. All at once half its heads reared up and let out this awful sound—a screeching roar that felt like a battering ram against my ears. I covered them as best I could, but it was no real help; the hurt lingered behind my eyes.

Artemis rubbed at my shoulder. I took a breath. How on earth was I supposed to help if I was so debilitated by the thing roaring? She said I could stay here, but I was already so in over my head.

I looked up at her.

Instead of paying attention to the presentation—which the Queen had not stopped giving during the creature's roaring—Artemis was focused on me.

She squeezed my hand.

Shit. I really did have to try, didn't I? I couldn't let her down. She believed in me. Had to be for a reason, right?

"...Applying flaming lances here and here," said the Gray-Eyed Queen. She was pointing here and there on the massive hydra doll. To my surprise and delight she was making the Passion and War dolls fly about like actors in a martial arts movie. Was there a bit of whimsy buried under that cool exterior?

"If we cauterize them in this way, we should only need to sever about half the heads, and that will allow the twins a chance to fire upon its heart unimpeded."

"How are they getting to the heart?" I asked.

Shit. I spoke out of turn. I could feel her stare on me, flaying me, but I had already done the deed, so I couldn't back down. I stood there and tried to act like I hadn't just stuck my bloody hand in a pool of sharks.

"That will be my job," she answered. Though there was no trace of anger to her, somehow I felt as if the tip of her spear was against my throat. "While War is distracting it with flaming lances and severed heads, I will crack the creature's ribs and peel back its skin, allowing for the shot."

"He will darken the skies," said Artemis.

"And she will bring the silver starfall," her brother added.

It was a lot easier to make sense of their relationship when they didn't get along.

"So it will be," said the Gray-Eyed Queen. "Is everyone clear on their role?"

As the gods broke to ready for the fight, Artemis took my hand and led me to the very edge of the cliff.

I grew up in a high-rise. Heights don't bother me. Still, looking down at the churning sea below us and the hydra island not far off, I felt unreal.

"Is this the real world?" I asked. I was staring at the hydra again—at its collection of heads, its hypnotic dance. "The air feels different here. But it can't be the real world, can it? People would have noticed something like this. It's gigantic."

"We are in your world, yes," she said. She looked to the hydra, too. Her chest rose and fell with a rare breath. "Humans will see what they wish to see. Once, they saw these beasts for what they are. Somewhere along the line that changed. Iphigenia."

"Yes?"

"Prepare my arrows, please," she said.

I appreciated that she said please. There, by the edge of the dizzying cliff, I knelt down on the marble and got out her quiver. She'd given me a bundle of arrows to carry separately from them, too.

Looking at them all laid out, I was beginning to understand why they were in separate bundles. Some were as long as my arm without an arrowhead to be seen; some were short, with flat broad heads. While most of them gleamed silver, there were a few tipped with a sickly green light, and there were some the pitch black of a new moon sky.

"Which ones do you need?" I asked her.

Artemis patted my head. "You will know. I have faith in you."

She was putting an awful lot of faith in someone who, until a few months ago, did nothing but play video games and run tech support for a corporation. Picking the arrows she'd use against a beast like this...

My eyes went to the hydra. From our perch it could not hurt us, but that did not stop it from *menacing* us. Again and again its many heads roared at us. Thanks to the fruit, I no longer needed to cover my ears—but a headache was starting to form between my ears all the same.

How had it gotten there? No one had told me that much. Did Mythic Beasts crop up randomly, like natural disasters? Were there any warning signs for them? Or had someone already dropped it here?

An image came into my head: the King of Gods wrestling this thing and flinging it onto the island. Afterward, her muscles pulsing with the blood of her exertion, she slaps her hands on her thighs and calls for a drink.

It wasn't so simple as that. Couldn't have been so simple as that. But I still had the question in the back of my head.

Unfortunately my job here wasn't to answer questions—it was to figure out which arrows Artemis would need.

I ran my fingers along them. How many to take? If I wanted to be cheeky I could throw them all into the quiver. But that wouldn't impress her, and she wouldn't like that joke very much. I had to be careful.

Right. So, if this was a boss battle, which items would I take? How many? Of course, this was some kind of nightmarish game without health bars or anything, so I couldn't take any health items. High difficulty, high reward.

First came the basic arrows. We'd need a fair few of them so that Artemis could attack without having to worry too much about wasting a precious resource. I went with six of them.

We'd need a couple of situational ones, too. I picked up one of the broadheads and turned it in the light. In that tiny little flash I saw the deep gashes this thing would leave in its wake—that the arrowhead would expand as Artemis willed it.

Two of those, then.

Next came the narrow ones. When I lifted those, I saw them sinking deep into muscle and bone. Two of those, too.

I ran my fingers over the rest of them, too. The source of these visions was a little obscure to me, but I wasn't going to question it. How could I, with everything else I'd seen? Maybe this was that tiny little drop of godly blood in me finally waking up. As I went from arrow to arrow I admit a bit of giddiness came over me, and I was smiling seeing their real purposes…

Until I got to the last two.

The last two arrows were not silver like the rest of the lot. These were the black ones I'd seen earlier. Where the rest were smooth and cold to the touch, these were rough, with a crackled surface not unlike paint beginning to peel. Here and there were uncomfortable soft swells along its length. I could probably dig my nail in and see the crescent pressed into the surface, if I wanted. But I didn't.

Because the second I tried to focus on these arrows, I saw them biting into the throats of people running for their lives. I saw the arrowheads dig deep. The shaft wobbled and dissolved, a black spike now embedding itself into the veins of its target. A horror dawned on me as I realized these were not really arrows at all but syringes for some unseen disease.

It was not the injury that would kill these people. It was the disease that she'd given them—she and her brother, together.

I could see them, when I closed my eyes. Her hands were my hands, and they fired these arrows over and over into the crowd.

My hand hovered over the arrow. As the vision passed, I turned toward Artemis. My mouth hung open; my shoulders shook.

"What... What did I just see?" I asked.

She knelt down next to me. The beast roared, but I could hardly hear it over the din of my worries.

"Hm. Niobe," she said. "That was the last time I used these."

I packed the two into the quiver. Whatever horror they would unleash, it was one they'd probably need to win the fight against this hydra. But my hand shook as I did, and when I handed the quiver to Artemis, it was sharper than I thought it would be.

But Artemis didn't make a big deal out of it. She took the quiver and stood, and she offered me a hand. The same hand I had just seen firing those horrible arrows.

The same hand that had been my steadiness throughout this whole experience, my reassurance. The realest thing in this place.

I stared at it: the dirt beneath her fingernails, their sharp gleam; her callused skin; the palm that had so often touched my cheek.

I wasn't an idiot. I hope by now that much is clear. I've dealt with gods all my life, and I know more than most what they're capable of. More than once four people went into a meeting with my father and only he came out. The details of what happened were always kept from me—but I knew what it came down to.

They'd upset the gods, and the gods had taken their vengeance.

Artemis didn't like people. She did her best to stay away from them whenever she could. The first time I had seen her, when I was laid upon that tree stump altar, I thought the same was going to happen to me. I thought I was going to die.

I thought she—the apex predator that she is—was going to eat me. When I first met her she was no different from the hydra to me: a creature I could not understand and whose existence made mine fragile.

I still saw that now, as she reached out to me. The softness I'd come to know so well from her for a moment faded, and I saw the Huntress for what she was: a being who could destroy me with a touch, powerful and impossibly above me.

What had she done before we met? What would she continue to do when we were apart? I was her handmaiden.

Could I have handed her the arrows she'd used against Niobe?

"Iphigenia," she said. "You have fears."

She always knew me so well. I nodded, my tongue resting against the roof of my mouth.

"In your fondness you have forgotten my nature," she said.

And, again, I nodded.

She knelt down. She pressed her forehead against mine. It was the closest I'd ever come to seeing her face—really seeing it. The bright moons of her eyes made it impossible to focus on anything else, but I could see the suggestions of her features there. The shadows of them.

"Iphigenia," she said. "Listen to me, little deer."

Something in the name snapped me from my silence; I looked to her and nodded. "I'm listening."

"Good," she said. She cleared my hair from my face.

"I have known the taste of blood from the day I was born. I will know it until the day I die. It is right, and good, for other people to fear me," she said. "But not you."

She took my hand in hers. I could not fight off the image of the hand that fired the arrows—but there was the other hand, too. The one that taught me to fire a bow, the one that caught me when I fell, the one that started fires, and the one that tied me up with such delicate care. Her hand.

"While I live, no predator shall harm you, no beast will mark you, and no night will be without the light of the moon to guide you. You are my handmaiden. I grant to you the softest parts of myself, and leave them in your safekeeping."

I opened my mouth again. "I've never been more afraid of anyone than I've been of you. But I don't think I've ever loved anyone else this way, either."

A warm, soft sound from her. She cupped my cheek and drew me up with her to stand once more. "I am birth and death alike," she said. "Iphigenia. Give me my bow, and strap my quiver to my shoulder. When I bring you one of the beast's heads, I will tell you what became of Niobe."

I needed something to do. Left to my own devices I would spiral into uncertainty, and she knew this. After that night at the pit, she'd always known this. She had been with me every step of the way to show me the things that needed doing—and to let me handle them however I liked.

I was confused by what I'd seen, but it wasn't what we needed to talk about now. Not with the other gods around and a beast so close by.

So I did as she asked, and I did it happily: I picked up her bow and I laid it in her hands; I walked around her and fastened her quiver across her broad shoulders. She did not need me. Not in the real sense. If she had wanted to, she could have done this herself.

But she wanted me to do it—and I wanted to do it for her. I wanted to fuss over exactly where her quiver sat against her hip. I wanted to check that her chiton was tied correctly. I wanted to serve her.

Girding her was part of the test, but that was hardly a thought at the time, if I'm being honest. The whole thing was pretext. What it meant to dress her in that moment was more than simply proving my worth as a handmaiden to someone who would likely never live with us.

It was about trust.

Her quiver hanging at her hip. An armguard I'd made myself for her with the hide of the boar we'd killed together. It was plain and without adornments, and I had only my own hopes and dreams that it would not disintegrate during the hunt. Normally she ran around barefoot, but I had made shoes for her from the same leather—makeshift and soft enough that she could feel the earth beneath her. A flower crown made from only the night-blooming blossoms I had found in my travels. The rope that she'd used on me only hours ago lashed to her belt opposite the quiver.

Simple things. She never needed any of them, really, except the quiver. But she wanted me to dress her. She wanted me to do it. This woman who had so enjoyed adorning me with rope—I wanted to adorn her, too.

And in exchange, she rested that hand on my head again.

"Good work, little deer," she said.

"Are you two quite done?"

Her brother's voice was an unwelcome interjection, but if it was going to be anyone at all interrupting us, it was probably best that it was him. I couldn't imagine what War would have said.

"Yes, we are," said Artemis.

We called for Wisdom. She had to evaluate the work I'd done, after all. Had to decide whether or not I officially qualified for handmaidenship. As the Gray-Eyed Queen paced around my mistress, I found myself having two thoughts.

The first was that many people would have been terrified to be in my position. Wisdom is famously vindictive; it does not take much to upset her. And though she had woven me the chiton I now wore, she did take issue with Artemis skirting the Law. She could, if she chose, find some way to fail me no matter how well I had done. Gods are fickle.

The second thought: I didn't care if she did. No matter what Wisdom thought of us, no matter what anyone did—I was Artemis's handmaiden. And if she wanted me dead because of that, then I was ready to take this all the way up to her father if I needed.

Eventually the silence broke. Wisdom hummed to herself. Though I did not meet her shining eyes, I felt them upon me.

"You do not fear me," she said.

"No, my lady," I answered. "I do not. I have done my duty, and I stand by it."

She leveled her spear at my throat. I did not move. Next to me, Artemis growled. Still I did not move. But if I'm being honest, maybe I smiled a little.

"The champions who fight on our behalf—the demigods who war now against the foreign Courts—all fear me."

"And so they are right to," I said. "But I know death well, at this point, and while I'm not ready to welcome it just yet, it no longer scares me. You have said I may continue on in Artemis's service if I can gird her, arm her, and clean what she brings to me."

"If you died and found yourself reborn," answered Wisdom. The spear did not move. I was conscious of the others watching me. "Have you?"

"Lady Wisdom," I said, "if you had told me months ago that I would be standing here with your spear at my throat and not a trace of fear, and without wanting to die, I would have been struck down as a liar on the spot. But I'm not lying. All of you know that. You can sense lies as Artemis can sense the phases of the moon. I have shed my old life like a snake sheds its skin, and whatever this new life brings me, I will hunt it."

Silence again, broken only by the waves and the roaring of the hydra. I thought about the champions Wisdom mentioned. At the start of this they had all seemed so impossibly strong, so blessed. But they were not here. Whatever happened in their war was not my concern—not unless it bothered Artemis. And I knew she did not care.

The war my father had sacrificed me for didn't interest me at all.

There were so many other things I wanted to do with my new life.

"What will it be?" I asked Wisdom. "Will you sacrifice me here?"

And I met her eyes, then, and let them pierce me. I could live through that. I knew I could.

"No," she said. "I do not sacrifice handmaidens."

The spear lowered. I looked to Artemis and she looked to me, and we did not in that moment need words to share in our satisfaction. My great hunter looked to the hydra with a nod. "Then let us hunt," she said. "I have promised my handmaiden a head."

And as she began to turn away, I called after her:

"Don't bring me a head. I want the heart."

Chapter Thirteen

I stood right there on the edge of the cliff, and I watched as the gods got to work. Let me tell you: the whole time I was in Artemis's Domain I hadn't touched my phone except for the occasional photo. It was off most of the time to try to conserve battery, and I'd done surprisingly well at that. I was at maybe 5 percent now.

Sitting on the cliff face I wanted nothing more than an extra battery so I could document as much of this as I could.

No one would believe me if I told them what I saw.

Passion alone was the stuff of a UFO enthusiast's wet dreams. I mean, she was zipping about around the snapping heads of the hydra as if she'd memorized its attack patterns somehow. When one head snapped for her, she dove; when another came at her from below, she barrel-rolled right over it. Her flaming wings scoured the hydra's scales, earning a howl in pain every time they touched. And that was before you factored in her arrows. She was firing them off so quickly her arms were a blur of blazing red motion.

I couldn't get a picture of her—not a clear one—but the video was something out of another world. If only I had signal. What would Ori think if I sent him this? Did he even know I was alive? I hoped that he did. Even if he didn't, I wasn't about to pass up the opportunity to be the coolest sister ever. A one-of-a-kind video of the gods at work. With their faces covered, it'd be safe for any of us to watch.

And there was so much to watch. Aside from Passion's burning hail of arrows, there was her stepfather's impressive combat skills. War had nothing to keep him in the air. He had no wings, no enchanted cloak, nothing of the sort. Instead he had planted himself on the island in front of the beast. As tall and broad as he was, from this vantage point he was so small that I had to lean over to see him.

But it was worth the effort. Four heads beset him, one on each side. When one lunged at him he would raise his shield and jam it between the beast's teeth. Then he'd drive the tip of his spear into the hollow below its jaw, where neck met head. A mighty howl would leave him as he'd lean in. Then he'd pull the spear like a lever. A spray of verdant blood coated him and his armor alike, and with a great bellowing laugh he'd turn to face the next attacker.

It wasn't always so easy for him. As the headless stump of the last one writhed behind him, he turned his attention away to a new target. And that target responded to his aggression by vomiting acid at him, an awful jet of steaming green, which he avoided only by the grace of Artemis hauling him out of place at the last moment.

But he never did stop laughing. Not as the next head spawned, not as the one after that. Before too long he was surrounded by a dozen of them, and I swear to you he looked more alive than when he started. He beat his shield with his spear.

"Come on! Show me some fun!" he bellowed so loud I heard him clear over the waves and the roars. And the music.

Music was the King of Song's job. If he could find the right song, he might be able to placate the beast long enough for the others to get some good hits in. It was a good bit of strategy. You always want to stack as many debuffs as possible on a boss to make them easier to deal with. But most people didn't look so pompous about it.

He had no wings to keep him in the air, but what he *did* have was a flaming chariot, pulled by a great disk of gold. Wherever it went the light followed; a ribbon of dawn itself wrapping around and between the gnashing heads of the hydra. There he stood with his lyre strumming away. I couldn't understand a word of the song he was singing, but each syllable hit my ears like a war drum. Hearing him, it was impossible to sit still; I had to pace, I had to move.

So I did. And that, as you may recognize, is *horrible* for your angles. My footage was all shitty now, jittery and unfocused, as I moved this way and that along the edge of the cliff.

My heart pounded. I couldn't keep my hands still. The unseen drums wouldn't allow it. I balanced my phone beneath the straps of my chiton. With it laid flat against my chest I could still get footage while I...

What was I going to do, anyway? What had come over me? My palms were stiff with pulsing blood. Fight. I had to fight, somehow, had to keep moving, had to...

The war hymn drove me to draw my own bow from its carrier and nock an arrow I knew damn well wouldn't hit a thing. But there was no alternative. Every muscle in my body was bent toward it, everything in me united for the singular purpose of this fight.

I drew back the bow. The distance between me and the hydra was too great to cross by any arrow. I knew it. I mean, I could hardly see War fighting for his life down there. How could I possibly hit?

Yet the music whispered to me: *What if you did? Can you really sit here and do nothing when there's glory to be had?*

I lined the plain, unassuming arrowhead up with the thing's torso—then angled a lot higher. A lot. When I loosed the arrow, it went so far and so fast that for a moment I lost track of it. Had it gotten lost in the faint clouds of sea spray? Had it already gone so far astray?

But my eyes caught sight of a streak of silver shooting like a star across the sky, straight for the hydra, and it was not one that had come from Artemis's bow. She was too far to the east, and this arrow had come from...

Well.

Where I was standing.

I looked at my hands. It couldn't be. I was a mortal, like any other. Artemis had spent *so long* teaching me to shoot. There was no way.

The ribbon of gold light passed me, and soon in its wake came the King of Song. I could have sworn he was glancing at me as he passed.

That fucker. He knew.

Maybe it was the music that was lending me these powers—but was it? I'd gotten those visions from Artemis's arrows before he started this song. Was it the fruit? Was it something else?

I didn't know. But I did know that I should help as much as I could.

I picked up another arrow. My own pile again—not Artemis's. Even with this music in my ear whispering that I could do anything I put my mind to, I wasn't dumb. Firing one of those might have some side effects I'd never be able to predict.

I nocked another one of my plain arrows. At its tip I watched the others fight: War's lance now aflame, driven deep into the core of a severed head; Artemis running along the beast's necks with a deer's grace; the Gray-Eyed Queen climbing the creature from behind.

Artemis nocked and fired. Just as I'd seen in my vision the head of her arrow expanded to a crescent as wide as a ship. Wherever the silver touched it sliced flesh. An absolute torrent of green blood coated the fighters as Artemis severed four heads and an arm with a single arrow.

When my heart pounded this time it had little to do with the King of Song's music. I could swear that, despite the distance, I saw her looking at me.

No—I couldn't let her down. I loosed another arrow at the aching side of the beast, at its pulsing wounds. The silver streaked straight to its target. A glimmer of light heralded another cry of pain from the hydra.

And it was then that the Gray-Eyed Queen struck. From her perch on the back of the creature she drove her spear deep between its bones. Calm she stood in the storm of horrible pain, of writhing flesh and agonies. As the heads turned toward her, Passion shot their eyes with burning arrows and War drove his flaming lance into the bases of their necks.

The Gray-Eyed Queen cut the beast's flesh like cloth for a pattern. Careful, precise, without erring at all—wherever her spear went, the skin there was parted from the bone beneath.

The beast's heart was open to the world—but it wasn't what I had expected. In place of a great organ, glistening and grisly, I saw a pulsing orb of green.

Artemis jumped from one of the creature's heads to her brother's chariot. There, balanced on the precipice of it, she drew back her great moon bow to its full extent. And the arrow she'd nocked?

It was black.

I drew again. I wanted to be with her, somehow, I wanted to do this with her even if I was only a mostly human.

She and I fired at the same moment.

A streak of black, a streak of silver, and a streak of gold from her brother's own bow. All three strands twisted together as they pierced the glowing heart of the creature.

I will remember the sound it made until the day I die. I will remember the cries echoing, each one doubled and tripled by the new heads, as life left the hydra. I will remember all this and more.

But most of all, I will remember the moment I realized what I had done.

You'll think that this was a glorious thing we did. And it was, in its own way. But it took the beast a long while to die. Even with the arrows piercing its heart, with its many necks cauterized, with a hole the size of a school bus in its torso, it kept breathing. It kept fighting.

It didn't have too long left to fight, thankfully. Artemis was too kindhearted for that. No matter what anyone said about her—and they said plenty of things about her—she hated to see an animal in pain. That the animal in question was a mythic beast didn't change matters much in her estimation.

One by one she went from neck to neck, severing it and helping Passion to cauterize them before they could regrow. Her brother played a cool-water lament to placate the creature, to stop it from crying out as much in agony. Eventually there was only one head left.

Other people would have stopped there for a moment. War would have. I know in my heart that he would have given a long speech, a grandstanding thing to memorialize the struggle of the gods against a terrible and fearsome foe.

But Artemis understood what I did.

The real struggle was that of the mythic beast.

Even now, with the King of Song himself playing a piece so beautiful that the Gray-Eyed Queen was shedding glistening tears beneath her plumed helmet, the hydra was trying to live. There wasn't much it could do but whine and paw at Artemis, but that is what it did.

And she gave it the mercy it so clearly wanted.

Her hunting dagger ended it in a single cut, and the monster went limp. Passion was with her in an instant to burn away any possibility of regeneration.

On that island in some far-off sea stood nothing that breathed. Only the five gods, coated in the verdant blood of their kill, and the corpse of something unbelievable.

Artemis returned to me on her brother's chariot. As promised, she brought with her the heart of the beast—or, at least, a chunk of it small enough to fit at her side. When they made landfall on the cliff, she rushed toward me as if she'd been away at war for years. She hadn't bothered washing herself off at all in the sea water. When she held me tight my cheeks got smeared with the creature's blood.

Maybe I should have thought it was gross, and I think a part of me did. You can't exactly enjoy being smushed up against something so wet and cold and slippery. The blood didn't feel like blood at all—it reminded me of cooking oil instead. Thick and unctuous and never quite sticking to anything.

"You did so well," she said. "I knew you'd figure it out."

"Artemis..."

I had so many things I wanted to ask her. There was this pride swelling in my heart, but in its shadow lurked the sharp-toothed dog of fear. I'd never had *powers* before. How could I have? And what did it mean that I had them now, after seeing what I had seen?

In the end I went for the easiest thing to say. "I'm...kind of scared, to be honest."

I didn't need to say anything else. She knew what I needed—even if it was something I thought was too much to ask for from her.

Without another word she scooped me up in her arms. With one hand she picked up the chunk of the beast's heart and with the other alone she supported all of my weight.

"Queen of the Wild—" started War, but I never got to hear the end of it.

Artemis leaped into the dark—and when we landed, we were home.

None of it felt real.

The ligature marks against my skin. The mythic blood that pooled in them. The goddess holding me in her arms. The divine arrows rattling around in my quiver—and the knowledge that I'd shot one of them with my own two hands.

Something switched in me. I'd gotten so used to the past few months of wilderness living. Sure, it was ridiculous; sure, I was spending every moment with a god. But there was a comfort to it. The unbelievable happened step-by-step. I was always allowed to get used to something.

Everything that was happening now was... It was just so much. Like a bunch of voices shouting at once drowning out any individual word.

"Iphigenia," she said to me, her lips against my scalp, "you're safe."

"Did that really happen?" I asked her. But it didn't feel like I was asking her. My lips didn't feel like they were moving. Not that they were numb or anything like that—it was more that I heard my own voice as if it belonged to someone else. Like I was watching a movie. There was part of me that wanted so badly to dig my nails into my skin and try to cling to whatever it was I *could* feel without reservation.

"It did," she said. Artemis carried me back to the last camp we'd set up together. She set me down on the stump she'd used to watch me.

And then the god knelt in front of me. With her bloodied hands on either side of my face she turned me toward her. The crescents of her eyes were wider, thinner, hardly there at all.

"You have seen so much today," she said. "You have done so much. There are many whose lives will never approach what you've experienced in this one day. I am prouder of you than I have words to say, little deer. You were so good for me."

The beast's blood against my skin, cold and slippery; Artemis's rough hands; the smell of the hunt and the smell of the fires we'd long extinguished. The wind through the leaves around us. So much to focus on.

So much of it paling in comparison to her words, her attention.

"Can you tell me what you're afraid of?" she said.

My lips stuck together. Could I? There were so many little fears. So many questions.

"I-I don't know," I stammered. "There's...Artemis, what did I do up there? What did *you* do? I don't know what any of it means."

A hum of understanding. She took my hand in hers, rubbing her thumb along the back of it. "You fear the things you do not know."

I nodded. Even that felt strangely distant—more like I was wiggling a joystick to look up and down than I was moving my actual head.

"I feel weird. So much has happened, and I just...I need some time to think."

She ran her hands through my hair. Blood clumped the strands together, but I didn't care. I knew she was trying.

"You will have all the time you need," she said. "I'll tend the fire, the camp. Will you be able to rest?"

That answer came quickly to me. I shook my head. Too much knocking around inside my skull. Too much to think about.

"Hm," she said. "Would you want to sleep, if you could?"

The thought was as impossible as any six other things I'd done today. Much as I wanted to dismiss it out of hand, I knew I shouldn't. Artemis didn't deserve me being rude to her.

"I, uh. Yeah. If I could. But I just don't think it's going to happen. There's been—I can't just stop thinking, Artemis. I really wish I could," I said.

I worried that I'd been a little too direct with a god. I should have known to have more faith in my liege.

"Iphigenia," she said. "There is someone I want to ask to help you. I think you deserve it. But I will need time to do so. Can you stay here, alone, while I ask them?"

"Haven't you already done—"

She touched her fingers to my lips. The hydra's blood slipped into the space between my teeth and my lips. In the end it was this sour taste that pulled me back into my body. I had no choice in the matter, either. It was *so* sour that it might as well have reached out and grabbed me by the hair. It was not a gentle sort of grounding; I screwed my eyes shut and wriggled.

Never in my life had I seen her react so quickly as she did then. The woman I loved so dearly became little more than a blur of silver-dark as she grabbed my canteen and held it out to me. The crescents of her eyes were so wide and full that I could see the curve of her cheekbones beneath them, the most I'd ever seen of her face.

"Iphigenia, listen to me. Rinse and spit," she said. "Keep doing it until you can't taste it anymore."

I tried to do as I was told, though to be honest my lower lip tingled like a motherfucker. I had to hold it shut. And of course I was already covered in blood, so it only got worse. But after ten minutes or so of sputtering I was starting to taste something other than the bottom of a barrel of Warheads.

The whole while she held me, the whole while she looked down on me with horrible intensity. If I didn't know her so well I might have been terrified. But the more time passed without anything awful happening the more she seemed to relax, and eventually I felt the tension in her leave.

"Ew," I said. "I bet... that never happened to any of the other heroes..."

"Not ours," Artemis said, "but some of the other Courts. Foreigners." She tucked a shock of hair away from my face. "I'm sorry. How are you feeling? Did you swallow any of it?"

I couldn't help but notice a small rise in her voice. If I had swallowed some of it, what would happen? The blood of a mythic beast could be made into a poison that would kill a god. What would it have done to me, if I had gotten any in a wound?

Before I could answer, she was dabbing at my face with a bit of fur we'd used for blankets.

"Feeling... fine, I guess," I said. "Nothing's on fire. Tasted awful, though. Like chugging concentrated lemon juice or something."

A hum. She kept cleaning me off. There was a quiet insistence to her hand as she worked.

"Tell me if anything changes," she said. It wasn't a question.

"I will," I said. "Artemis, you really have done so much for me already. You don't need to go getting me some magical way to sleep."

"Can't, now," she said. "We should keep an eye on you tonight."

I sighed. "It would be really bad if I swallowed any of the blood, wouldn't it?"

She hummed again—though this time it was a little lower than usual. "It could be a lot of things."

"What happened to the others?" I asked. "The ones from other Courts who had done this sort of thing."

She leaned back. There wasn't much clean space left on the fur she'd been using to dab away the blood. We'd need a real piece of cloth for that—and that wasn't something we were liable to get here in her Domain.

"One learned the language of birds. Killed a dragon. Became a hero," she said. "Others...become aggressive. Rabid."

Her eyes didn't leave mine. I appreciated that. I appreciated, too, that she didn't bother trying to sugarcoat this at all.

I looked down at my hand. Which would it be for me? A rabid anger, or more of whatever it was I had done on the cliffside? Maybe someone else would have been more worried about the dying part of things, but it didn't scare me. If anything I was worried that Artemis would have to look after me if things got bad—and worried about who would look after my family.

"If I make it through the night, will I be okay?"

There were her eyes again, this time full and round. "I can't say. Probably. That's as far as I can go."

This time I was the one who hummed. "Well," I said. "At least it's something to focus on for a while."

She squeezed my hand. "Would you like to hear the story?"

I lifted a brow. There was a nervousness to her voice as she spoke. Like a deer that had heard a hunter not far off. Was it the poison that worried her—or was it whatever story she was about to tell me?

She must have sensed what was on my mind. Artemis had a way of doing that. Not literally, of course, but she was very good at sensing someone's emotions. So she pulled me close to her and sat me on her lap. With her arms wrapped around my waist and her head on my shoulder, I knew I was as safe as safe could be. Even if I wasn't entirely sure what I was about to hear.

"It is your family's story. They have not told you. Could not tell you. The Law forbade it, so that you would not follow in your ancestor's footsteps."

I tensed. The man in the pit—his aching voice. His *hunger*.

"I will tell it only if you want to hear it. But if you want to hear it, Iphigenia, I will tell it. You deserve to know."

Did I want to know, though? Whatever it was that had led to that man's imprisonment had also led to the curse placed on my family. The reason I had spent my entire life prior to this point in a high-rise was because of whatever had happened in this story.

Did I want to know? Would it make a difference if I did?

You can't learn from your history if you don't know any of it—and there's always something to learn from history. If I buried my head in the sand, I was no better than the rest of the family. My father sacrificed his own daughter. It takes evil in your blood to do that.

I had to know what the evil was in mine.

"Okay," I said. "You can tell me."

And so she began.

A Story

A lament for the fallen, the falling, and those yet to tumble to the depths—sing this for me, muse. Your sister calls on you to lend her humble tongue the moon's own silver. So rarely do I call on you that I have almost forgotten the words, but here already I find your guiding hands. Do not leave me alone in the forest of meaning. Show to me the hunter's mark of beauty, and the trail of truth that will lead me to my quarry.

The trail leads us to a truth often spoken: My father has sired a great many bastards.

Some of these bastards you have come to know well. Stories abound of Heracles's great deeds and worthy accomplishments, though they leave off the manner of his death and his many struggles. You have heard of Dionysius, too, my sibling, the spirit of mystery and revelry. Some may even call my brother and me bastards, and they would not be wrong in saying so.

But when we speak of *this* bastard, we turn our attention not to the skies where my family and I have come to dwell, but to the earth below.

There was a man named Tantalus. His father, as I said, was my own; his mother was a mortal woman named Pluto.

Every morning my brother pulls his chariot across the sky. The sun goes with him and bathes all the mortals in its golden light. Warmth and life he offers, as I offer secrecy and comfort.

I tell you now that there was never a more wretched man to walk beneath my brother's sun and my own crescent moon than this Tantalus.

It was many years before we discovered this about him. Father does not always claim her bastards, and with mortals, it can be many years before their godly features begin to show. We did not know he existed until he wandered into the Court. He used no door to do this; he eschewed any normal route. Instead, he had coaxed the branches of an olive tree into growing in a circle and stepped through that thrice, backward, to find himself among us.

My father knew him for her own the moment she laid eyes upon him.

"Look, children, for our number grows! My son Tantalus has found his way here. Let us have a feast to celebrate his ingenuity!"

So it was proclaimed, and so it was done. We fetched all we could to offer as fine a feast as we might offer to any hero. The Queen of Gods was incensed by the arrival of yet another bastard, but she bore this with grace and kindness, for she knew that Tantalus could not have picked his parents. The fault was my father's.

Let he who proclaims the feast less than abundant speak to my arrows. Succulent meats had we, and ambrosia, and all the things that may whet a mortal's appetite. Wine, fresh fruit, cheeses, and all we could find for a mortal to eat.

Yet it was not enough for Tantalus to be welcomed this way. He demanded yet more food.

"Father," he said, "for so long I have gone without your love. Would you truly deny me another plate of food?"

So it went. He asked for plate after plate of food and consumed them all. And at the end of this feast, my father clapped his shoulder and sent him on his way.

He returned to us again and again. Each time he ate more than the last. I had my suspicions of this when he never grew rounder—and when he returned always hungry. Those who sup on ambrosia do not feel the call of hunger for months. Why, then, was he eating so much?

I voiced my suspicions to my brother, who voiced them to Wisdom, who told us that we had the right of it. The next time Tantalus turned up, we watched him closely—and discovered that he was hiding the food in his many-pocketed robes.

"What is the meaning of this?" my father asked him.

"Father, I have done only as any king would do for their beloved people: I have provided to them that which you have provided to me," he said.

This was as a rock in a horse's hoof to me; it could only bode trouble. But my father adored him. Here was a man who was so dedicated to his people that his generosity had outstripped his sense. Who could look on that ambition and hate him? So my father proclaimed, and forgave him, and sent him on his way with baskets full of ambrosia.

It was then that the Queen began to truly seethe over the matter. And who could blame her? Here was a demigod who refused to depart his world for our own, who took what *she* offered him gladly, and made no offer of his own in turn. She said to us that, should he besmirch our names, we should not hesitate to strike at him.

It did not take long for such an insult to occur. One day, Tantalus returned to the Court with a package he struggled to hold aloft. It was nearly the same size as he was.

"Siblings, beloved family, I have finally brought all of you a gift to repay your kindness," he said. "Here is a meat most rare, a thing seen only within the bounds of my kingdom. As you have allowed my kingdom to feast on ambrosia, we have grown wealthy enough to offer you this much of it, treated in oils that would beggar all but the present company, spiced to perfection. I swear on my own divine blood that there is no meal quite like this one."

He placed the package on our table and uncovered it.

He had not lied. It was anointed in fragrant oils and fresh herbs, and the spices prickled the nostrils. Yet I knew the moment I laid eyes on it what it was I was beholding. Though the Hearth is not my realm, no god has handled more flesh than I have.

And that was no prey animal. It was not venison, nor duck, nor beef, nor the flesh of any bird I knew. All the spices of the world could not have fooled me. There was a rankness to it that could only have one source.

Miasma. The noxious fumes that follow those who kill their own family.

Tantalus had served us his own family. There he was, standing at the table, carving off thin slices of meat to serve us. He practically shoved it in our faces.

As the Queen had given me leave to attack within her Court, I nocked an arrow and fired on him immediately. I pinned his feet to the spot where he stood.

"Father," I said, "say the word and I shall kill him."

But my father shook her head.

"Death is too fine a gift for one such as this," she said. "Let me speak with your uncle, and together we will devise a punishment."

So it was. The punishment they devised is one you know well already: Deep in the confines of a cave belonging to two Courts, both disinterested in his plight, we would confine Tantalus. In knee-deep water we would leave him, with all the fruit he desired hanging overhead. But when he reached for the water he would find that it would recede before him—and when he reached for the fruit, it would never so much as graze his fingertips.

We left him in this cave for eternity because he had killed his son and tried to feed him to us.

You may wonder what drove him to do such a thing. We did. It was Wisdom who pried the answer from his mind. When she told us what it was he was thinking, we all wished that she hadn't.

There was no great desperation that drove this action. There was no malice, no hatred. Indeed, so far as we could tell, he felt not even a trickle of love for the son that he had butchered.

He simply wanted to know whether the gods were as infallible as we seemed to him. He wanted to test us.

That is the man that you saw in the cave. He would sacrifice you, too, if he could.

But let us not turn aside from the child. What were we to do with his remains? Killed for so little reason, in such an unjust fashion—was there nothing we could do to give him a second chance at life? His father's crimes were not his own. He should not need to suffer for them.

No one had attempted anything of the like before. This was not merely reversing disease or removing a wound; this was rebuilding a body entire. My brother toiled for ten days and ten nights alongside the Fates themselves. He wore his hands raw. His golden skin was sallow with effort when next I saw him. But it was done.

Pelops breathed anew.

I shall tell you of him, but first I will tell you what became of the other children of Tantalus. A spat over inheritance saw the two younger sons kill the eldest. A family already tainted by the fog of kinslaying was now deeply immersed within it. Whenever they breathed, any of them, they breathed in this corruption. It seeped into their lungs like rot creeps along the veins.

Which made the words of his only daughter all the more galling.

Tantalus's only daughter was a woman named Niobe. She married a king. This alone should have contented her. But there was more: Her husband was just and kind, and loved her as truly as any man could. And with that she could have contented herself—but there was more. She and her husband had together fourteen children, seven boys and seven girls, all of whom lived to adulthood, all strong and hale, with minds as quick as their steps. Any one of these children would have been a boon.

And yet there was more she wanted. Like her father, she was always reaching for another fruit. It was custom in those days to celebrate the gods openly—and it so happened that one day in particular was set aside for the celebration of my mother. One year, Niobe saw the procession celebrating my good mother and all that she had done.

Something in this rankled her.

She pulled aside her husband and asked him why my mother should be the one worshipped. Yes, Leto had granted to the world the Queen of the Wild, the Lady of the Moon, the Protector of Children; yes, Leto had raised also the King of Song, the Lord of the Sun, the Bringer of Cures. But she had fourteen of her own children, and any one of them was a match for my brother and me. And was her grandfather not the very King of Gods? Never mind what had become of her father; she was just as worthy of veneration.

Being that this was my mother's day of veneration, she heard all words said in the vicinity of her idols. The moment they came to her ears she summoned us to the Court of Earth, where she had come to reside.

My mother is the best of myself and my brother at once—as charming and kind as he is, yes, but my singular determination comes from her as well. It was the combination of these two that so beguiled my father. When we went to her that day, it was not the warm, bright countenance that greeted us. It was the dark one, black-veiled and full of cold wrath.

"My children," she said to us. "I have suffered insults from the Queen of Gods, from my siblings, and from those who claim to love me. Yet I persist in the name of being your mother, raising you, caring for you as I have these long centuries. This woman Niobe has besmirched all three of us in one fell blow. I, who have asked nothing of you, ask that you avenge us."

"Avenge us?" said my brother. "How shall we do that? Shall we strike her blind, or mute, or change her to a form more suited?"

My brother grasps poetry as easily as he does the skirts he chases. Hidden meanings often reveal themselves to him in verse. When it comes to people, matters are different. He refuses to see the darkness—and it is this, I think, that will get him killed one day.

But until then he has me to mind the darkness for him. And as our mother gave us our orders, I filled my quiver with the black arrows you have seen, for I knew well what she was asking of us. I remembered the evil that Tantalus had done. This woman who had spoken so freely of her boons made no mention of what her father had done, nor the tragedy that had befallen her brother.

"Apollo," said our mother, "follow your sister's example in this matter."

He looked to me, and I knew in that moment that he did not approve of this course of action. I could not say that I approved of it entirely myself. But in all our years, our mother had never asked for anything of this kind before—and I had little to tie me to mortals in those days.

"Mother," said my brother. "Are you certain of this? All of them?"

"I am certain," said our mother. "I call on your love of me and your dutiful natures. Too long have I suffered insults. If I begin to suffer them even from mortals, or near-mortals, then I lose what little I have left to me aside the two of you."

Reputation was no laughing matter among the gods. A Domain could fade if not given the proper attention. It did not happen often. Many of us took precautions not only for ourselves but for others. If a Domain did begin to fade, they often sought a place within a larger Court that could sustain them.

My mother had no Court of her own, and even her title was one of contention. The Queen of Gods felt that she should rightly be the Queen of Children, too, but our father said otherwise. Still it made matters tense enough that she was the only one of our kind addressed by name more often than by title.

In contrast to this, my brother and I both could have sustained a Court, even then. Our Domains had been powerful since the moment I delivered him from our mother.

I thought of her fading. I thought of her wandering around the Court of Earth begging for what ambrosia she could be given, and I knew it was not an acceptable outcome. She deserved more after everything she'd been through.

So I slung the arrows across my back, took my brother's hand, and pulled him through the veil between worlds to the land where Niobe dwelled.

She and her family were gathered for dinner.

My brother, his hands trembling at his lyre, offered them mercy. He played a strain of music to catch their attention and then said: "Let Niobe, the braggart Queen, renounce the words she has said. Let her look upon our splendor and that of our children and realize the error of her ways. If she does this, we shall leave."

All eyes fell on the Queen.

Niobe stood from her place next to her husband. When she beheld us it was with Tantalus's eyes, cunning and dark. "You will try to strike us down. But your father's blood is in our veins, too, and you will find that we fight just as fiercely."

Thus she sealed the fate of her family.

I will spare you the details of it. Suffice it to say that she was wrong—it was no fight at all. Niobe thought that we would fight nobly. She expected a confrontation alike to those with our brother Heracles, or any of the noble warriors who oft took to the field in those days.

But I am not the Queen of War. I am no tactician. I am the Huntress. And to hunt you must always know the quickest way to end your quarry. To do otherwise cuts against the core of my being. I do not cause unnecessary suffering.

Niobe had cloaked her children in beautiful armor. Their

godly constitutions meant that they could have, if they liked, fought us for quite some time. Their sword arms were strong, their shields polished and shining, their armor forged from star metal. To kill them we would have needed to sever all their limbs and watched them bleed. That is what their grandfather had done to their uncle. That was the boon of their godly blood: Wounds were painful but almost always survivable.

But there was mortal in their blood just as much as there was divinity. And it was this that we targeted.

The black arrows carry with them all the poison of illness. A single one alone is enough to fell any mortal who is struck. In only a day they will rot away as their body begins to fail.

So it was that we shot all fourteen of them, my brother and I. One by one they fell to the ground overcome with weakness. They would die before the day was through—and without ever waking again.

We left Niobe to her misery.

There is one last tragedy that befell your ancestors. I had nothing to do with it and heard the story only secondhand from the others.

Pelops recovered from his resurrection. He had grown to be a strong, ambitious man. If the deaths of his nieces and nephews troubled him, he showed no sign of it. He had set his sights on the daughter of a particular king. As was common at the time, this king had been granted an oracle that his son-in-law would kill him. Thus he had slain everyone who had asked for his daughter's hand. All along the road to his kingdom he had mounted their heads as warning to anyone foolish enough to attempt it.

Pelops was a fool.

He challenged this king to a chariot race for the girl's hand. The king accepted the challenge. He hired the best horses and the finest chariot he could find, and all the kingdom gathered to watch the race.

But Pelops did not content himself with a fair race: He cheated. He and his friend snuck into the king's stable at night and sabotaged the royal chariot. Nor did he content himself with simply cheating. He had caught the eye of the King of Waves more than once.

"Great lord of the thundering waters and horses, will you grant unto me a token of your affection? Give me a team of horses that cannot be beaten."

Poseidon did not refuse him this—on the condition that Pelops grant him a night together. Pelops agreed, and so the horses were given to him.

On the day of the race, the king's chariot shattered in two. He fell and scrambled to safety, but there was no stopping Pelops's divine horses. They trampled him to death. Some say it was an accident, but I have my own thoughts on the matter.

I told you there was a tragedy. It is not the death of Pelops, nor the death of the king. Instead, the friend Pelops had conspired with to sabotage the chariot was the true subject of the princess's affections. She loved him in the true way, without reservation, and anyone who looked on them could see this.

As did Pelops.

On the night of his wedding Pelops struck down his friend and co-conspirator. And as he died, this friend proclaimed that fortune would never come to the House of Pelops without misfortune in its wake, a dog as hungry for a meal as the accursed family was for what did not belong to them.

The truth of this was concealed for many years. When at last the princess discovered what Pelops had done to win her, she ended her own life.

So it has been for your family. So it shall be until the curse is washed from you. The reason you serve us—the reason every Heir of Pelops is given to the service of the Courts—is to keep the curse at bay by currying our favor.

I wanted more for you than this.

And that, Iphigenia, is why I saved you.

Chapter Fourteen

She told me that story over the course of a single night. Some people fall asleep when they hear someone talk like that. The rhythm of the words is like the rocking of a crib guiding them gently, gently, toward death's younger sibling. Artemis let each bit of it hang in the morning air. Memories left out on a line to dry.

I didn't know what to make of them. The memories she'd left out here were old. I couldn't be sure who they were meant to fit. Sure, they were hers. But did they still fit? Was she trying to give them to me?

She told me the story, and then she let the silence lead.

I leaned my head against her shoulders. She wrapped an arm around my waist. The air smelled of the meat we'd roasted and I'd pecked at. She hadn't touched it at all. When it was the two of us alone like this, we didn't like to pretend.

We didn't like to pretend.

I held the hands that had fired black arrows on my ancestors.

I laid my head on the shoulders that had borne the burden of this knowledge.

What could I have to say to her about any of it? The hydra's blood covered us both.

Fourteen people running for their lives. A man cutting up his own son. A friend's betrayal, and a wife's suicide.

Some of it one could say was her fault. She did not need to fire the arrows. But if my own mother had asked me to defend her in that way, what would I have done? So many times my family had asked me to do things I hated. But I did them, because I was the Heir of Pelops, and I didn't want it to fall to my siblings.

It was the same for her. We both knew it. If she had not killed Niobe's family, then her mother would have had to do it herself.

I looked at the blood smeared across my hands, across hers. Something in me was already starting to change. Part of it was knowing that we were the same, and that we were different.

The same acid green covered us. It could poison me—but it wouldn't poison her.

The idea was already forming in my head. The plan that would lead me to speaking with you, and asking for your help. That was the other change in me—the realization that I had a way forward. A map painted in green ink. In the morning, I told her about it.

"Iphigenia."

I was tending to the fire when she spoke in the tone she only ever used when she was about to leave. The sun had risen on our little camp. While the night was her Domain, it seemed her family could call on her as they wished during the day.

It had to be them. She wouldn't leave me otherwise.

"Duty calls, hm?" I asked. I slapped my hands against my thighs. "Do you think I'm clear from the poison?"

She tangled her fingers in my hair. "Should be," she said. "When I return in the evening, I'll bring more ambrosia and a better cure."

I tilted my head toward her touch. She trailed her fingers down from my scalp along the back of my neck. The rise and fall of my vertebrae were valleys that she sought to map.

"Will you be all right, Iphigenia, if I leave you for the day? Say the word, and I will stay at your side."

"I can manage," I said. "But there's something I want from you."

"Name it," she said. A promise in two words.

I let myself fall back against her. When I tilted my head up, I stared her dead in the eyes. Niobe I was not—but I knew now that there was divinity in my blood, too, and I wanted to wake it.

"Let me go back to the mortal world," I said. "It doesn't have to be today. Doesn't have to be all the time. I can part-time it. Might even be easier that way, to be honest. But I want to go back."

The shadows of her face moved. My own private velvet dark sky.

"You do not miss the mortal world."

I smirked. "I don't, no. Not as much as I thought I would.

But there's something I need to do, and I want the space to be able to do it. I think I've earned that."

"So you have," she answered. "I will grant this to you, for a price."

"There's always a price when it comes to the gods isn't there?" I said. I smiled up at her. "Come on then, let's hear it."

"I will give you something to wear. You will wear it every day. And if I call, you will come," she said.

A cool, level voice. Her hand tracing a circle around the base of my throat. I thought of my ligature marks. "Something to miss you by?"

She dug her nail in along the line of my collarbone. I drew a sharp breath. It wasn't enough to break the skin, so delicate was she with her touch. But it was enough for the pressure, the promise, the pain.

"Yes," she said. And as she traced my collarbone I felt a cool metal start to form beneath her finger, cold as river water. When at last she withdrew her hand from my neck there was a small metal collar in its wake—a crescent of silver. "When you need me, touch this, and I will hear what you say."

My tongue stuck to the roof of my mouth. I let my hand hover over the collar. It was beautiful—there were no other words that could begin to describe it. A circle with no beginning and no end. Cold enough against my skin to draw my notice but not enough for any real pain.

The cold froze me in the present moment. I took a breath. I was really doing this. The Domain that had been so kind to me, that had provided so much for me, was no longer going to be home. Loud music and honking cars would wake me instead of the sun and the cries of the animals around us. I would sleep on a plush bed instead of a collection of furs and straw. Instead of catching my food I would order it on my phone and have it delivered to my doorstep.

Hell, I'd have a door.

A few months ago, all of this would have excited me. On that first night I would have given anything to be able to head back home. Cut off all my hair, offer my blood, whatever it would have taken. All of that for a charge for my phone, four walls, and guaranteed meals.

I didn't need those things now. I missed them less than I thought. Looking around the camp, I kept thinking: *Oh, the snow shoes I was making are only half done. I'll have to dry out more cord to keep up that job. Maybe I should make a little shelter for the firewood. I can't forget to cure the strips of venison I hadn't gotten around to eating.*

So many things to do. Things I would have thought of as work, once upon a time. Here I was with my palms itching and water at my eyes at the thought of leaving it behind.

But worst of all was looking on Artemis.

"Iphigenia," she said, her hands on my shoulders, "this will always be your home. Tell me you know that."

I bit my lip. "I know. When you have the chance—I know you don't need to eat the same way I do, but there's all this venison and I would really hate for it to go to waste, so if you could find something to do with it…"

"I will," she said.

"And there's all of the ashes, too. We can't just leave them there. They've got to be disposed off properly. The fire's been going for such a long time now, I bet it's a pock on the ground there, when we put it out."

"You're worrying about the wrong things." Artemis spoke plain and simple. Each word hit its mark. I took another breath and looked down as she continued. "Worry about yourself. That is what I want."

A god can say what they want the same way they breathe: They do not have to. It all comes so naturally to them. My gut wanted to argue that there was just so much to worry over, that maybe I should take an extra day—

But I remembered that there was god in my blood, too. That there was something important I needed to do.

This place was home. The bough that had tripped me that first hunting trip, the mountain I hadn't finished climbing, the bear I'd gotten by on my own. All of my traps laid out along the river and in piles of leaves. The stump we'd carved out, the fire I'd set, the furs I loved best. And, of course, the tree where she had tied me up and introduced me to a self I hadn't known.

What did the high-rise have that compared?

I would come back here. I knew I would. The sooner I could finish my little task, the sooner I could go back to figuring out how in the fuck you're meant to set hairpin trigger traps.

Divinity and love guided my hand. I cupped her cheek with my mostly mortal hand.

"I'm going to miss you so much," I said.

She covered my hand with hers. "You will come when I call,"

she said. Then, a squeeze. "And I will call. Do not forget whose handmaiden you are."

"Yours," I said.

Her cheeks rose against my hand. She was smiling at me. How did it look, that smile of hers? I wondered if she'd have sharp teeth. Would she rake them against my skin some day? The rope had left such pretty marks, such lasting proclamations. What would it feel like to have a bite mark...?

"When will you leave?" she said.

"Soon, but not today. Tomorrow, or the day after," I said. My reasons were...not entirely altruistic. "There's still plenty to take care of here—"

"You want to be tied up again," she said.

I smiled, and laughed, because I could no more deny her than I could deny the moon. "Maybe."

She tilted my head up toward her. As she did, she rested the palm of her hand against my throat.

"Say it properly."

Fluttering in my stomach. Now I was *really* thinking about those teeth. "I want you to tie me up."

Artemis pulled me closer by the throat, a gentle pull that nonetheless left little doubt of her strength.

"You have until moonrise to consider what *properly* means," she said. "I know you won't disappoint me, little deer."

Our own private eternity slipped over us as she held me in place. I was so lost in staring at her, in considering the best way to say what it was I wished to say, that when she disappeared I did not notice it. One moment she was there, and the next she was gone. The silver eyes and shadowed face that so beguiled me became gold and white aftcrimages suspended against the endless blue sky.

I had plenty of time to think.

There were plans that needed making. I had all sorts of details to iron out about what it was I was going to do when I got back to Oz. Would I stay at the high-rise or someplace near it? What was I going to do for money? Did I need any, with how short a trip I was planning to take? Maybe I should ask Artemis to leave me in the bush; maybe that would feel more natural to me now.

But truth be told, I wasn't thinking of any of that. Details, details, details. All as slippery as eels.

One night before I returned to the world of the living. What would Artemis make of it?

As night came upon the Huntress's Domain, I put out our fire. To do this I hauled buckets to the stream, filled them with water, and hauled them back. Some might say this wasn't an efficient use of my time. I'd tell those people that few things help someone focus better than carrying large amounts of water a good distance away. Every muscle in your body gets bent toward the task. There's no room for anything else while you're carrying all that.

And, okay, sure. Maybe I was wondering if I'd walk face-first into another of her traps. Maybe I wanted to make myself a bit of a target.

What can I say? There's something to being *pursued*. This whole forest was as much a part of her as any of her limbs; nothing happened here without her willing it. Every branch that raked against my skin was her hand; every howl in the distance was a promise from her to me; every breeze was her whispering in my ear.

Find the right words. A simple assignment.

Less so when the anticipation was building in me. When my body remembered so well the way I'd felt with her.

I have to admit that when I threw the water on the fire there was a part of me that was shocked I'd made it that far. The water hissed; steam rose in a great veil around the camp. Cold didn't wait its turn to steal in. The difference in temperature was immediate. I might as well have jumped face-first into the water myself.

I'd already spent plenty of time there washing up. I knew that she wouldn't touch me, and I didn't want her to. But...well, the last time I'd been such a mess. I didn't want to be a mess this time. The flowing water had so shocked me that I'd spent ten minutes doubled over with my hands desperately cupping myself to keep the water from touching my clit. With how wound up I'd gotten myself it was *maddening* to feel the water running against me.

I could have gotten myself off then. She was as much the water as she was her own corporeal self. Wouldn't it be the same as the time we'd shared together?

But she'd asked me not to disappoint her, and I knew deep in my heart that what Artemis really wanted was a hunt. It would be no fun for her if I wasn't on edge when she tracked me down.

So—I'd washed up very carefully, and I'd made the whole trek back, and when I threw the water on the fire I thought to myself: This is really it.

Darkness rolled over the camp. The light left me more dazzled than I knew. Though I knew this clearing better than I knew my room back at the high-rise, I had to wait for my eyes to adjust before I tried to navigate. The sheets of yellow and orange that remained in my sight took their sweet time in fading away. Standing there in the cold dark my heart began to race.

When the moon rises, she'd said.

It was high in the sky now.

Where was she hiding? In the wild there were always eyes on you; there was always something alive that wanted you dead. But at that moment?

Oh, the eyes were like arrowheads.

I took a breath. Shakier than I would have liked. My body knew what my mind was too shy to admit: She was here. I could feel it in the cool air, in the quiet, in the way the wind moved around me. My anticipation was easy for her to scent. How much longer did I have before she descended on me?

Her weight against my back. Ropes tying my wrists together. Her free hand wandering here and there as she tied her knots. Her breath against my neck, heavy and cool; the edge of her armor grazing against my bare skin.

All of it was so real to me. So close.

I stared into the smoldering fire not because I wanted to but because I was not seeing the flaming remnants at all. All I could imagine was her.

And then I heard her voice, and the tension in me creaked higher. It was only a single word. One syllable, spoken with rough need, whispered in my ear on the winds themselves.

"*Run.*"

My desire-clumsy legs beat against the ground before my mind could catch up. In the dark of the forest my own hand was only a suggestion against the velvet black; the boughs and roots that had vexed me in the day would spell disaster here. To run through the night was to invite disaster.

And oh, how I longed for that disaster.

Ducking beneath the branches I knew to expect, I dashed, my feet pounding with every hit against the springy earth. All around the leaves crunched, the wood creaked, the Domain sighed with life. Unseen growls heralded the glowing eyes of a pack of wolves.

My heart caught as I beheld their silver pelts—and it became a war drum when as one their eyes landed on me.

I turned and ran.

Behind me the wolves ran in their packs, behind me the barks and snarls of hunger and need. A thousand questions bounced around inside my skull. What to do? Where to go?

Thinking was only going to lead to bad places. There was about as much space for thought as there was space between the lead wolf's jaws and my hands. I had instincts. I needed to trust them.

A breath. Up ahead was a familiar tree. The one I'd scraped the mushrooms off all that time ago. If it was light out I could probably still see the places where I'd been too clumsy with the knife and accidentally carved into it.

That tree was safe.

I jumped toward it with all the power I could muster. There was a branch at the very top of my reach; my palm scraped against the rough wood as I scrambled to get a hold. The same mushrooms that had sustained me through my early days now served as steps up toward safety.

They were shitty steps, let me tell you. Couldn't bear any weight at all. The second I bore down on them the fungus tore out from under me, and had I not already gotten my arms around the branch I would have dropped straight into the waiting mouths of the beasts.

Breathing heavily, the wolves on their hind legs to bite at my heels, I summoned all the strength I could muster to pull myself up. Two meters off the ground, I stared down at them.

Gleaming teeth. Bright silver eyes. Coats that shone in the dark. Their claws raking against the bark of the oak tree as they tried to climb as best they could—but each time they tried they sank back down onto the earth.

Bite and snarl and growl and howl, they couldn't reach me.

Perched on the tree, I grinned. The part of me that's caught a chat ban on several games wanted to roast them for their inability to climb a tree...but I couldn't have done this a couple months ago, either. And there were other things to worry about.

Like where Artemis was going to come—

I didn't have time to finish the thought. The wolves I'd been watching gathered together all at once, like magnets snapping together, fading into a weave of shadow and light that reforged itself—

Into Artemis.

Before I could react she was on me. Light as a star's regrets she shot onto the branch and straddled me. Her massive shape—antlers, bulk, godhood—was a darkness greater than night itself. As her hand clamped down over my mouth it stifled a whimper.

"Climbing was clever," she said. Her breath was cool against my ears; my nose full of the musky scent of her. "But I've got you now, little deer."

A rush of blood shot straight to my groin. She was pressed so tight against me.

"I could let you go," she said. "Let you try again. Would you like that, I wonder—testing yourself against me? Or..."

She took my wrists in her hand and she pinned them above my head.

"Maybe you'd prefer if I trussed up my catch and watched her squirm for me...?"

Questions demand answers. It's hard to give them when your godly master is bearing down on you. There was *so much* to focus on. Had we ever been this close before? Had I ever felt her body like this? She was *pinning* me. I could try to lift my hands if I wanted—but I knew it would be no use.

And that was so *dizzying*. To be held like this. To put myself in someone's hands not as a sacrifice but as a willing participant.

Her other hand laid against my throat. Every breath I took came because she did not close that hand. I could not move it if I tried. I could not pry my way to freedom. In a way I was doomed to be her plaything here.

But only because I wanted to be. If I said the word, she would carry me down with a doe's own gentleness.

"Iphigenia," she said. She tilted my head to look at her—the darkness of her face, the moons of her eyes. "Be a good prize and answer my questions for me. I know you can. Focus."

I didn't want to focus. I wanted to stay here forever. But I wanted to be good for her, and so I tried as hard as I could to think of anything but the way her knee was perilously close to my crotch.

"Tie me up," I prayed to her.

And the god? Oh, the god answered.

Torn fabric. A blindfold tied around my head, and her own belt lashing my hands to the branch. Then, as my heart pounded anew in my ears, I felt something at the very edge of my mouth. Something hard and leathery.

...A bit? Like for a horse?

"I want you to listen to me. Can you do that for me?" she said.

Oh, I was starting to shake a little already. Just what did she have planned? What was that thing? Was she really going to truss me up and leave me totally defenseless, without even a way to shout or scream?

How I hoped she would.

"I'm listening," I said. And I was. Mostly.

"If you need me to stop, you will pray for it. All you need

to do is address a thought to me, and I will hear it," she said. "Nod if you understand me."

Every breath I took made me all the more conscious of where we were. Of how close she was. I could feel her eyes on me.

I nodded.

"There's my prize," she said, and another wave of anticipation rolled through me. "Open your mouth for me."

Not that she needed to tell me. The second she spoke again I'd already gotten myself ready for her. She slid the bit between my lips, then coaxed my mouth closed around it. I heard the whisper of leather and felt a set of straps tighten to hold it in place.

I knew it would be an interesting sensation, but I wasn't prepared for just how *exposed* I felt. Whenever I took a breath now—and I was breathing heavily—it naturally came through my mouth. It was already open, after all. Thanks to the bit keeping me from shutting it all the way and making my tongue rise in my mouth, even the steadiest breath would have come out as loudly and shamelessly as possible.

Panting. That was the word for it. I was panting like an animal as she undressed me.

Gentleness was a distant afterthought. Though I knew her to be patient and deliberate, there was little of that now. The wolves reigned.

Her sharp nails grazed my skin as she tore the binds of my chiton. As it fell away from my shoulders she peeled it back and revealed me to the night that was her, the breeze against my cold stiff nipples that was her, the hands and eyes that were hers.

Another stupid animal breath from me. Spit built up in the back of my mouth. It made me sound all the more desperate, all the more in need, and we'd only just begun. It was the loop of hearing myself making it all so much the stronger.

Only when she'd let my chiton fall to the ground beneath us—only when I was naked before the god—did she continue her work. Rough cord against my skin at the shoulders. She ran it along the length of my body. How was she going to lash me to the branch in truth? I knew the hands were only the start of things—

Her hand on my thigh. Coaxing me up.

"You will writhe for me tonight," she said.

Before I could catch my breath she looped the cord between my legs. I gasped and whined at the contact of it against me; the unyielding pressure that I knew was only going to get more intense. Her careful clawed hands slid the rope beneath my back and up over the other shoulder...only to loop it between my legs again.

Another ratchet in the pressure and I was already doing as she asked of me. My breaths came heavy and needy.

I will writhe as much as you want, I thought. *I want you to watch me.*

A deep growl from her. Had she heard me?

She must have. Her hands moved fast now, tying new cord around that which she'd just secured. Though she was no spider, she wove this web with a natural expertise. Rope surrounded my breasts, applying enough pressure to set the blood within them tingling; rope bit into my thighs, each new coil both better distributing the weight and tying me closer to the branch. There was enough space for me to wriggle—but only barely, and only because she was lashing the harness she built for me to the branch. That way I could move.

And move I did.

With every new loop my breath came a little sharper. The pressure against my clit from the rope only made things worse—whenever she adjusted any of the ropes, that one would shift just slightly. A few centimeters that felt like her loving hand coaxing the pleasure out of me.

I whimpered and whined as she worked. The pressure was building up bit by bit. A pot simmering to a boil.

"You're holding on so well," she said. Her hand trailed along the length of my body, but only along the paths forged by the ropes. "I thought you'd have given in by now. But you don't want to do that just yet, do you?"

The next time she spoke her breath washed over my ear.

"You want to cum only when I tell you, don't you?"

The amount of control it took not to cum when she said that! I didn't know I had it in me. I took a shaky breath, my spit dribbling down the side of my mouth. The gag was making it all overflow. What a mess I must have been, and yet here she was whispering things to me like this. Making me *want* like this.

"Hold on a little longer. You're going to have to earn it," she said.

There were few things I wanted more at that moment. You could have offered me a million dollars and I would have chosen to try to hold on. Even though the pressure at the base of my spine was almost painful, even though I could hardly think, even though I was a pathetic mess tied against the branch beneath her...

I was going to hold on.

The ropes were just the start. As I lay there at her mercy, she slid a nail beneath them, pressing just so against my skin. Enough to hurt—but not enough to harm. And the contrast when the rope came back down over the red?

Pressure, pressure, pressure.

"Such pretty sounds," she breathed into my ear. "Tell me how much you like it. Go on, try."

And I did. My tongue worked to try and speak, to say, "I love being your pet," but it was no use. Too clumsy. It came out a wordless, whiny garble.

She laughed. Her hand against my throat, a wide rough palm and absolute care.

"Good effort," she said. "Keep trying to talk. I want to hear you."

There were so many things I wanted to say—but I soon found myself overwhelmed in trying to say them. The second I opened my mouth again there was something cold against my collarbone. Her nails, again? I had no idea what it was. My mind scrambled to fill in the blanks, and that only made it all the more maddening; I had no idea what was about to happen. My attention was split up between the prick of cold at my collar, the building pressure between my legs, the rope against my skin.

I was gasping. Shuddering beneath her as she traced these cold shapes on my body.

Please, I thought, as the cold traced the blood-hot skin of my thighs. *Please, I don't know how much longer—*

"Say it out loud."

Oh, that—

No, no, I wasn't going to call her names in my head even if the idea of having to shape a word around the bit was driving me up the wall. She wanted to see me try. She wanted to see me struggle.

And I wanted to struggle for her.

"Prlrree…"

"Almost."

A sharp breath. The cold tracing its way from one thigh to another, back up along my stomach to my nipples.

"Prrll…."

Circling each nipple in turn—a sharp, cold tip. An arrowhead? A knife? Or simply some unseen ice?

"Almost, Iphigenia. I know you can do it."

Up along the delicate skin of my neck, so close to my face, so close to me—

"*Please*," I managed, mangled though it was.

The cold pulled away, and she leaned back, though I heard her low rumble of satisfaction.

"Let me see you cum," she said.

And there, in the trees, I did.

Afterward, she untied me and carried me down herself. With my head against her chest, she stroked my hair and dabbed away all the sweat that'd accumulated there. In the heady daze of what came after I wasn't sure where she had taken me—only that anywhere she took me was safer for having her in it.

She cleaned me with careful attention. Like her most treasured possession, she lavished me, washing and drying and leaving me new. The Goddess of the Hunt even went so far as to help me back into my chiton.

It was a while before I could think straight—but all of this was such a pleasant dream that I didn't mind. So deep and so pure was the calm I felt from being a mess in her arms that I felt sleep coming and had no choice but to welcome it.

Yet just before the sleep took me I felt her lips against mine, and heard her voice.

"Beloved of the night, remember always your home."

Chapter Fifteen

To tell you the truth, I'm not certain it's a good thing for people with divine blood to spend a lot of time in the Courts. I think something happens to us when we do. Maybe that's why my family was never permitted to return to them directly—we had to keep to this high-rise with its tenuous connections. If we got too close to the real thing, we'd start to change.

The first day I woke up back in the "real" world I lay there in bed for hours. I can't describe to you how good a *bed* felt. Not just the plush fabric and the warm blankets, but the safety of it. The way it yielded to me. Wrapped in sheets, I knew for certain that I was no longer in the world of scrambling for my next meal. I'd returned to the place where I could summon food to my doorstep in less than an hour.

Now, there were questions. Where was I? Whose place was this? How was my family?

I could answer some of them. I had a sliver of charge left on my phone. Enough to google "Pelops Corp." and click some news updates.

Agamemnon Pelops: Interview with Greatness.

Dad was fine. Don't know what else I expected. My chest went tight at the sight of him beneath the headline. There he was with his "serious" mug, the one that made people think he was stuffy. He wasn't. When it was the two of us, he would always joke around with me about our situation. "We're the most well-traveled recluses in the world," he'd say.

Some days, he'd tell me we were going on a tour of the world. "Stop playing your games and come along." Whenever I went he'd have a huge flight of beers set up, or a series of charcuterie boards. Once it was a hamburger from every country he could manage. Each one would have the little flag next to it. We'd make our way around the kitchen, and we'd try each one and pretend we were in that place. Together.

He understood me. He understood how much it sucked to watch my friends do whatever they wanted while I was stuck cleaning up family messes. If I wanted to go to an arcade, he'd have one of the rooms adorned with old game cabinets and top-of-the-line gear alike. We had a deli, a little library, all sorts of things. Because I asked for them. Because I wanted to feel normal.

I looked at the photo of him beneath the headline. He was in his favorite suit, wearing his favorite watch. I didn't recognize the hammered-copper wall behind him—but it wasn't unusual for him to have conference rooms redecorated. He got restless. I would know.

"How could you have sacrificed me?" I asked the photo.

I didn't wait to hear the silence that followed. Instead I scrolled through. Interviewers loved to make us out to be a family-oriented company when they could; we were well known for our reclusive tendencies, so reporters loved to break the story that we could be normal. They broke it about three times a year. Nothing was more normal than a family, so we'd always get mentioned.

There.

"There are those who worry your personal life will get in the way of your ability to run Pelops Corp. There've been more stories about your divorce than there have been about your acumen lately. What do you have to say?"

Divorce?

The word stared back at me, pixels on a screen shattering the clay feet of my life.

Divorce?

Why—why would she ever? They got along so well. Other people's parents argued, but mine only ever had tiffs here and there. Dad adored my mum. Bought her whatever she wanted, too, and would never stop talking about how useless he'd be without her. He wasn't wrong. What Dad had in business sense, he completely lacked in relating to other people. That was where Mum came in. Whether it was remembering a client's birthday and sending an appropriate gift or knowing just when to bring up an insecurity to really needle a rival, she'd saved him more times than I could count.

He hung on her every word. So often I would walk into my father's office and he'd be visiting my mother, instead, even with his schedule so packed. He always made time to wander over and dote on her.

So why...?

"My divorce is a personal tragedy, I won't deny that. My wife mended the pieces of my heart together when we met; she shattered it again when she asked for a divorce. I wish I could say that I'm clear minded. But I'm not. I live in the shadow of that pain, and I imagine I will for a long while. I have to figure out who I am without her."

She divorced him?

That was—but why? My fingers were cold as I scrolled a little further. Come on, 2 percent battery, just a little longer...

"All I can say is that it's thrown other things into focus. My relationship with my two beautiful children, Orestes and Elektra..."

"Do you get to see them often?"

"Orestes, yes."

Of course he'd see Orestes often. With me gone, he was the heir. He was trapped in the high-rise just as much as I'd been— Mum couldn't get him out of there without risking a vengeance bloodier and more complete than any a human could manage.

My jaw hurt, and the pain was radiating up to my temples. I couldn't bear to read anything about him anymore.

I needed to figure out where my siblings were. I needed to

speak to them, and I needed to get us out of this mess once and for all. Too many of us had paid for our ancestors' hubris.

We could change things. I knew we could. All I had to do was get to them, and I could fix it all. The answer lay in a small vial tied to the belt of my chiton. Artemis hadn't taken it from me. Whether that was because she didn't see it or because she approved of what I was up to, I had no idea. But she would have known what it was when she saw it.

Beneath the comfortable sheets I sucked in a breath.

The first order of business was finding a phone charger.

You can't trust a god to decorate a human home. They're going to make the kinds of mistakes you didn't even know were possible.

This place, for example. I had a bed, yes, with lovely sheets and a clean mattress and eight kinds of blankets. It was more cloud than bed. But I didn't have any pillows.

There were bowls of fruit laid out on a rough wooden counter. Lots of different kinds: berries, bananas, mangos, persimmons. All gleaming fresh. But I didn't have a fridge, and the oven jammed into a corner of the cabin was probably older than my grandparents.

There were cabinets, but nothing in them. I had ten different spatulas but only a single set of silverware. And I mean literal, actual silver silverware. It was way more ornate than anything else in the cabin.

I had one metal bowl, ten plates of strange sizes and shapes, a collection of knives that would have made any edgy teenager blush, a single towel, and a stack of gossip magazines from the nineties. There was a *gramophone* here. But don't get excited thinking there were any records—there weren't.

Every single thing I found was baffling, and every single thing I lacked all the more so.

Which is to say, of course, that by the time I tried to turn on the light and discovered there was no electricity, I wasn't surprised.

A phone charger? I'd be lucky if I found anything newer than a rotary in this place. Wherever it was.

I hadn't bothered throwing open the windows. In the center of the living room—which was also the kitchen, and the dining room, and the bedroom—there was a glass panel in the ceiling. Plenty of light got in that way. I knew with a glance that it was a little after two in the afternoon. Felt weird to do that without trees blocking the way, but it was nice to have the skill.

Other than the time, I didn't have much to go on. The magazines were Australian, so I had that going for me. Artemis hadn't left me too far from home. But then, just what was this place? It wasn't like her to hole up in some place that had a roof.

It wasn't until I actually stopped to focus that I realized there was one very big clue as to where I was: the sound of water.

I had been so focused on tearing the place apart that I hadn't registered it. Background noise, so far as I was concerned. Was I really by the water? My breath caught in my throat and I ran over to the window.

When I tore open the curtains, what I saw was *beautiful*. Ocean.

Ocean, as far as the eye could see. A hazy blue, with the sun threading gold through the waves, right outside my window. So far as I could tell the cottage was on the end of some kind of pier. I saw the edge of the wooden platform beneath it, saw a few barrels of who knows what circled with rope. But that was all I saw—except the water.

I ran to the next window. That one had less of the ocean to show me. Instead, there was a thicket of trees and brush. I could see the wood beneath the cabin there, too, but below that I could see the rich white of a sandy beach.

You could have knocked me over with a feather. This place was *beautiful*. And it was mine?

In my chiton I ran to the door and threw it open. I had to know what I was dealing with, had to know how to try and get home.

I was right about the pier. And about the beach, and the woods.

So far as I could tell, I was on my own little private island. I could see the curve of it when I went out to the edge of the pier. The buckets, as it happened, held fishing supplies: nets, traps, rods, line. Someone had also set up a telescope pointing to the east. Looking back at the house, I could see a beach big enough for a leisurely walk. At the end of it was the mouth of a small cave. Behind the house was... well, I didn't want to call it a forest. It wasn't very big. A copse of trees, more like, but enough that you could walk through them for a little while.

Well.

No store down the street, no internet, no electricity. And no idea which way to go to get to civilization. If I was lucky, there'd be a boat here. My hopes were not high. You'd think a boat would be lashed to the pier if anything, after all. It was not.

The list was already starting to form in my head. I'd make my own boat, then, and I'd use the telescope to figure out where I was going. I hadn't seen much of the wildlife here—but I did have all that fruit. If I could find some ambrosia hidden within the bowls I could probably make it a month or two without having to worry about food. Shelter was taken care of, and it wasn't exactly cold, so I didn't need a fire immediately...

All of it fell into place.

The first order of business was getting my phone charged, sure. But there were a lot of steps I'd need to take to get there.

And I wasn't afraid of taking them.

I could sit here and tell you the story of how I built my own boat and learned to sail so that I could get back to my family. You've already heard me talk so much about that sort of thing, though. If I spend any more time telling you about how important it is to properly conserve your energy when you're not sure where your next meal is coming from, you're going to scream.

So I won't.

Here's the big picture: It took me more than a week. Speaking of conserving energy, I had to be careful with mine. Not only did I have little idea what I was going to have to eat—there wasn't much in the way of fresh water. I had to boil the salt out of the sea water around me. If you've ever had the misfortune to have to do that, I commend you. If you've managed to avoid it, try to make sure it stays that way.

I rationed out my godly fruits, boiled my water, and did a lot of experimenting when it came to woodworking. It's surprisingly hard to lash logs together in a way that won't see them trying to run away from one another when you put them on the water. Might as well be like coworkers the second five o'clock hits for all the time they want to spend together.

My first two attempts floated off into the great blue without me. None of my swearing could bring them back.

After that I started making models first. The third ship—*Fuckface III*, if you must know—was a whole lot better. Except I didn't make a rudder, so when I realized I couldn't steer the damn thing I had to abandon the raft and swim back to shore.

Fuckface IV had a rudder, but no sail. I took it out for a spin and liked it but saw room for improvement. Turned it into my little fishing raft while I figured out how the hell I was going to make a sail out of what I had on the island.

Fuckface 4.5 (I had to abandon the Roman numerals) was my key to victory. So was diligent repurposing of those wonderful, precious, too-good bedsheets. Artemis had given me such comforts, and here I was turning them to survivalist ends. They weren't even *good* sails, not hardy at all. If there was any roughness out there, they were going to tear.

Still, I was pretty sure she'd approve. And not just because I told her I was going to do it.

I spoke to her during the nights. With the moon high in the sky, I knew that she could hear me—and that she'd be listening for me, too. So I would go out to the edge of the pier and talk to her from there, staring up at the moon that was her. I'd tell her how the day had gone. What my schemes were.

Most of the time there would be no direct response. I think she knew how important it was to me to try to take care of this on my own. I was in the human world now, and I wanted to be able to get by in it. What was all that training we'd gone through for if not this exact situation? Besides, there were plenty of things she needed to take care of, I was sure, without me around to babysit. She was probably lazing around up there in her Domain, relishing the chance to be unmasked again.

But there were some nights a cloud would pass across the moon and, when the light returned, I'd find her sitting next to me.

We didn't talk about my plans when she showed up. Both of us knew that there was one reason she'd turn up in person—she wanted to be near me. She wanted to be able to hold me as much as I wanted to be held.

On those nights she taught me all sorts of interesting knots I could use for nautical purposes. And *other* purposes.

I liked the other purposes better. I never felt so alive as when the sun hit me in the morning and I still wore the marks she'd left on me.

Anyway, like I said, I got the raft working. Got the telescope on board, too, so that if I fucked up using the stars I could try to use it to get back on track.

All in all, it took me about a month and a half just to get on the water in a real way.

Let me tell you—after all that effort it was a little anticlimatic how close the nearest shore was. Turned out it was only a day and a half away. Here I was prepared for a weeklong journey, stocked up on fresh water and fruits, and then...I don't want to say it was *right there*. It wasn't. But it wasn't *far*. Maybe that was part of Artemis's thinking when she'd given me that cabin: a place that was close to other people, but not overly so. Another one of her little tests.

I looked down at my hands. So much more callused than they'd ever been. There was a time I would have said they were gross, even. But I loved them now. They let me do so many things.

A month and seventeen days after my triumphant return to the human world, I brought *Fuckface 4.5* to a beach, hid it beneath a pier, and scrambled up toward civilization.

Wild animals are unpredictable.

You can get to know them and their habits, though. If a bear is feeding, you don't want to go anywhere near it. Wolves are looking for an easy meal, so you have to make sure you don't look like one. A stag will run from a fight most of the time. They won't always *keep* to these behaviors, and that's where people end up getting into trouble, but for the most part you can figure out where you are in relation to a wild animal pretty quick. There are rules.

There aren't any for people. People are worse in every way.

(Except you. We're best mates. But then, you're not really human anymore either, are you?)

I had thought of this moment for so long. Early on in my service, I would imagine what it would be like to go back home. To be around people again.

But the second I started walking up the shore, my teeth hurt. Music blasted from a dozen speakers, all blaring different songs at full blast. The chattering of the beachgoing crowd was thicker than any cloud of bugs I'd had to deal with back in Artemis's Domain. I made it only a few steps on the plush white sand before my foot scraped against a broken beer bottle. If it hadn't been for the sandals Artemis had given me, I would have been limping a red trail up to the little surf shop not far up the shore.

It was so *strange*. Other people! I kept catching strands of their conversations. Dinner plans. Reminiscences about ragers past. Silly jokes. Awkward conversations that would never lead to a second date. Life was all around me, just as it had been in the forests, but it was *different* here.

I knew the rules there. I wasn't sure I knew them here anymore. The chiton I'd been so proud to receive was out of place at a beach.

But I touched the delicate silver collar against my throat, and the bumps along my wrists, and I remembered that I had something others did not.

It was like moving through unknown woods. You had to go quickly and quietly, and you had to be aware of your surroundings.

So—the little surf shack, with its brightly colored signage, became my destination. I opened the creaking door and shivered as the aircon hit my skin. The radio was playing here, too; Top 40 stuff that I couldn't place for the life of me. On the newsstands were gossip rags announcing break-ups and make-ups featuring people I didn't know. Even the snacks that had been so familiar to me stared back at me from the shelves with new flavors.

I wandered the aisles in search of my mythical quarry. Eventually, I remembered that they don't tend to keep chargers out in the front of the shop—they're too likely to be stolen. So to the service desk I went.

And there he was: the first person I was going to speak to in who knows how long. A spotty teenager who could not care less that I was in his store. He was too busy playing gacha games on his phone to even realize I'd shown up.

"Excuse me?" I said.

"Yeah yeah, what do you want?" he said. But then he looked at me, really looked at me. Took in the chiton and the quiver and the bow and the knife. His eyes widened. "Is this some kind of costume?"

His voice cracked a little. Was he scared of me? "No. I just need a phone charger."

He swallowed. "What kind of charger?"

I took my phone out of my pocket. He flinched. But then he laughed. "Mate, I gotta check the archives for that. No wonder you're all dressed up like a bloody gladiator if you've got an artifact like that!"

"I'm not a gladiator," I said. I fought the urge to pinch my nose. "Do you have it or not?"

By now the other people in the shop were staring at me, too. A mother hurried her kid away from us. I heard the shutter of someone's phone taking my photo. Whatever. The internet was just another Court.

The kid ducked away to take a look for the charger. I leaned against the counter and looked out onto this world I'd returned to. The unknown faces on the covers of the magazines.

And then I saw it:

My mother's face.

She and Ellie were hiding in a corner insert of one of the celebrity gossip rags. I hadn't noticed them at first, given the size of it. As the boy continued his search, I walked to the rack and picked it up.

Clytemnestra Pelops responds to her husband's accusations: He knows why I left, and so do my children.

It wasn't the aircon that was leaving me frozen. I flipped to the page with shaking hands. There was my mother in a single-page interview. Alongside it was an image of her on her favorite dining chair, the one that looked like a throne. The photographer had draped this golden silk across her that only made her look more regal.

"Did what I could. I can get you the cord but not the brick. Think the café down the way has some outlets if you're really in need. We've got some portable chargers that might help— Hey, you okay, Maximus?"

"It's Greek. Not Roman," I said. I had to shake the thoughts away. Without a thought I picked up the magazine and the cord alike and started walking out of the shop.

"Hey!" he shouted.

And it was then I remembered that most insidious, most human creation: money.

I had two options here. I could keep going and see if he'd call the cops on a woman who was clearly armored and a little weird, or I could plead my case. Not that I had much to offer. What would I even give him?

I stopped. Turned. Went back to the counter.

"I'm gonna level with you mate. Got no cash," I said.

He groaned and threw his head back. "Nothing? You're just wandering around in a costume like that without a single dollar? Not even a credit card? We take Apple Pay, you know, if you need to charge your phone before you use it—"

I did have my cards saved on my phone, now that I thought about it. But I didn't want to stay here. A lifetime spent in the spotlight taught me there's nothing worse than people staring at you. Despite all the days in the wilderness, I felt a twinge of old fears about paparazzi photos showing up on the internet.

"I've got nothing. Been away on a trip and just got back. I mean, I can bring you some fish if you want, but that's about the size of it."

He shook his head. "I don't get paid enough to deal with whatever you clearly have going on," he said. "Just take the cord and get out."

"Magazine, too?" I said, rapping my knuckle against it.
"Why not. Why the fuck not," he said.
It was all the permission I needed.

Money is hard to come by, but if you look the way that I do and speak the way I know how to speak, you can usually make do. Advantages to living the life I have, I guess. Most of the time I didn't like to think about them. I was a woman showing up in the middle of town in a weird costume, but I wasn't Black or Indigenous, and I'd had the schooling to be able to pass for some eccentric weirdo. A lot of people would have been kicked out of a café for much less. A mixed-race woman with light skin who spoke a certain way? Probably just out on a lark.

Like I said, I didn't *like* knowing any of that. But I knew it. And when it came to my plan, I was grateful for the cover my privilege gave me.

I could get to the café the kid mentioned without much trouble. It was the café *itself* that was the annoying part.

Maybe it's regular to you by now, but let me tell you—there's few things louder than a café around lunchtime. The conversations I heard overlapping outside were happening here, too, but there were ten times more of them. More disjointed, too. Every few words I'd hear, there'd be a shout from one of the baristas. Flat white, americano, six-word-long order I couldn't follow. By the time they settled that, the voices I'd heard had melded into the mass.

It was a nightmare. The rustle of wind through leaves brought you only the information you needed to know: It was windy and you were near trees. This place made me want to unscrew my ears.

But I needed an outlet, so there was nothing for it. I found a table and holed up there. If I was lucky, no one would ask me if I'd ordered anything. Or... A couple got up across from me. They left their cups behind. Civilized people would have balked at scooping up their trash for my own nefarious uses, but I wasn't civilized anymore.

With an empty, lipstick-covered cup in hand, I was totally blending in. Never mind the outfit.

My phone took forever to charge. Got warm, too, like a stone that I'd left in the fire. I tapped my too-long nails against the surface of the screen as the questions danced around in my head with the plans.

Text them? Call them? Just show up? Maybe I could get a rideshare from here to the high-rise. Wasn't sure where I was. I could probably afford it, though, once my phone was on. As long as my cards hadn't been canceled.

Shit. I was dead, wasn't I? Legally speaking.

I tapped my nails on the screen again. *Come on...*

"Refill, ma'am?"

My hand went to my bow out of reflex—the hostess had surprised me into action. I just barely managed to tamp down the fight part of fight or flight and took a breath. What kind of place offered refills?

"Uh, yeah sure," I said. I handed her the cup, and she picked it up and walked off.

Weird. Whatever.

More important: the phone logo was on screen again. Seconds later, my phone wheezed its way back to life. My lock screen stared back at me: a silly photo of me and my siblings in matching animal onesies. I was a deer, Ellie a cat, and Ori a wolf. My breath caught. We all looked so *young*.

No use dwelling. I unlocked it and waited for notifications to come in. There'd be a ton of them. I had all of the company IT accounts linked to my phone for remote support. There was no way they'd have remembered to deactivate all my backups. And, well, maybe I'd have other notifications, too. Not that I could imagine it.

Sure enough, the second I got signal my phone started to go off like mad. I had to mute it or else it would have vibrated clean off the table. When the hostess came back with whatever it was I'd ordered she found me playing hot potato with the damn thing trying to sort through the notifications as they came. Eighty percent of them were pure nonsense: ticket requests and follow-up requests and pointless newsletters the company sent to every employee no matter what.

But there were some that were worth burning my fingertips to read.

The sibling group chat. Ellie and Ori were still using it?

The corners of my eyes were as hot as the phone in my hands.

I took a shaking breath as I opened it up. Messages poured in. Dozens of them. I kept trying to scroll up to catch up on everything I'd missed, but new messages would come in, snapping me to the bottom. Memes, mostly. Stuff about the games we'd played together, or jokes about never leaving your room.

> Thought Iph would like this.
> Sharing this here for big sis.
> Made me think of her.

Oh, no, no, no. I scrolled up higher and higher. Did my parents really tell them I was dead? I was a memory to them already. How long had it been? My hands shook as I tried to read the dates. When I did, the phone fell from my hands with a clatter.

Three sets of birthday posts. Three Christmases. Three Halloweens.

It had been three years since I'd died.

No wonder they were mourning me. No wonder none of the articles about my family mentioned me. Thirty-six months or more had passed. Hundreds of sunsets and sunrises. For me it had felt like half a year at the most. How had this happened?

Artemis wouldn't have hurt me in this way if she'd known. That didn't stop me from laying my hands against the cold metal at my throat.

So *long*. What if they didn't believe me when I showed up? What if it was already too late?

No. I couldn't let myself give in, not when I'd gotten so far on my own. I didn't spend all that fucking time building a boat for nothing.

I was going to save my family.

Another breath. My skin against the metal. I wasn't the same girl I had been when I'd died that night. I was no sacrifice.

I could do this.

> You guys have shitty taste in memes. I don't understand what half of these are even referencing. No sense of timelessness, smh. You've all gotten weird without me.

I hit Send without thinking. Then I realized I probably shouldn't break the news of my living to them by commenting on their dogwater taste in memes.

> It's Iph. For real, I promise. We need to talk, and it has to be just us.

You'd think that if your supposedly dead sister messaged you from beyond the grave, you'd answer instantly. My siblings are built different, I guess. I was holed up in that café for another hour before the answer came in.

> Prove it.

Orestes was the one who had sent it in. I imagined him hiding away from our father in one of the empty offices.

Good of them to ask me to prove it. I would have too, in their position. I picked up the magazine I'd just bought and made sure the date was visible, then took a selfie and sent it off.

I stared at the phone and waited. The Wild had changed me. What if it'd been too long? Maybe they wouldn't recognize me anymore. Stupid. Why wouldn't they? It wasn't as if I had a ton of scars now or anything. Just nerves.

Breathe, Iph.

I stared and stared and waited and waited.

Ding.

My phone slipped out of my hands as I picked it up again. This time it was Ellie who answered.

> It's really you? Dad said you were dead. We went to your funeral. How can it be you?

My funeral? These poor kids.

I swallowed, hard, at the thought of what they must be going through.

> He said he was forced to sacrifice you. That you died to protect us from the Queen of the Wild.

Orestes this time.

I slammed my hand on the table. The rattle set everyone

staring at me, but I didn't care. That was the lie that he had fed them?

Can we FaceTime? I sent back.

It took a little while for the response to come through. Maybe they had to make sure the coast was clear? I wasn't going to press. But with every second that passed, my heart hurt a little more. It was beating so fast I thought it would burst right there in my chest—this quest of mine dying out with my last breath.

I was about to talk to my siblings again. Maybe.

When the ringing started, I grabbed my phone like a bear snatching a fish from the river. My hands shook and I took a breath. *You can do this. Big sis time.*

I answered the call.

Two squares stared back at me when I answered. In one there was a young man with long hair and a worrying set of circles beneath his eyes; in the other was a young woman with dyed black hair and thick eyeshadow. Her mascara was starting to run at the sight of me, and his eyes were wide as could be.

I sobbed. Sure, the other people in this café probably thought I was some kind of emotional wreck cosplayer, but they didn't even cross my mind. I *was* an emotional cosplayer. But I wasn't a wreck. I'd broken myself apart and put myself back together and I had earned this. I needed it.

But oh, how they'd changed. My precious little siblings. How could three years change so much? Orestes was a completely different guy now. If his name hadn't popped up and he hadn't looked so much like our uncles, I never would have recognized him.

"H-hey guys," I said. My voice cracked. "I'm so happy to see you. I missed you so much."

"It really is you isn't it? It's Iph," said Ellie. Hearing her sob made me feel better about the streaks of tears starting to run down my face.

"Yeah, it's me. But man alive, is that really the two of you? Have you gotten into the Cure or something, El?" I said. If I made her laugh, maybe this would all feel less awkward.

"Fuckin' kill me for mourning my big sister, you asshole," said Elektra. But she was laughing as I said it, and I felt a lightness start to form in my chest.

We could do this. I could save them.

"What happened? Where have you been?" Ori's voice wasn't what I'd expected, either. Way deeper now, though there was a bit of a creak to it that he hadn't managed to shake.

"I can't talk about that here," I said. There were people watching; I could feel them. "What I can say is that there's more to the story than Dad told you. And that I really, really need to talk to the two of you. In person."

"Why didn't you say anything sooner?" said Orestes. He'd not given me a chance to breathe.

"Because I was visiting with Guests," I answered. It'd have to do; I couldn't exactly start talking about the secret parallel world of gods in front of a bunch of rugby mums and creative writing majors. "There's more to it than that, but I promise you this is the first time I've been back on this side in…"

"Three years," said Ellie. "We thought you were—"

"I know," I said. "But please. There's a lot the two of you don't know, and I'm worried about you. You're both mad I haven't reached out sooner, and I get that. I'd be furious if I were you. But I promise that if you give me a chance to really explain, a whole lot of things about our lives are going to start making sense."

Silence on the other side. Were they texting each other? Probably. It hurt, but I let them have their space to chat. This was a lot for them to take in.

"I can sneak into the arcade in the middle of the night. If Ellie can get there, I think that's our best bet," said Orestes.

Ah. He couldn't leave. Of course he couldn't.

Something passed over Ellie's face. "Can I tell Mum, Iph?"

My chest twisted. Shit. If we told her, she might want to get involved. Truth be told, I'd rather keep this to just my siblings and me. Might get messy otherwise. But... my mother had left a man she loved dearly because of what he'd done to me. She was a little strict, sure, and she'd always seemed to like the others more than me. I understood that, though. I was the heir. My life was so different from hers that she never stood a chance to relate. Seeing me move through the years must have been awful for her. Ellie and Ori were easier. Normal.

I took a breath.

She deserved to know.

"Yeah. Yeah, I think that's probably for the best," I said.

"Can I call her over now? She's in the other room," said Ellie. Orestes winced. She continued: "I'll tell her she can't be weird about it, Ori. That you don't have a choice in being where you are."

"Maybe she'll get it the fiftieth time you tell her," Orestes said.

"Ori, I'm so sorry," I said. "When I get back, you won't have to worry about that anymore. We're going to fix it."

He narrowed his eyes. I wasn't sure what to make of the look on his face—or the anger I saw behind his eyes. My little brother could trash-talk with the best of them, but how often had I seen him angry? Not like this. Not before this moment.

"You had better," he said. Then, after a beat: "Go get her. It's important enough that maybe she won't flip her shit."

I didn't protest, though Ellie didn't wait to see if I did before setting her phone down and going to get Mum. Orestes and I looked at each other in the quiet.

"I took photos for you," I said.

It was weak. Maybe even glib, given everything that had happened. He'd been cooped up in a high-rise for three years without the ability to leave, and here I was offering pictures.

But I needed to say *something*. I wanted him to understand that I had been thinking of the two of them.

"Show me in person," he said. He crossed his arms, then sighed. "I don't know how you did this, Iph."

"It's easier when you're born with it," I said. "When you only know sunlight from the roof of a building and wind from an open window, you don't long for much more than that. Besides—I had the two of you to look after."

There was more I wanted to say. It was risky, though. Maybe it would only upset him more. But I needed to get it out.

"Whenever it was getting hard to deal with, I told myself

that at least the two of you would never have to deal with it. That you would be able to live your nice, normal lives doing whatever you wanted. To be honest, I hated the idea of having to run the business one day. But I would have."

"Yeah, well," Orestes said, waving his hand, "you fucked off, and now I'm here."

"I didn't fuck off," I said. Keep it level, Iph. No use arguing. He had good reason to be mad, and I didn't want to draw any more attention. "And you're not going to be there much longer. Not if I can help it."

He let out a long sigh. "So you're coming back home? Becoming the heir again, is that it?"

Before I could answer I heard the clamor of a door. Ellie was coming back. Orestes pulled his hoodie up and drew the strings tight.

"She's gone, Elektra. Whoever you're speaking to is a scammer. I thought I raised you better than to give them the time of day."

That was Mum, all right. Hearing her going on like that was comforting in its own way. A bit of what used to be normal. Think I preferred the wolves howling when it came down to it, though. You always knew where you were with the wolves.

"Just give me a chance, okay? Just look at the screen." Ellie picked up the phone and turned it toward her and Mum. "Hey, Iphy. Hey, Ori."

Do you know what the strangest feeling in the world is?

The thing that makes you feel more like an adult than anything else?

Seeing your parents age.

Three years. That was all it had been. Yet there was more gray in her hair than I remembered. New lines, too, graven between her brows when she frowned. When I saw her like this, it took me a moment to register that she was my mother at all. Before then she was another well-to-do woman who had seen and carried too much to bear.

And she'd gotten that way because of what had happened to me. My mother was severe. She'd never been *exhausted*.

When she saw me, she covered her mouth. The gasp that left her seemed to weaken her; Ellie had to lean over and hold her up to keep her from toppling over.

"Iphigenia?"

"Hi, Mum. I'm sorry about the shock. I know this is a lot," I said. I wiped at my eyes. This was so *weird*. I shouldn't be seeing my mum *cry*. "I-if you need proof that it's me or whatever, I get it. Uh... When I was six, you let me have one of the chocolates from a box the Court of Flame sent Dad. I took a bite out of it and spat it out right there on the spot."

"God, it really is you," she said. She reached out to touch the screen, and I reflexively shied away from her hand. Hadn't quite prepared for that one. The bears were easier to deal with than all of this emotional stuff.

"Yeah. Look, there's a lot I have to explain, and I know things are bad with you and Dad," I said. Through sniffles—but I said it. "I don't need to go into all of that right now. Really, I don't. But if you could get Ellie to the high-rise tonight, I'd be grateful. I need to speak to the three of you in person. And I promise you can ask me whatever you like then."

Silence. I couldn't read the look on her face. I doubt anyone could have. Then:

"Your clothes. She didn't kill you, did she?"

What is it about mothers always asking the questions you don't want to answer?

"No. She didn't," I said. "I'll explain. I promise I will. But can you make this happen, Mum?"

There was a set to her jaw, then. A sort of hard line. It reminded me of nothing so much as the axe we'd use to chop firewood in the clearing.

"Nothing would stop me. Not even your father."

Chapter Sixteen

My phone was to the human world as my gifted knife had been to the Domain. I couldn't imagine what I had done before I had it.

The meeting was set for the high-rise after midnight. With a destination in mind and a bank account as fathomless as the Court of the Deep, I could manage it. You don't want to know how much I paid for a ride. *Why didn't you just rent a car and drive?* you might think. But I didn't have any ID, obviously, and even if we ignore that, I had spent my entire life in a single building. Of course I can't fucking drive.

The ride was a couple of hours long. I sat there in the back of the sensibly sized SUV as the driver tried to chitchat with me. Kept asking me about my costume, trying to talk about the latest gossip. Had I heard that so and so had been caught cheating on that actor on the set of their latest movie? And they had to finish the whole picture with all the drama going on?

I hadn't. And, truth be told, I didn't really care. Not about what had happened and not about keeping up the appearance.

A series of noncommittal grunts was the best he got out of me. Eventually he turned the radio on, and that was that.

The whole time I was texting my siblings. I had so much to show them. The photos would have to wait until I'd had time to introduce them—it wouldn't be a great idea to show them beautiful vistas beyond human imagination when they were still processing that I was alive.

I asked them what they'd been up to. Ellie was a lot more willing to talk about that than Orestes. Seems the divorce proceedings were taking up a lot of Mum and Dad's time. Ellie had to change schools thanks to all the chatter about it. She didn't mind very much; there was a better fashion-oriented program at the new place. While she didn't outright say she missed Dad, she did talk about how much easier things were when she could get everything she might need all in one place.

Orestes's answer was a punch. Work. What else?

Outside, the Australian coast sparkled in the evening sun. Purple and orange danced along the horizon; rich white were the crests of the waves. Hundreds of wheels against asphalt sounded like their very own river, one that I'd found myself drifting down. If I rolled the window down, the warm winter air came in to the car like a torrent. Motor oil, sea spray, the driver's favorite air freshener.

I used to dream of these simple pleasures and sensations. I would have *loved* talking to this man about absolute nonsense if this had happened sooner.

But now, the thought persisted: *Orestes lost all this.*

The driver dropped me off not far from the high-rise. Seeing it jutting out against the skyline was surreal all on its own; despite living in the damn thing as long as I had and looking out onto the city from it, I hadn't realized how it looked from the outside. I stood there on the pavement looking up at it like the world's most strangely dressed tourist. More than one person shoved me aside as they made their way through the downtown streets.

It was a little after midnight when I arrived. The only places open were clubs and convenience stores. The former were going to be closing soon. And, if I was being honest, being inside a nightclub would have done my tits right in. I mean, imagine! All that loud music, the bodies pressed so close together! I barely had the fortitude to survive a car ride with someone. Being shoved into a stranger's armpit by the sick beats of pop starlets had less than zero appeal.

I wasn't feeling the stores very much, either. Before I'd abandoned my house back on the island, I'd taken the fruits along with me in my bag. I ate one as I circled the block. It'd feed me for most of the night.

The only real question was how I'd get in without alerting my father that I was here. Fortunately, I'd thought about that one. Pelops Corp. had a rock-solid policy that anyone in a strange outfit and intricate mask was rushed right through security. They had to be intricate, though. You couldn't show up in a Ghostface outfit and hope to be let in.

I'd had *plenty* of time to carve on the island. The mask I'd come up with was a delicate wooden thing carved from fragrant wood. A network of stars and moons made up the decorations. I hadn't managed to find much in the way of dyes or paints, so I put all the effort I could into the carving itself. Ridges here and there, a series of interconnected borders, whatever I could manage. The result was... pretty good, if I did say so myself. It looked a bit like one of those sandalwood fans you get as gifts sometimes. Except a little thicker.

With a mask and my get-up, there was no way I'd have any trouble getting in. All the more so since I was showing up in the middle of the night with no warning. That was how Guests tended to do things.

Better than that, too—if my father saw the photo of a chiton-wearing, bow-wielding masked stranger, it might scare him.

After all—Artemis was bound by the Law never to hurt him or a member of his family again. But one of her handmaidens?

Oh, her handmaidens could do what they liked.

As I touched the collar with moonlight on my back, I felt the cool comfort of her regard on me. I stopped short in my aimless pacing.

"My lady," I said. "I'm doing something important."

She couldn't manifest outside of the high-rise—not without specific permission. But she didn't need to. The moonlight spoke to me in her stead. Every word wrapped around me like a bracing night breeze.

"Little deer. Have you finally started your hunt?" she asked.

The collar felt cool. Her hand. I smiled, my hand rising to the metal.

"Yeah," I said. "More of a rescue, really, but yeah."

The wind carried a growl in my ear—the prideful sound she'd let out when I managed to fire a bow right or identified the right kind of mushroom.

"You will not have need of me," she said.

"And if I get you into trouble?" I asked. It had been in the back of my mind. "If the others don't like what I'm going to do?"

"Do you care?"

The words hung in the air. I could swear that I saw a smiling shimmer in the moonlight.

I laughed. "I don't think I do," I said.

The wind went quiet. My heart, however, took a while to catch up. Having her so near me...

She could have stopped me. If she had wanted to, she could have whispered *crescent* in my ear, and I would have turned around. Not that it would have changed my goals at all, but I would have talked about it with her. I would have found a way forward together. But she didn't.

I looked at the lobby of the high-rise—at the guard sitting behind the desk watching his shows with a doner kebab laid out in front of him.

I was going home.

After all of this, when my family was safe—I'd head back to the Wild, and I would rest again in her arms.

Ellie and my mother arrived first.

They parked a ways away, and when they approached, I only recognized them thanks to Ellie's choice of footwear. Hoodies and sweatpants were excellent disguises for those looking to avoid notice. All the more so when they were the boxy no-name kind, whose roughness you can see from a glance. With her hair tied back and a cap pulled low to hide her face, you'd be hard pressed to recognize her.

Except, of course, that Ellie would rather be caught dead than wear anything like sensible footwear. So there she was wearing a set of designer trainers meant to look like ninja tabi. Easily cost more than some people made in a month.

It was a little obnoxious—but it made me smile in its own way. It was very her. And more than that, it meant I was close enough to hug my sister for the first time since I'd "died."

The second I realized it was her, I ran over and threw my arms around her. She squeezed me tight. In the warm hug, she started to sob against me. I had maybe a second to process that before my mother joined in. There she went, smoothing my hair, checking me over for bruises.

"It's really you."

I couldn't tell which one of them said it. Their voices had gotten too similar.

"Yeah," I said. "Thank you both for coming."

Ellie wiped at her nose as she pulled away. "Ori's still in there. We're going to have to get to him."

"Your father's forbidden me from entering outside of pre-arranged visits," she said. "You... You look like quite the little messenger. I'm sure there won't be any trouble."

Did they know what I was just from looking at me? Well, they couldn't know the half of it. I looked between them back to the front door.

"I can probably get Ellie in," I said. "If they think I'm a Guest, I can say that she's an attendant. They might buy it."

"In this outfit? You didn't tell me I was going to be so underdressed," Ellie countered. The giggles dulled the edge on the crack in her voice.

I waved a hand. "I can make it a bit more convincing, let me just..."

Artemis had given me a bag to store things in when I was gathering. More than anyone should be able to store. I usually kept a deerskin in there in case I needed a blanket, or a tarp, or a thing to lie on... Lot of uses for deerskin when you have one.

Like disguising your little sister.

"Is that a fuckin'—What is that? It smells!"

"Yeah, nature's smelly. Put up with it for a little while, and you hardly notice anymore," I said. I wrapped it around her like a warrior's cloak.

"Where did you even get this—"

"I skinned it myself."

"You *what*?!" She jolted backward as I finished tying the thing in place. "You *skinned* it? W-with your hands?"

"Elektra, please stop making a scene," said our mother. "Your sister's come back from the dead with a new skill. One part of that sentence is a lot more shocking than the other."

Grinning with a parent-sponsored victory, I took off Ellie's hat and yoinked her hood down. "Let your hair dangle out. They'll buy that. But don't wear a cap. Don't think they even allow those at Court."

Poor Ellie was standing there pulling the most offended face in the world. Like a cat dropped into a tub full of water. If she had to wear that deerskin for long, she was going to chuck it at me, I could feel it.

But with the hood pulled over, she did look...well, she looked weird. And that was probably enough to get us by.

"Iphigenia," said my mother. "It may be a while before I can join the three of you, and there may be...trouble. If you don't see me by four, leave with your sister."

I raised a brow. Hm. Whatever bad blood there was between her and Dad had to be worse than I thought. "Is...is it because of what happened to me?"

She hugged me tight, then set both hands on my shoulders. "I will never forgive a man who sacrificed my daughter for his own ambitions. Even if it turned out that you were all right. Never," she said. "I want you to know that I had no idea what it was he was planning to do. I wouldn't have allowed it."

I bit my lip. There'd been enough crying already. But...it was good to know that she'd been thinking of me. That she was angry for me.

"I would have carried you out of that high-rise myself if I

had to. I tried to do that with your brother, but security tore him away from me."

"It's why they don't talk," added Ellie.

My mother nodded. "It's complicated. I won't pretend that it isn't. But it isn't *your* problem, Iphigenia. It's your father's bed, and he's going to lie in it. Let me handle that part, all right?"

There was something caught in my throat. So much I wanted to say. Instead I just... muttered an agreement.

"We... um... We should get going," I said to Ellie.

"That's right. Stay focused. I'll talk with you soon," said my mother. "And Iphigenia?"

I'd already turned to leave, but I stopped when she called.

"Wherever you've been... it's been good for you."

The first step was the guard. When I walked up to him with Ellie in tow, I kept myself as straight-backed as I could. My time in the woods taught me to walk without making a sound, and that's what I attempted to do here. With the bow in my hand, I liked to think I looked the part of a godly emissary.

He would be the judge of that, though. As he studied me, my forearm twitched. I was all too conscious of the bowstring against my fingers, of which arrowheads in particular I'd brought along. Would he question me? Would I be ready if he did?

"You're one of the Guests, aren't you," he said.

"Yes," I answered. I tilted my head toward Ellie. "With an attendant."

I was never going to nail Artemis's ridiculous accent, but I could try. Keep things a little stilted, a little unnatural.

"Business with the big man, then?" he said. "Or the young one?"

"Private business," I answered. Since when was it policy to ask? People got killed for that in the old days.

He raised his hands and waved. "Far be it from me to get in the way, just trying to direct you," he said. "Go on, then."

Ellie was smart enough to keep quiet. He let the turnstiles up for us, and we wandered onto the lift together—two sisters on a mission.

The doors shut in front of us. I snap-shot an arrow into the camera. Ellie jumped and cursed. A burst of sparks and a small shower of glass rained down on us. Ellie's jump put her out of the way of the shrapnel, at least.

"Iphy, what the fuck?!" she said. "We're not in a fucking spy movie!"

"Longer it takes for Dad to realize we're doing something weird, the easier this will be," I said. "Besides, now we can talk. I meant what I said, Ellie. I'm getting us out of this. All of us."

"By shooting arrows at things?!" she said. Her voice cracked.

"I need you to trust me," I said. "And to hit the button for the arcade. Forgot which floor it's on."

Ellie stared at me. In the shadow of her eyes I could have read a lot of things, if I tried. Maybe it was fear, or maybe it was admiration. Maybe it was just confusion. I didn't know, and I didn't have time to worry about it. As long as she followed me, we could talk this through at the end.

She hit the third floor button, and the lift lurched to life.

I used to know these walls so well. I could navigate them in the dark with my hands full. Had to do it more than once. You wouldn't believe how often an IT job means swapping out monitors for people when they're not using them. If you happen to sleep where you work, the easiest time to do that is the middle of the night. And so, lots of wandering the lonely halls at night blasting whatever music you like.

I couldn't do any of that now. Not that I knew exactly where to go.

Ellie did, though. She'd been here a lot more recently than I had—and I bet she didn't have to memorize the layout of several godly biomes. The forest had overwritten my mental map of this place like Solar Beam overwrites Vine Whip. No space for the old anymore.

"Are you going to shoot out all these cameras, too?" she asked as we stepped out onto the third floor. A reception desk sat dead ahead of us. Unmanned, given the hour.

"If I can remember where they are, yeah," I said. "This is important."

"What the hell were you doing wherever you were?" she said. "You're acting like you're a ranger now."

I rolled my shoulders. "I'm something like that," I said.

A door on our right, one that needed a keycard. Ellie took one from her hoodie and tapped it against the lock. It whirred open. We pressed on into the dark corridor.

The third floor was where we kept the rec rooms, from what I remembered. Up ahead we saw the signs for the indoor fitness center—down the hall to the right. Gym, football pitch, indoor pool. Anything you could want to work out was down that way. We weren't interested in going down that way—but neither were the guards.

The arcade was the prime post for any of our security guards. They fought over it all the time. Since no one tended to be in the building after hours but family members and gods, you could get away with playing all the games you wanted most shifts. Not that anyone would ever beat my high scores. Anyway, while we probably wouldn't encounter anyone in the hallways, there would *definitely* be someone on the lookout in the arcade.

And I couldn't really afford someone hearing us, or trying to stop us, or any of that.

Ellie led the way. I let her take point while I reached into my quiver. The important vial I kept on me, but in the front flap of the pocket I'd stashed something Artemis and I had cooked up for dealing with predators we didn't want to kill but needed to pacify. I spread the thick, silvery paste onto one of the narrow arrowheads.

Hunting animals was one thing. That was survival. This was…

My fingers trembled more than I would have liked to admit.

A breath. I could do this. I would be as gentle as I could, and gentle did not mean powerless. It did not mean undetermined.

To hunt was to assert your own right to life. Your own *need* for life. I understood that now—why it had been so important for me to learn these things, why Artemis had insisted I try on my own at first.

When my father offered me on the altar, I was fine with dying. I would have accepted whatever came to me.

Now?

Now I knew what I wanted, and I knew that I could get it, if only I was brave enough to follow through. I wanted to live. I knew I could.

I nocked the arrow. Whatever poor sod we were going to encounter down here—well, I'd aim for the leg, and he'd be out before he hit the floor. This much paste was enough to keep a bear asleep.

Down the hall, to the left. The faint lights of the arcade came up ahead of us. So did the music. Someone was playing one of the fighting games—and I knew for damn sure it wouldn't be Orestes. He hated those.

Ellie came to the big glass panel of the arcade. I peeked inside and saw the guard there. Sure enough, he was hunched over a cabinet. Combos flowed from his hands as his character flew across the screen and landed a knock-up punch. Excellent work, to be honest. Too bad he was about to lose the match thanks to outside interference.

When Ellie opened the door, I shot the arrow. A sharp cry of pain left him as he crumpled onto the ground. The arrow had gotten him in the calf, and a spurt of blood covered the coin slot on the machine. But he didn't shout for long. Maybe two seconds after we heard him collapse to the ground, we heard him start to snore.

Ellie turned toward me. The question was plain in her eyes: *What the fuck?*

"He's asleep, and it wasn't a kill shot, I promise. He'll be fine," I said. "The paste thickens and blocks any blood flow. Go look for yourself if you want."

"Iphy..."

I winced. Why did she have to speak to me in that tone? Like I was flying off the handle. Well, maybe I was. This wasn't normal. But it needed to be done!

"Ellie, I'm still your sister," I said.

She hummed. "It isn't a ranger. I was wrong. You're acting like one of them."

"Does that scare you?" I said. I watched the guard on the floor, the rise and fall of his chest. He really would be all right—I'd caught him on the outside of the thigh. When this was all over, he'd have a neat scar and a story for his mates.

"If I'm honest? A little, yeah," said Ellie. "Everything's happening so quick."

"I know," I said. I laid a hand on her shoulder. "We'll be done soon. We just need to get Ori. Where do you think he's waiting for us?"

"Probably by the air hockey machines. You know how much he loves those," Ellie said. She could hardly look at me, and I could hardly blame her. This really was a lot to take in all at once.

"All right. How about you go over there first? I'll meet up with you," I said. I nocked another arrow, this one broadheaded. There was a winking red light in the corner I needed to do something about.

"You're not going to kill him, are you?" she said.

I winced. But it wasn't unreasonable. With him on the ground and me asking her to step away, it must have seemed an awful lot like a mercy kill situation.

"No, I'm going to try to get him out of sight," I said. I wanted to tell her that I didn't kill things unless I needed to eat, but I had the feeling that wouldn't have gone over well. The sort of thing Artemis would say without a second thought.

She sighed. "All right, fine. As long as you promise you're not going to hurt him," she said.

I thanked her as she rushed off down the twisting aisles. Rhythm games up ahead of us, gambling to the right. The lights painted us in a panoply of colors. The guard at my feet was drooling onto the nostalgic, acid-trip carpet.

First, the camera. Another snap shot took it out. I scanned the room for any more lights and didn't find any. Good. Slinging the bow back into its holder, I hooked my arms under the guard's pits and started dragging him out of the way.

We had this imported Japanese spaceship game. A team-based bullet hell game, *Space Invaders* on steroids, you know the type. Pretty swanky—the whole thing was set up to look like four cockpits lined up next to each other. They even closed down if you wanted.

Right now, I wanted them to.

I hauled him up and into a cockpit, then made sure that his seat belt was nice and secure for his flight.

With that settled, I just had to find my siblings. Now, the air hockey tables... Where were they? I had to shut my eyes just to think—there were so many lights and sounds. So *much*. How had this place felt like home to me once?

In a minute or two it came to me. They were down with the other classic arcade games: Skee ball, the racehorse games, all of that sort of stuff. The less electronic portion of things. I ducked down the aisles. Before long, I could hear them talking.

"She totally shot him, Ori. No hesitation, just *shhhp*—arrow in his leg. I don't know what's going on."

"You're sure?"

"You think I'd fucking imagine that?"

"I don't know. I don't know what any of this is, El. Is that... Is it really her?"

"Maybe the better question is what's happened to her," said Ellie.

My chest hurt. Would this still be worth it if my siblings thought I was some kind of weird monster at the end of it?

Yeah. Yeah, it would be, if they could be free.

"El, Ori," I called. They didn't need to know how much I'd heard. "Are we all set?"

I heard them shifting. As I came around the corner of an old-fashioned rail-gun hunting game, I saw the two of them huddled over by an air hockey table.

My brother had to be two meters tall now. Gods, I'd missed

way too much. I wanted to run over and hug him, but with what I had just heard, it didn't feel right. I settled for standing awkwardly nearby and seeing what he did.

And what he didn't do was hug me.

"Iphy," he said. "Is it true that you—"

"Yeah," I said. "I told you, I really need to talk to the two of you alone."

Orestes took a step toward me. I couldn't help but notice that as he did, he made sure to block Ellie from my view. "You aren't going to hurt us, are you? You're not like Them?"

"I don't eat people, if that's what you're asking," I said. I hadn't planned for this part of things to hurt so much. In my head, it had been so easy. "Look, I know that this is a lot. You're dealing with a ton of revelations all in one day, and they don't exactly make sense for you. Your sister is back from the dead, and she's shooting people with arrows. Showed up in a weird outfit and made weird demands. It's weird! I know it is. But let me talk. I can explain, now that it's just us."

His eyes searched mine. I wasn't going to back down—but I set down the bow so they'd feel safer.

Tension came off his shoulders.

"Let's hear it, then. Start explaining. What happened to you, and why are you acting this way?"

I stood. There was a lot to say and not a ton of time. I'd been working through this speech in my head since the car ride over.

"Dad sacrificed me for the sake of politics," I said. It had to start there, with the barest, most upsetting fact of the matter. "He led me to the Court of the Wild, handed me over, and told me that I had to die for the sake of some war that has nothing to do with any of us. That if I didn't die, we'd lose."

My voice was starting to crack. I kept going.

"The Queen of the Wild told him that if he gave up what was dearest to him, she would stay her arrows from interfering in the war. And she told him that because she knew that he would give me up. Because our family has always been this way. For generations and generations we've been this way. Our ancestors have killed their children or gotten them killed more than once, and it just... it just keeps happening. She knew he wouldn't hesitate."

I thought of her, then. I thought of her seeing me in that hoodie, malnourished and pale, and thinking that I deserved to live. Did she love me then? Or did she come to love me as I grew?

"I went willingly. I agreed to die. I said that I would do whatever it took to keep the two of you safe, and I told the Queen of the Wild it was okay, I didn't mind."

How much had it hurt her when I said those words? I took a breath.

"You agreed to die?" said Ellie. "But... You..."

"Why didn't you tell us?" said Orestes.

"There wasn't any time. I couldn't talk to anyone about it. I had to make the decision then and there," I said. I sniffled. "The Queen saw that I didn't fear death. That I would have sacrificed myself for my family without even knowing our past. And she took pity on me, so she..."

How to even describe it? Best to say what she would say.

"She saved me. She took me on as her handmaiden. So that's where I've been, the past three years. In the Court of the Wild, with her. Learning to survive, to hunt, all that. For me, it's only been a few months."

I let it rest there for a second—I knew they'd have questions. Orestes opened and closed his hand.

"So…you've been off having some kind of adventure?" he said.

"Call it that if you like. Dad really did plan to kill me, and she really did agree initially. But once she saved me, we had to figure out a way to keep us both alive. We settled on rebirth, I guess you could call it. If my old self died, it would still count by the letter of the Law. Wisdom wasn't going to accept that without a little convincing, so I had to pass a test. That meant studying. So I've learned a lot about myself, and about her. About…." Probably better not to break it to them that the Queen took *handmaiden* further than most people would and I loved when she did. "About our family. Did you know, we're cursed because Tantalus cut up his son, Pelops, and tried to serve him to the gods?"

Ellie went pale; Orestes's nostrils flared. He was trying so hard to look tough, but I knew his stomach was turning.

"No one's ever told us that."

"Because it's *horrible*. Because if we knew, none of us would want to be the Heir of Pelops. Stuck here our whole lives, and for what? For the sake of working off the debt that bastard, his siblings, and his son racked up. The other gods think we need supervision. That we're all going to turn out that way, so we might as well serve them."

"But why us?" said Ellie. "Why not other families who have done terrible things? Why do we have to—"

"We have their blood," I said. "Tantalus was a bastard of the King of the Gods. That's the real fuck of it: We're like Them, deep down. All of us are. That's why they put one of us in containment each generation."

Another breath.

"But that's why I'm here. I can free us."

Silence in the arcade—or, at least, what passed for it. The music and the sound effects from the games kept right on playing. Orestes and Ellie looked at each other.

It was Orestes who spoke.

"How?"

I held up the flask of green. "This is the blood of a hydra. A mythic beast. I hunted it with Art and the others, and they didn't see me get it. The other day I got some of it in my mouth. Gave us both a hell of a scare, but when I woke up in the morning I felt lighter. I think it kills the part of us that's tied to the curse. If we all anoint ourselves with this, then we can break the contract our ancestors agreed to. We can be free. Rebirth has always been the secret."

"You hunted a *hydra*?"

"What did you just call her—"

I waved my free hand. "I can show you," I said. I pulled out my phone and opened up the photos I'd taken. Sure enough, there they were—the masked gods in the midst of their combat, and my face looking back into the selfie camera.

"Holy shit," said Ellie. "That thing...It's the size of a mountain—"

"That's War, and Wisdom, and...That really is you, isn't it?" Orestes said. There was a soft wonder that had crept into his voice.

"Sure is," I said. I stashed the phone. "I won't lie. It is dangerous. The blood has a kind of venom to it that...Well, things can go badly. But I was covered in it myself, and I made it through. Plus, I got some ambrosia from Art. It should help you stay whole."

"I don't like that you said 'whole,'" Ellie said. "Are we talking, like, acid, or...?"

"We're talking a lot of things," I said. "It's risky, but I think it's worth it. I'm sick and tired of—"

"Iphigenia. I have to admit, I wasn't expecting to see you again."

All three of us stood taller. As Orestes had stepped in front of Elektra, I stepped in front of the two of them, another arrow already nocked.

When I turned I saw my father.

He was in one of his favorite suits, despite the hour, and the arcade lights made his jet-black eyes shine like ink. On either side of him were two more guards—each armed to the teeth, each staring us down.

We didn't have long to act.

"Run," I told the others.

"We're not leaving you," said Ellie. She planted herself behind me, even though I could hear her starting to hyperventilate.

"Orestes, take her away from here," I said. My brother, now not so little, scooped up Ellie and turned tail. Good. He knew this place pretty well. Maybe he could find somewhere to hide out for a while.

In the meantime, I had this to deal with.

One of the guards stepped forward after my siblings. I didn't hesitate in shooting this one, either; I loosed an arrow at his calves and nailed them together. He toppled over in pain. The screams were like screws driven into my temples; my stomach twisted. I didn't *want* to have to hurt people. But I wasn't letting him get at them. I couldn't.

Maybe someday I'd forget what it sounded like.

My father's face wrenched in horror at what I'd done. "Is this what's become of you? A murderer?"

Murderer.

The word lit a fuse inside me. My chest went hot, my ears tingled. "Murderer? He's going to be fine. It's a clean wound. It'll heal up all right. I'm no murderer. But you?"

I stepped toward him, the bow in hand.

What did it mean that he stepped back?

What did it mean that I kept going, anyway? That I wanted to see him step back again, and again, until his cowardly back was against the wall and he was forced to confront what he had done?

"You."

A step forward.

"Tried."

A step back.

"To."

A step forward.

"Sacrifice me!"

His back hit a cabinet; he started. The remaining guard put an arm between us, and I batted it away.

"You're gonna let me talk to him. Especially since he came all this way," I said. Every word was dizzying, the rush of this confrontation carrying me forward like a rope tied to a runaway car. "That's what you want, isn't it? You want to know that it's me. Well, it is. Surprise. I'm alive."

His eyes narrowed as I took another step forward. The bow stayed in hand. I nocked another arrow from the quiver in case the guard tried anything.

"You can't have known the pressure I was under," he said.

The child in me wanted to scream. "Yeah? So you're saying there's a kind of pressure where it's okay to serve your kid up to a man-eating god on a silver platter?"

"That's not what I meant," he cut in.

"But it's what you did," I said. I paced around him and the cabinet he was up against. The guard kept his eyes on me; let him. If I loosed it, he wouldn't be able to stop me. My arrows were too fast. "Some war breaks out between two Courts, some distant thing, and rather than keep your fucking brown nose out of it, you decide you need to get involved. We're a fucking international logistics and trade company, not an army!"

My throat hurt with all the shouting I was doing, but I didn't stop. Couldn't if I tried.

"You never told me about the rest of our family," I said. "I guess you didn't want to put the thought into my head that a father could ever sacrifice his children. But you knew, didn't you?"

The tears bit into the corners of my eyes.

"You knew the whole fucking time what kind of people we came from. What sort of life I'd have. And you never tried to find any way out of it. You just accepted the system for what it was. And it wasn't enough for you to lay a single child upon that altar, oh no. You lined up Orestes for it when I was gone. *Bastard* isn't a strong enough word. We're your *children*!"

Spit flew from my mouth as I spoke, and I made no move to stop it. He didn't move, either. The whole while he stood there and watched me go on.

My chest rose and fell, the bellows stoking the great flame of my anger. I clamped my jaw shut so tight it hurt.

"What do you have to say for yourself?" I said. "Where's Mum?"

"It wasn't an easy decision." His voice wavered. "Do you think I've been able to sleep since I last saw you? Do you think I'm proud of what I've done?"

Anger kept hold of my throat; I could think of nothing to say to stop him.

"What were my options, Iphigenia? Put yourself in my position. Either you sacrifice your favorite daughter or your family loses everything. *Generations* of sacrifices, of lives lived in gilded cages, all gone in an instant. Your grandfather's work, your great-grandmother's. All of our money and all of our fame and all of our good names. What was I meant to do?"

"You said parents tend to protect their children. You told me that knowing what you were about to do to me."

He held his head in his hand. "I know."

"Tell me the truth: if it had been me or you, who would you have chosen?"

"It wasn't that simple—"

"I'm making it that simple!" I shouted. "If you could have died instead of me, what would you have done?"

"The family will always need an heir, Iphigenia," he said. "No matter which one of us died."

And it hit me then what had happened. He said it himself: no matter which one of us died.

He had thought about it. The sacrifice was of whatever he held the most dear, and I knew how much he valued his own life. He could have been the one on the altar.

He chose me. Like Tantalus he would have cut me to pieces and served me to the gods. Sacrificing himself, finding another way out of the curse, making some kind of bargain that could save us—none of that had ever really been in the cards.

He chose himself and the curse instead of my family and freedom.

I couldn't take it anymore. Not from the man who had raised me like a lamb to the fucking slaughter.

I loosed the arrow. It bit into the cabinet right by his eye. I could see some of the dust end up on his eyelid.

The guard went for me the second I fired. A big man lunging at you can be hard to avoid. I tried to jump out of the way, but I trained as a hunter, not a fighter. He got his arms around my waist and lifted me up in the air—

Only for a bolt of silver to strike him straight through the chest.

He fell to the ground and I—

Fell into her arms.

"Iphigenia." When she said it, it was all gentleness and care. *I'm sorry*, that name said. *I had to come.*

She set me down on the ground so lightly that my feet didn't even register the contact.

My father looked from me to the god at my side. I could see it registering on his face—the predicament that he'd gotten himself into.

With Artemis here, there wasn't any reason for fear or regret. I swallowed it all down. Someone was already dead because they'd gone for me. There'd be time to reckon with the consequences later.

"Where's Mum?" I said.

"You have to call off your attack—"

"Shut the *fuck* up and tell me where my mother is. Or did you sacrifice her, too?" I said. My voice broke, and I didn't care, didn't care at all. Artemis, standing at my side, rested a hand on my shoulder. But she didn't intervene. She didn't steer me one way or the other.

She trusted me.

My father was a different story. There was little of the man who raised me in the way he was staring at me now. No wonder. I'd never in my life done anything like this. All those times he'd taken me around this prison, knowing full well the kind of life that awaited me at the end of it...

To him I had always been a sacrifice. It just so happened to work out more literally than he expected. I was always going to be the one trapped in the high-rise, I was always going to be the one with no future except what I'd been given. He'd lived that life himself and never once imagined better for me.

How could I have been so naïve?

"I love you, Iphy. You have to know that," he said. He reached for my hand, and I slapped his wrist away.

"Funny way of showing it," I said. Anger had me in a vise; it was hard to breathe. I drew back the bow and leveled it at his face. "Answer the question."

It was only then that Artemis turned toward me. A soft, simple gesture. There was no word to stop me. Only concern. The cool metal of her collar was ice against the fire. I did my best to focus on it.

"Please answer," I said.

I waited. One breath, two, three. I stared him down, blinking as little as I could, as the guard bled out next to us. Though there was godly blood in my veins, I was no idol of war; the tension of the bow wore on my muscles. I could hold it only a few seconds longer. When my grip inevitably gave out, would I bother to turn the bow away from him?

The bow creaked. I gritted my teeth.

One breath, two—

"Put the bow down, Iphigenia. Killing your own father is a burden you shouldn't have to bear."

I turned. My mother was shambling toward us. Shambling truly was the word—my heart fell right into my stomach at the sight of dark red on her gown. A wound she'd done her best to stanch with all the pressure a single hand could give. Yet though she was already pale from the blood loss, I'd never seen her eyes more determined. And in her other hand?

Oh, in her other hand was a golden axe.

At first I had no idea where it had come from. Where the fuck would we keep something like that? But as I studied it, the answer came to me. It wasn't one I liked.

See, there was blood all along the business end of the axe. Blood that was already turning brown. And the wound on my mother's side...

"Mum?" I said. "Mum, are you—did he try to—"

As I lowered the bow and turned toward her, my father's survival instinct kicked in. His only decently developed one, it seemed. I heard him make a break for it behind me.

And then I heard the low growl of Artemis going after him.

For now, that was Artemis's responsibility. As I approached my mother, all I wanted to do was throw my arms around her. She waved me off. It was enough to clear my head and make me try to think what we'd even do about a fucking axe wound—but none of the first aid I'd learned applied to something like this. And I didn't even know a ton, just how to do stitches, and my mother was—

Scrambling, reaching through my packs for something,

anything that might help, my hands closed around the fruit. Ambrosia. I'd brought enough for my siblings... If I used some to save my mother, would there be enough for us?

"Mum, I'm so sorry," I stammered. My hands were cold and shaking but still I pressed them against the wound. "I—we need to get you help, you're hurt so bad."

"He's gonna hurt worse in a minute," she said. And with a surprising amount of strength, she shoved me out of the way.

I turned. Artemis had caught him—my father, the two-time murderer. A pathetic excuse for a man even now trying to scrape his way to freedom. She had him pinned by the throat, her knee pressed against his diaphragm.

And there was my mother, advancing with the axe.

"Mum," I said. "Mum, what are you gonna do?"

"What I should have done the second I realized what he'd done to you," she answered. The axe scraped against the bad carpet.

This had to be some kind of fever dream. When I had been the one about to kill him it had seemed right. What about this made it seem so horrible?

"A daughter for a company. For a curse," my mother said. She was in front of him now. The golden axe reflected his own face back at him—his own terror. "What a wretched man."

Artemis's head swung around, like an owl's, her eyes landing on mine. A question lay there. *Do I stop her?* she seemed to ask.

I couldn't feel my fingertips. My tongue stuck to the roof of my mouth. The sweat was rolling down my forehead in sheets, and nothing felt real. The hydra paled in comparison to the thing I was about to witness.

But could I stop it?

He had tried to kill her. He had tried to kill her daughter. And with her bleeding out the way she was, would there be any other chance for her to get her revenge?

When you're hunting, you have to keep a lot of things in mind. One of them is that you have to kill with one shot—or get as close to that as you can. Most of the time that's because you don't want the animal to suffer. No one who hunts humanely is there to watch an animal bleed out.

But there's another reason, too.

If you shoot only to wound, the animal will do everything in its power either to get away from you or to make your life a living hell. Deer are lovely creatures—but an angry stag? They'll put their antlers through your skull without a thought. It won't mean anything to them. They won't think of your family, or the good you might have done. They think about survival.

When you wound an animal you have to kill it. Anything else is cruelty.

My father had offered me to the slaughter. He hadn't had the guts to kill me himself, only to offer me to someone who he thought would do the job. When it came to my mother, though...he wounded. He *aimed* to wound her.

Out in the Court of the Wild, he would have been torn apart for this.

Why should this be any different?

Artemis asked me a question in perfect silence. Standing there, hot from anger and cool from disbelief, I answered it without a word.

The golden axe raised high in the air.

I turned away as it fell. And when I did, the darkness came upon me—the velvet that was her embrace, the black that enveloped all. In the whole of the world there was only her embrace and the smell of her. Safety and comfort.

I had hoped to spare you from this, Artemis whispered to me. It was like the wind—I knew she wasn't really speaking. The dark was. But I heard it all the same, and I allowed myself to sob knowing no one would see.

"I know. But I had to save them," I said. "It... It isn't your fault."

A low hum. She held me tighter in that cloud of darkness. *You have. They are free of him.*

Snot started to dribble down my nose. Oh, I was really sobbing now. "I—You have to help my mum, if you can. Your brother could save her? I have fruit, but only enough for my siblings, and I need it for—"

Iphigenia.

A word, a prayer, a balm. The sound that left me was ugly and small and childish, and she held it, held me, without a worry. I felt her rough hand clearing away my tears.

Go to your siblings. I will tend to your mother. Cleanse them of the curse, and they shall find shelter with us.

"You'll save her?"

For you, I would have saved even him, she answered.

The dark flickered around me. When I blinked, it was gone.

Only the long hallway that led toward my siblings. Only this, and her hand on the small of my back, urging me to go.

I found them in my old room. Of all the rooms in the high-rise, they picked that one. I was grateful for it. In the aftermath of what had happened, I wasn't thinking about where I was going. My feet led the way, and the rest of me followed. Of course I ended up there.

Orestes was at the door. When I knocked he shouted, "Who's there?" and I had to tell him in my weak voice that it was me.

He knew there was something wrong immediately. They opened the door and let me in, and I just sat there in my old chair. My old things looked back on me. My figures, my collectibles. They'd left everything just as it had been. But the dust said they hadn't been back here, and there was this awful stale taste to the air, and no one had bothered caring for my miserable little houseplants.

"He's dead, isn't he?" Ellie said.

And there was no hiding it, not with shock setting in the way that it had, so I nodded.

"Did you...?" asked Orestes.

"No," I said. "He tried to kill Mum, and she killed him."

Silence. My PC's fan whirred away. No one had remembered to turn it off, either. If I jostled the mouse it would wake up and ask for a password I no longer knew.

"Is she okay?" said Ellie.

I bit my lip and nodded. "Yeah. That much I can promise you," I said. "Artemis is taking care of her now."

Another wave of silence. We sat there, none of us knowing what to say, before I got together the brain cells to remember that I'd come here to cleanse them.

I pulled the vial from my pocket and held it in hand. The cold glass warmed against my skin.

"I still have the hydra blood," I said. Focus. "If we don't cleanse you guys now, the curse might spread."

I glanced at Orestes. He was staring intently at my hand.

"If we do this, I'm free?" he said.

I nodded. "But you might die."

He didn't hesitate. He took the bottle right from my hands. "Just tell me what I need to do. I'm not spending another second in this place if I don't have to."

Chapter Seventeen

On that night it felt like the world had come to an end. Deep in the thicket of my sorrows, I could see no way through to the clearing. Here was a ditch of regret, over there the brambles of my aimless anger, and behind me a stream of frustrations that I couldn't possibly hope to ford. There was no way out. I'd done all this for the sake of saving my siblings, and I had.

But my father was dead now, and my mother had killed him.

How do you find a way to keep going after that?

Here's what I've learned. Maybe it's something you already know.

You don't find a way to keep going. Life, and time, continue. The sun rises the next morning regardless of whether you want it to. This whole thing, living, breathing, *being alive*, is an arrow that's already in the air. We're headed straight toward a target, and there's nothing we can do to stop it.

As time goes on, as you're pulled through the air along the arrow, it starts to hurt less. You get used to the winds. You find your balance. And it happens without you realizing it. There's never any day where you wake up and you think, *Wow, I sure am cured of all that grief.* It doesn't work like that.

But every day it gets a little easier to make it out of bed. Every day it's a little easier to feed yourself. Eventually your stomach rumbles all on its own, without you having to remind yourself that you're hungry.

You go *through* these things. The arrowhead punches through the parchment, or the target, or whatever the case may be. Sometimes the arrowhead's a little dulled after. But it keeps going.

We keep going.

Cleansing my siblings was easier than I thought it would be. I anointed them with the hydra blood, and I announced what I was doing.

"Let this blood poison and kill the curse upon the House of Pelops," I said.

It felt like the right thing to say. The words were there for me when I reached for them. The parts of me that were a god must have wanted to help. After I'd spoken, my palms burned, and the blood began to glow an acid green. The glow lasted for a few hours. And then...

Well, then it was done. Ori and Ellie said they felt lighter. I had already been cleansed when the hydra blood touched me the first time, so I knew what it was like.

I stayed with them through the night. Artemis was with us,

too; I felt her cool presence in the metal against my throat. But she waited outside my bedroom door and did not intrude. Our own personal guard in case anything else should go wrong.

In the morning, when the employees arrived to work and the guard shift changed, they found my father's body. They did *not* find my mother. Nor did they find us.

By then, I'd already opened the door and invited Artemis into the room. She was so big that her antlers knocked against my once-precious figurines and sent them scattering to the floor. The shadows she used to conceal her face were darker than usual. Was that her mood, or her concern for my siblings?

"This is Artemis," I said to my siblings. "She's my— Well, I'm her handmaiden. I've been living with her in her Domain this whole time."

"You're the one who tried to kill her," said Ori. He was sitting on my computer desk, his head bowed beneath the loft bed. "I guess you wanted to make up for it, didn't you?"

"Ori, don't be so mean to Iphy's girlfriend," said Ellie.

"She's not—It's—" I stammered. I had so many other things to worry about, and yet I still felt the need to make the correction. Not that I could call the right word to mind.

Artemis laid a hand on my shoulder again. "Something like that," she said.

And that felt... right. A welcome respite from the oppressive weight of everything else that had gone on. *Girlfriend* was a little too casual, but we weren't married. She was my mistress, and I was her handmaiden. Wherever and whenever she needed me, I would be there. But so, too, would she—always watching over, always protecting.

It felt weird to say that to my siblings, though.

"Girlfriend or not, I still think it was shitty of you to try to kill her," said Orestes. "She might have forgiven you, but I haven't."

"Think what you like," said Artemis, "but I never intended to kill her. I wanted to free her, as she has freed you."

Ori crossed his arms. He was getting ready to counterargue, but we didn't have time for that.

"She's on our side, Orestes. And she's willing to let us hide out with her for a while until all of this blows over," I said. We hadn't talked about that part of things—but I knew she wouldn't mind. I was pretty sure it was why she'd come at all. "That way you two don't have to deal with any questioning. We'll have time to figure out our next steps."

"And if we're gone for a year?" said Orestes. "You've been gone for *three*, and you said it wasn't even that long for you."

"I'll go back and forth," I said. "Split my time between the realms. Everyone already thinks I'm dead, anyway, so it'll be easier for me to get settled. And once I am, you guys can come back full time."

Ellie hugged herself tight. When she looked up at me, I could tell how much all of this was wearing on her. "Yeah. Sure. If it gets us out of this place, then I don't mind."

Orestes turned toward her. I thought he might argue. Instead, I saw the lines of his tension soften, and he sighed.

"Might be good for a few days, I guess. Are we going to have to be roughing it, though?"

"'Fraid so," I said. "You're going to learn all about woodcraft over there."

He groaned. But in the end, he didn't argue.

My mother was there when we arrived. So was the King of Song. He was tending to her wounds with his own two hands. I can't tell you how surreal it is to see a god on his knees to bandage your mum. As much as I hated him, I had to admit he was doing us a solid with this.

We talked. I mean, it took us a while to get there. At first it was just tearful embraces and promises that things were going to be okay. But eventually, after a few hours, we did talk.

And my mother said that she was leaving.

"Why?" I asked. I was incredulous; the word left me like the scrape of metal. "After all we've done—you're leaving? But we're all together here—"

She took my head in her hands. "Someone needs to take the fall, Iph. Otherwise there are going to be questions the three of you can't answer. I'll go back and take responsibility for all of it."

Ellie was sobbing. I couldn't blame her. I wanted to cry, too. But I couldn't with the other two also here. I took a steadying breath and hugged Ellie. She didn't deserve to feel alone.

"Why's it have to be you?" Ellie said.

"Because it should have been me a lot earlier than this," she said. She looked down at her hands. "I should have realized what sort of man he was sooner. And I never should have let the three of you be raised the way you were. He told me that was the way things had always been done in the family and I…accepted it without question. There were so many things I *should* have questioned. A whole life spent in a single building is no life to live, no matter how plush. I should have tried to find a way to get you out of it. I…"

She looked up to the sky.

"I have to take responsibility for all of it if I'm going to take responsibility for any of it."

We tried to argue with her. At least, Ellie and I did. What good did this do us, to let her go and watch her get locked up? To see her name all over the news? Society didn't treat female murderers very well, no matter the cause. And there was no way that the full story would ever be printed. She was going to be torn to shreds out there—and that's not counting the jail time.

If we let her go, we might not ever see her again.

But the thing is—we weren't really *letting* her go. She was her own woman. Nothing we could do would stop her. Oh, we could trap her here, or try to keep her from walking off, but that'd be a horrible thing to do to someone. It'd make us no better than our father.

Orestes was the first one to get there. The moment she announced her plan he locked eyes with her and said, "All right."

It took Ellie and me a while to get there. But we did.

The arrow stayed in flight.

Mum went back home. I walked her back myself. We left the Court of the Wild and ended up on that same little island. It was only then that I realized I'd left the damn boat on the shore—so I had to make us a new one. Once you've made the first four, the fifth is a snap; I wasted no time in the making of it. Nor in the sailing.

When we made it to the shore, she called the police. I waited with her until the sirens approached. As they closed in, she squeezed my hand.

"If you told me a year ago my daughter would have made us a raft and sailed us straight to the cops, I would have laughed."

"To be fair, I think anyone would. Sounds fucking ridiculous," I said. I wasn't crying. I think I'd left all my tears for the Courts. The night before we left, I'd bawled my eyes out. But now?

There was no use for it. My mother wouldn't feel any better if I was in tears when I saw her off.

"Will you look after your siblings for me, Iphigenia?" she said. "They've been through more than anyone should. You're the only one who could understand. Please look after them."

The cars were closing in. We could hear the sirens grow louder.

"Yeah. Of course," I said. "I don't want them to suffer anymore. Even if I am worried about them."

"That's the thing—you're always going to worry about them," said Mum. She wiped at her eyes. "All you can do is set them up so you worry less. And I'll worry less with you there."

A police car rounded the corner of the street. If I stayed much longer, they'd see me with her. She knew that as well as I did. Another squeeze of the hand.

"Go on. No sense in you sticking around. Your girlfriend can only save you so many times," she said.

I stood. With one last hug I left her—but I didn't wander too far off. From a little hidey hole beneath the pier, where I'd stashed the raft, I watched the police arrest my mother and did nothing to stop them.

My siblings are shit survivalists.

I don't mean that they're beginners, mind you. I mean that they're shit. I think I must have told Ori sixteen times that you have to be sure to douse a fire if you're stepping away from it without anyone there to watch it. What does he keep doing? Leaving it unattended for hours and hours. Ellie refuses to help with any of our catches, which I can't blame her for, but her foraging always contains at least one poisonous mushroom or berry. I'm beginning to think she has some kind of sixth sense for things that'll kill us.

But I was a shit survivalist for a long while, too. It takes time to get better. As Artemis told me so long ago, you have to want it. You have to try.

And this just wasn't their end goal. They aren't trying to impress an unknowable god; they're trying to get by until they can go back home.

Artemis does her best to get along with them—but they don't trust her, and I can't make them. No matter my affection for her and absolute trust that she'd never harm us, she *is* a god. I know well how the hands that hold me close can kill and clean. I'm accustomed to it. I love that about her—knowing that this fearsome being is soft for me.

Ori doesn't trust her, but he does like hunting with her. We go out in the mornings sometimes. She's taught him how to fire a bow, and he isn't a half bad shot.

Ellie doesn't trust her, but she does like learning about the wildlife. She'll leave out food for them sometimes, and just when she has a question about what sort of deer it is she's seeing, Artemis will be there to answer it. Never as a surprise—always as a whisper.

They're getting by all right. I'm looking after them, just as I promised. Whenever that big lug walks away from the fire, I'm the one to put it out. And whenever Ellie finds something in the traps and doesn't want to deal with it, she calls me, and I clean it out.

After every five days in the Wild, I go back to the mortal world for a little while. I think I'm starting to work out the time differences well enough that I'm not missed for too long. I can go a whole week in the mortal world before anyone realizes I've taken off back home.

Well, anyone except Artemis.

She always knows when I've left.

And, sure enough, whenever I make my way back to that little cabin, she'll be there that very night. With the way things are right now, we don't get a lot of time on our own—but we make the most of it. And having a cabin means we have a place to store things or set them up. There are hooks in the ceiling.

It's way nicer to be suspended from those than from a tree branch, you know?

Sometimes she calls on me for handmaiden duties. Serious ones, I mean. Most of the time it's for hunts like the one with the hydra—a bunch of gods get together to kill a beast one of them managed to track down. Sometimes, though, she brings me to the Courts with her. The others think I'm amusing. Wisdom tried to argue that I shouldn't be let in those spaces since I'm not her Oathsworn, but the King of Song pointed out that technically there are no rules against handmaidens, and Artemis's grandfather said that there was enough of my blood to count as kin. That was that. No more arguments.

I haven't seen her face. I don't mind it. Maybe one day, when she does offer me an oath, I will. But I'm not in any rush. What we have together isn't what most people have. We're different. I'm all right with our relationship being all our own.

When I'm in the mortal world, I find work as a wilderness guide. Lots of people need those, and at this point I can navigate most places pretty well. Worldwide service, believe it or not. I can go anywhere nature reigns just by asking Artemis to drop me off there. Sometimes she makes me pay for it later, but it's never a price I balk at paying.

And speaking of pay—boy, does this job pay *well*. It turns out that a friendly guide to the most dangerous places on Earth is in pretty high demand. I've saved up a pretty penny doing this. Enough to get the cabin some internet.

Which is, of course, how I met you.

Epilogue

I've known you for as long as we've been in hiding. As I told you this story, you might've even remembered the headlines of my father's murder, or my mother's trial, or whatever. We've made a lot of true crime YouTubers a *lot* of money. People speculate about her reasons, or what happened to the kids, or what happened to me. I've listened to videos that suggest I was offered up in a demonic sacrifice. In most cases that would be flat-out wrong, but in mine, well…

I don't mind what people say about me. I don't! In a lot of ways, the Iph that was sacrificed that night is dead and gone. I like the new one a lot more. Sure, I still have trouble sleeping, and some days it's hard to get out of bed. But I can do it now. The depression might be loud, but the things that need doing are louder, and whenever I falter, there's my family and Art there to remind me why I do what I do.

I'm happy now. Really. Nothing brings me more joy than being out in the woods and being useful to my family or Artie. Even being dragged to Court is nice for that—she's so bad at dealing with people, and she's so fond of showing me off. I always feel like she wants me to be there.

But the favor I asked you for a while ago, before I started rambling like a video game commentary channel, is for my siblings.

You used to be a therapist before the whole business with Passion happened, right? And you worked with people in bad situations. I don't know if I would say Ori and Ellie are in a *bad* situation—they're cared for and looked after and all that—but I don't know if they're *happy*.

I want them to be happy, more than anything.

I know that it won't be easy. We've got to figure out if they come back as themselves, or if we have to come up with whole new identities for them. It's a choice they're going to have to make themselves—to leave everything behind like I did, or to try to make something of it, no matter what might come their way.

They have their own feelings about what happened. About me being gone so long, about Mum doing what she did, about our family and what it means for us to be tied to this lineage. They deserve someone to listen to those feelings and help them sort it out.

It can't be me. They deserve someone better equipped.

I figure—who's better than the newly minted God of Souls?

I know it's probably a weird thing to ask, and you might think I hooked you up with Passion so that all of this would happen, but I didn't know it was going to go that way. Really. And I never would have bothered you with this when you didn't know anything about the Courts. I'm coming to you because you can understand them now.

So, what do you say? Will you help out? I promise Artie and I will find some way to thank you for it. Artie and Passion aren't super close, but when I tell you she's behind me on this, I want you to believe it. Anything the moon touches, anything the Wild can offer you—whatever it takes, I'm willing to pay it. There's no sacrifice I'm not willing to make for my siblings.

How about it?

Iph, all you had to do was ask.

Acknowledgments

You would think acknowledgments get easier to write the more you do them. That's not quite true. There's an old saying that you never learn how to write a novel—only how to write *one particular* novel. Once you're done with that one you have to start all over again. Acknowledgments are the same.

This book took a *lot* of work to get off the ground. I've never been so stuck as I have been with this one. As such, my first thanks has to go to my editor, Sam Brody, for stepping up to deal with the absolute mess that I had made. She's been nothing but kind, supportive, and easy to work with. I can't thank her enough for her understanding and grace during a bit of a turbulent writing process.

My agent, Arley Sorg, has been a wonderful addition to the team. Insightful and caring, I've really appreciated having such a soothing presence. I can't wait for us to work on more projects together—I can already tell it's going to be a total level up.

A thank you to the rest of my team at Forever, as well: Leah Hultenschmidt, Caroline Green, and Lori Paximadis. It takes many hands to put a book together and this one would have been lesser without your contributions.

I was horribly stuck on this book for about a year—the longest I've ever been stuck on a project before. A single conversation with my friend Zee unraveled this massive Gordian Knot. It came apart so easily that I wondered how it had ever been a problem at all. Sometimes insurmountable problems really do come apart that easily. I wish the same for everyone reading this.

Lastly, I'd like to thank my partners, Charlie and Matt, without whom I would never be in a state to finish anything at all.

About the Author

K Arsenault Rivera was born in Mayaguez, Puerto Rico, and has been living in New York since the age of three.

At a compact four foot nine, K is a concentrated dose of geekery. She's incredibly passionate about her interests, some of which include Greek myths.

You can learn more at:
KArsenaultRivera.com
Instagram @ArsenaultRivera
Bluesky @ArsenaultRivera

RAISING READERS
Books Build Bright Futures

Thank you for reading this book and for being a reader of books in general. We are so grateful to share being part of a community of readers with you, and we hope you will join us in passing our love of books on to the next generation of readers.

Did you know that reading for enjoyment is the single biggest predictor of a child's future happiness and success?

More than family circumstances, parents' educational background, or income, reading impacts a child's future academic performance, emotional well-being, communication skills, economic security, ambition, and happiness.

Studies show that kids reading for enjoyment in the US is in rapid decline:

- In 2012, 53% of 9-year-olds read almost every day. Just 10 years later, in 2022, the number had fallen to 39%.
- In 2012, 27% of 13-year-olds read for fun daily. By 2023, that number was just 14%.

Together, we can commit to **Raising Readers** and change this trend. How?

- Read to children in your life daily.
- Model reading as a fun activity.
- Reduce screen time.
- Start a family, school, or community book club.
- Visit bookstores and libraries regularly.
- Listen to audiobooks.
- Read the book before you see the movie.
- Encourage your child to read aloud to a pet or stuffed animal.
- Give books as gifts.
- Donate books to families and communities in need.

Books build bright futures, and **Raising Readers** is our shared responsibility.

For more information, visit **JoinRaisingReaders.com**

Sources: National Endowment for the Arts, National Assessment of Educational Progress, WorldBookDay.com, Nielsen BookData's 2023 "Understanding the Children's Book Consumer"